RISING DRAGONFLY

Second Edition

JASON BUJNOCH

Rising Dragonfly, Second Edition, published August, 2021

Editorial and proofreading services: Highline Editorial, New York, NY; Cath Lauria

Interior layout and cover design: Howard P. Johnson

Photo Credits: Titlepage, Chapter Openers: Dragonfly, iStock by Getty Images

Front cover: Dragonfly, Depositphotos

 **SDP Publishing**

Published by SDP Publishing, an imprint of SDP Publishing Solutions, LLC.

To obtain permission(s) to use material from this work, please submit a written request to:

SDP Publishing
Permissions Department
PO Box 26, East Bridgewater, MA 02333
or email your request to info@SDPPublishing.com.

ISBN-13 (print): 978-1-7367204-0-0

ISBN-13 (e-book): 978-1-7367204-1-7

Library of Congress Control Number: 2021908803

For Clara and Ava, my captive audience.

He who rules by fear breeds fearlessness.

—*Shaolin Proverb*

Prologue

Brother Bill Cox, the urban greenhorn, biked the city streets in an ever-expanding pattern, seeking out landmarks and speaking to clergy and other non-profiteers about potential service opportunities. The number of homeless people was as shocking as the scenery was striking, in the parks along the tree-lined bayous at the toes of the high rises and skyscrapers. Houston was a Mecca to Brother Bill.

At a Gothic old church called La Estrella de Jahweh, Bill spoke to a Jaliscan monk who told him that he might want to *dress* like a holy man, while riding through these neighborhoods, if he wanted a little extra protection from God. The priest offered Bill a white Roman collar and a black shirt for free, but Bill politely refused the gifts at first. They really wouldn't match his shorts. But he accepted them after the padre insisted. *Seriously.*

Bill tottered along the wide, manicured trail beside Buffalo Bayou with his head on a swivel. When he had passed by this spot earlier, the sea fog had still been thick as smoke, the sculptures in the Art Park just formless shadows along the murky levee. But now the opaque mist was rising and burning off, so Bill could inspect his surroundings in better detail. Then he glimpsed something in his peripheral that sent a chill to his core and spread goosebumps over his bare arms and legs. Bill squeezed his handbrake and his bike shuddered to a halt.

He looked up the trail and back, avoiding eye contact with

the grisly thing out in the dark water. But for now he was all alone. How could no one have seen this yet? Because of the fog? Or had some city folks just passed on by, leaving someone else to deal with it?

The sun was fully up now, igniting the high, glass buildings of Downtown with its rosy corona. Bill could feel the skyscrapers glaring over his shoulder, like a cadre of curious saints.

He steeled his resolve and looked with purpose out across the waterway. And there it was, plain as day, a hunched human form wearing a shiny pink windbreaker—bobbing gently amid the jam of debris corralled by those long, floating "trash catchers" that were attached to the legs of the bridge. They kept garbage from drifting downstream into the Theatre District.

Bill lowered his kickstand and dismounted. Then he shuffled down to the bayou on a branch off the main trail that led to a set of concrete steps and a small dock for kayakers. He walked to the water's edge, shaded his eyes and focused out into the flotsam. It was a boy not a girl, a young man with a shadow on his jaw, a tattoo on his neck, and several earrings Bill could see now in the growing light. The kid was face down, in one of those poses only struck by the lifeless, but otherwise appeared to be intact. Bill sighed and mumbled a weak prayer that only the dead and the skyscraper saints could hear.

A tiny amphibian chirped repeatedly from a patch of purple flowers along the bank to the west, where a lone butterfly also hovered in search of nectar. It made the surrounding concrete feel sterile and corrupt. He inhaled deeply, just through his nose, letting his eyelids flutter and fall. It was going to rain soon. The frog in the brush was singing for it, and Brother Bill, native to the Gulf Coast, could smell it coming on the sea breeze. He dialed 911, lamenting that it took death to make life feel this lucid.

1

TING AND THE FRANKENBIKE

When the divers pulled the kid out of the bayou, he had no ID, no keys, no drugs, just sixteen twenty-dollar bills in a cheap money clip still tucked in his jeans pocket. So he hadn't been mugged. There was also a drowned phone in the pocket of his pink windbreaker. The mass of floating debris had kept the body buoyed largely out of the water, and the guy didn't appear to be that banged-up, except for one ugly bruise that pretty well covered the right side of his face. The senior diver asserted that the fatal blow was probably struck by a drifting, cut-away piece of tree stump, which the aqua-cops had also hauled ashore for closer inspection. The thick piece of floating timber had turned the thirty-foot dive into a fatal one.

"Looks like a user. Prob'ly wandered down from Montrose all jacked up on somethin' and felt like takin' a swim," Detective Jack Lamonte surmised.

"Yeah, we'll see what he was trippin' on when we get back the tox report. Maybe sometime after Christmas," added Detective Rick Martines, only half joking.

The hayseed who'd discovered the body was a preacher. Just moved to town from Oyster Prairie, a spot in the road about fifty miles south along the coast. They jotted down his info and let him go. So they had no witnesses to the incident, and they hadn't found anything of interest along the bridge or on the banks. The obligatory data had been recorded and the officials were starting to pack it up.

Detective Lamonte was a bit surprised but also relieved by the conspicuous lack of media presence. News people could usually home in on a corpse like cadaver dogs. And here they had a Caucasian body floating in Midtown, but they'd only had to snub one low-ranked print reporter from *The Houston Rag*. A nosy little hipster chick that called herself AKK.

Scanning the scene one last time before heading back up to the car, Lamonte saw something he hadn't noticed earlier—an odd stamp of fresh graffiti on the concrete bulkhead across the bayou. Jack walked closer at an angle so he could make out the words through the bridge pillars:

Viene sus Madre
Oceana

Jack Lamonte could grunt enough Tex-Mex Spanish to get his point across in the Barrio, but he couldn't read the stuff to save his life. Pointing across the bayou, he yelled over his shoulder to his partner, "Hey Rick, what the hell does that tag say over there? Doesn't look like typical gang-banger crap."

Detective Martines was twenty yards up the levee already, leaning on a bent sapling and using a stick to scrape mud off his boot. He looked up and hollered, "Huh?"

Jack faced him. "What the hell do I keep you around for? What does that say exactly over there? Doesn't look like a typical tagger." He pointed at the mural again. He read it out loud, butchering the pronunciation.

Rick flung the stick and walked back down toward his partner, where the mud was. He saw what Jack was talking about and had plenty of time to study it in route. It was just four words and he was wearing fresh contacts. "Uh, no. Hmm, don't look like gang bangers. *Viene sus madre oceana.*"

It was muggy beyond measure and Lamonte's skin was beaded in sweat. "Well, don't just read it to me, what the hell does it mean already?"

Rick glared at his partner. "Watch yourself, *bolillo*. It's pretty simple. It says like, 'your mother the ocean is coming.' Like, maybe a warning about the climate. Rising seas or something."

Jack smirked. "So it's like some kind of doomsday garbage. Some drunk Meskin hobo tryin' to be a prophet." He shook his head and turned to go.

"Yeah, just some *mojado borracho*." Rick spat on the ground, checked his boots and then his gold watch. Time to wrap this up and go grab some lunch.

蜻蛉

With no hit on the fingerprints or matching missing-person reports, Detective Lamonte figured the quickest way to ID this kid would be the wet phone they found in the pocket of his pink windbreaker. The thing was dead but he'd inspected it and asserted that it wasn't exactly saturated. Riding atop the flotsam, it had managed to settle above the water line. Jack had palmed the device at the scene, separated it from its battery and let the two components ride back to the office on the dashboard while he blasted them with the big sedan's defroster. Now back at his desk, he set down his burrito and his giant iced tea. He pulled the phone and battery from two separate pockets of his utility trousers.

Detective Martines had his doubts. While he unwrapped his lunch—also a forearm-sized, custom burrito from one of their favorite mom-and-pop taquerias—Rick said, "This little weirdo could have aliases for all we know or warrants out for God knows what. He's got some money, nice clothes, real diamond earrings, but no ID? Ten to one he's a dealer." He glanced at his partner over his computer screen. Their desks were pushed together so that they faced each other.

Detective Lamonte gave no reaction as he reassembled the phone, set it on his desk and pressed long and hard on the power button. Then he also proceeded to unwrap his lunch.

Rick Martines was staring out the window, chewing while he continued to speculate. "Cut off from mommy and daddy, too lazy to work, time to start stealin' or dealin'."

Lamonte took a bite just as the phone beeped, and a bit of onion jettisoned from the corner of his mouth as he said, "Yes!" He chewed hastily and swallowed as the phone's tiny screen powered up. "And now, we find out who the tattooed little weirdo is." The name SEAN materialized on the screen, along with a wallpaper pic of the skinny kid they'd hauled out of the water this morning. "I'm in."

The phone was a prepaid burner any bum could buy, totally disposable, with one battery bar left, and only five people in the contacts. Lamonte selected each one and jotted the name and number on his notepad in case the phone died again. There were no saved messages or texts. So he opted to contact the service provider and passed through a level of computer speak. Then he squeezed a customer-service person on the other end of the line for a proper name, with the threat of impeding a murder investigation: The kid was Sean Dorsey, or at least that's the name he'd given when he'd set up this phone.

"Stiff's name's Sean Dorsey," Lamonte said to Martines without looking up. He made a note, hung up the phone and began to inspect it once more. Not one text or voicemail was saved on the device, which pretty well verified Martines' assumption that the kid was a dealer. Plus, the phone was a throwaway. And who only had five people listed in their contacts? Lamonte scrolled down to *Mom* and hit TALK. The area code looked like Beaumont. It only rang once before a timid woman's voice came on and asked, "Sean?"

Jack cleared his throat. "No ma'am, this is Detective Lamonte with the Houston Police. Are you the mother of a young man named Sean Dorsey?" He didn't have time to beat around the bush. "Hello? Ma'am?"

"Yes, this is Maddy Dorsey. Is there some sort of trouble?"

Boom, Lamonte had verification on the stiff's name. "Are you driving right now? You're not on the road are you?"

"Uh, no, I'm at work."

"Are you seated comfortably, with coworkers nearby, friends maybe?"

"Well." Her breath caught. "Yes."

"I'm sorry to have to tell you this, ma'am, but we believe we found your son this morning, deceased. Now it doesn't appear that he suffered or anything, and uh, we just need somebody to come in and verify his identity." Jack gave her a moment then pressed on. "And we'd like to ask you a few questions if you don't mind, when you're ready. Ma'am, are you okay?"

She exhaled. "Yes, I'm okay. And you may not understand this, but I been prayin' so hard lately. And well, I'm actually a bit relieved. He's gone to be with God now." She sobbed but Jack thought he heard laughter too.

"Honestly I do understand, ma'am." He cleared his throat. "Now, where can I send an officer to come pick you up?"

"No, no, that won't be necessary. I'll be fine. Where do I need to go?"

"It'll be safer if I send an officer to come get you, ma'am.

Please, I insist." Lamonte jotted down Madeline Dorsey's info and hung up. "Poor woman. Couldn't tell if she was sad or happy or what. Little queer's prob'ly been worryin' her sick since the day he was born."

"I can believe that," Rick intoned.

"Lives in Beaumont. She'll be down at the cooler this afternoon for an ID." Jack hit TALK again, and up came the list of most recent calls. Right below *Mom* was *Ting*, and then *Nelly*, and that was it. This list had been cleared recently too, but not entirely. Lamonte's faint unibrow furrowed. This *Ting* would be the person Sean Dorsey had last dialed before he splashed down in the bayou. Jack selected the call, noting the time it was made— roughly the same as the approximate time of death. He scrolled down and selected the next most recent call, *Nelly*, which had been placed several hours before the call to *Ting*. "Ting," Lamonte said aloud.

"Huh?" said Rick.

"Ting," Lamonte repeated. "Like *thing* but without the *H*, that's who we're callin' right now. Ting."

"Must be Chinese," Martines hypothesized.

Jack thought he heard a ring on the other end, but then the cheap little phone finally gave out for good. The detective tried to resuscitate the thing by smashing some buttons, but he soon gave up and lobbed it into his gunmetal trash can, its destiny.

Lamonte whipped his cell out of its tiny holster with his left hand and transferred it to his right. The holster on his right side housed a blue steel, semi-automatic hog leg. He dialed Ting's number from his notes, put the phone to his ear and frowned at his cooling burrito. Outside, a silky drizzle fell like a curtain across the inner city.

蛉

When Marcus heard his phone ring, he was on his *Frankenbike* (a bruiser of a cruiser cannibalized from bicycles past) skidding down a grassy trail toward the base of the levee along Buffalo Bayou near the Waugh Street Bridge. Marcus was headed to his pad in the south end of the Houston Heights—a woodsy old neighborhood that had earned its name in the great Turn of the Century Flood.

Marcus normally wouldn't answer this call, but since he was right at the bridge and it had just started to rain, he rolled up underneath Waugh Street to take a respite. He fished his phone out of his backpack right as it stopped ringing. It showed that the missed call was from Sean; and a voicemail notification popped up along with it, but the voicemail was from last night. *Hmm.*

Movement caught Marcus's eye. Up to his left, at the top of the concrete bulkhead, sat a homeless dude reading a damp newspaper. He looked up and waved at Marcus, and Marcus pointed back at him as if they knew each other, because they did.

The phone rang again. But this time Marcus didn't recognize the number, and as a general rule he didn't take calls from unknown parties (and few from known ones). He had an odd feeling about the string of digits displayed on his outdated cell. So why did he feel so compelled to answer? He hit TALK but decided to use a trumped-up baritone voice as a last-minute precaution. "Hello?"

Jack Lamonte said, "Who's speaking?"

"Well uh, you called me. So I might better ask *you* that question." Marcus's counterfeit tone rang of the late, great Robert Goulet. "Hello?"

Jack's annoyance was palpable. "This is Detective Lamonte, the police. Who is this?"

"Uh, this is Marcus uh, Washington. Is there some sort of problem?" To say he regretted taking this call now would be a severe understatement. He could kick himself.

"I need to speak to the owner of *that* phone," the high-ranking cop demanded.

"Uh, speaking."

Lamonte stopped taking notes. "You said your name was Marcus Washington."

"My name *is* Marcus Washington."

"Then who is Ting?"

"Uh, I guess, I am, also."

"What's your full legal name, Mr. Washington?"

Marcus loathed this, but you can't just hang up on the cops. They can find you. "Well, my full name is Marcus Garvey Qīngtíng Washington but—"

"Marcus Jarvey what Washington?"

Marcus repeated himself. "Qīng-tíng."

"Shine-ting?"

"Perfect."

Lamonte frowned. "What is that, Chinese or something?"

"Uh, yup."

"So, you're Chinese."

"No, I'm American," Marcus corrected.

"I mean you're an *Asian American?*"

"Uh, I guess, sort of."

"What does that mean, you guess, sort of?"

"It means I guess I am part Asian. Are you a Cauc-asian American?"

"Just shut up and answer what I ask you," Lamonte said through his teeth.

"That sounds contradictory," Marcus replied matter-of-factly.

"Just *shut* your mouth."

Some people were destined to never get along. If he could teleport this goon down here under the bridge right now, Marcus would teach him some manners.

Lamonte finished jotting some details. "Alright, now then. You there? Hello?"

"Yeah, I'm still here, shutting my mouth."

The Detective sighed. "Mr. Washington, do you go by the name Ting or what?"

"Yeah, I guess. Some people I know call me Ting."

"So why didn't you tell me your name was Ting?"

"Because I don't *know* you."

Jack Lamonte gripped his phone like a mini handgun. "Listen buddy, this is getting me nowhere. I'm gonna need you to come in so we can talk face to face." He squeezed a tiny imaginary trigger.

Marcus felt another stab of regret. "What? You need me to come in? Am I under arrest or something?"

"Why? Should you be? If you were under arrest, you'd be sitting in front of me in handcuffs right now, pal."

Pal? Marcus inhaled deeply, closing his eyes, the sound of his breathing a gently breaking surf.

"Hey! You there?" Lamonte barked on the other end of the line.

"Yeah okay, when and where do you need me to be?"

"Well, it's after noon on a weekday, are you at work?" Lamonte asked, raising his brow.

"Uh, no, but—"

"I didn't think so. Just get here, and hurry up." The Detective rattled off the address and then he added, "And don't make me come lookin' for you." Lamonte holstered his phone and reached for the tinfoil U-boat that was his lunch. Rick Martines was grinning and nodding, chewing. Jack Lamonte told him to wipe his mouth.

"Freakin' fascist," Marcus said as he zipped his phone into his pack and slung it on. He glanced up at the homeless dude, who now appeared to be asleep with his head back on the rolled-up newspaper. As Ting turned to go, a fresh tag on the concrete across the bayou caught his attention. It was weird, a purplish gray color, and it didn't look like spray paint either. *Charcoal maybe?*

Ojos del Mundo
y Sol

Marcus dug out a stray ballpoint pen and a weathered notepad from the bottom of his backpack and copied the odd graffiti. He would have to ask Jaime about it.

For now, he was more concerned about his impromptu mandatory meeting with the cops. As he stuffed his pen and pad back into his pack and slung it on, a thought came to him unbidden. *I will* not *end up like my father.* Tíng frowned. That's not something he would say. It didn't even sound like his own voice, inside his head. He took a deep, cleansing breath, letting his eyelids flutter, centering himself. Then he stepped onto the pedals and cranked the Frankenbike toward home. Hopefully at least the rain would let up.

THE FLASH 'N POLICE

The rain wasn't letting up. Marcus stared out the window at the sinking terrain. He could almost hear the weeds growing taller amid the expanding puddles across his untended yard. He sighed heavily. It was time to make a decision. Unfortunately, he knew he was going to regret whatever decision he made. It was that type of situation.

What did the cops want from him anyway? They could've at least told him that much. And if he decided to just blow them off, *would* they come looking for him like they'd threatened to? And why had they called his phone and not even known who in the heck they were calling? Way too many unknowns.

Of course, if he was in real trouble, they wouldn't have bothered to call. They would have been waiting for him at his house, right? But he hadn't done anything wrong so why were they messing with him at all? And why were the cops always such a-holes, like he was some kind of criminal, like he was their enemy? Weren't they supposed to be civil servants? Marcus could not think of one civil interlude he'd ever had with a cop.

And the thing he was trying *not* to think of right now was

burning in the back of his mind like a hot shell casing: Tíng's mother had told him long ago that it was an off-duty cop that had killed his father. Of course, it had been ruled an accidental shooting—whatever that is—and the cop had just walked away, scot-free, no penalty, his name never even released.

Marcus closed his eyes and sought the internal bottomless pool that was so often his refuge. Over the course of several deep breathing cycles, a shroud of negativity dissipated into the void, and the dancing duelist opened his eyes more resolute. He'd done nothing wrong, so there was no need to worry.

Still, he had just returned from town and he wasn't making another trip back and forth in this weather, period. There was a contest this evening at work, so he'd planned on going in early to meet up with his friend Nelly, who was a perpetual contestant. Marcus wasn't going to be late because of the whim of some badge-wearing goon with an authority complex. Normally he would just throw on some sweats, stuff his uniform into his backpack and ride the Frankenbike in to work. But this rain was set in, and the gutters were already full. Marcus didn't own a car so his best alternative would be to take the bus, which would take ten times as long. *Ugh.* At least the buses had those bike racks on the front now, so he would take the Frankenbike along in case the rain stopped. He could ride it home later.

He wondered how long the cops would detain him, and the idea of dealing with the police inside one of their compounds threatened to fluster Tíng again. What if a police dog went off on his backpack? It contained zero contraband but he didn't trust handing it over to some government enforcer for inspection. Supposedly the dirty cops carried little baggies of street drugs; a little sleight of hand and you're busted. They take your freedom, put your name in their system, and they basically own you at that point. Deep, cleansing breaths.

Okay, so he would just leave his pack here. The bigger one,

his favorite that he typically used, was still wet from his ride home anyway. He would get dressed for work here and cover up with his water-resistant Kangol and trench coat. So, no sweats, or he would burn alive on the bus ride—too many layers. His work attire would be concealed well enough by his trench coat and boots anyway.

Marcus pulled on a fiery red leotard and a sequined, form-fitting dance panel. Then around his waist he wrapped a long, gossamer sash that shimmered like the aurora. He covered up with his long coat, and then stepped into his beet-red Doc Martens boots, which rose halfway to his knees. Topped off with the Kangol, the incognito entertainer checked himself in a full-length mirror affixed to the bathroom door. Finally, he tucked a satin eye mask and a pair of matching Bloch dance sneakers into his deep coat pockets. Then he checked the mirror one last time before heading down the stairs of his garage apartment.

It was still drizzling when Marcus stepped off the bus near a dreary multi-story building that reminded him of Darth Vader's helmet. He'd passed by this place countless times but had never been inside. And he swore after today that he never would be again. He grabbed the Frankenbike off the bus's front-end bicycle carrier and scanned the area for a bike rack. There wasn't one, so he quickly chained his wheels to a smallish tree and bounded to the top of the concrete steps. He slipped through the closest pair of glass double doors and into the shelter of the foyer. And there he stopped cold when he gazed upon the gauntlet of walk-through metal detectors, each with an attending policeman.

Marcus almost bailed that instant, but the thought that some meathead might "come looking for him" made him stay. A couple of cops were already checking him out anyway and he didn't have anything that would set off a metal detector except for a key, a phone, and a bill clip. So Marcus put these objects in the plastic bowl and passed through the ominous, rectangular portal, greatly relieved when the thing dinged instead of buzzed.

He was going for his things when a large officer with a portable weapon scanner held up his hand, looked directly at Marcus, and said, "Stop." The cop finished passing his wand all around some woman's vital areas and told her to go ahead. Then he pointed at Marcus and said, "Now you." The enforcer employed the beckoning-index-finger and said, "Come here."

The condescension made Tíng's cheeks tingle as he approached.

"You need to leave the trench coat on the hooks over by the entrance."

Marcus politely replied, "But I just passed through that metal detector."

The big-boned officer didn't debate with civilians. "If you're coming in here, then you remove the trench coat, and leave it in the foyer." The beefy lad pointed over to the long row of hooks, laden with all manner of dripping community apparel. He gripped his handheld metal detector as if it doubled as a truncheon.

The mock flames on Marcus's hidden bodysuit threatened to kindle for real. He had a mask and sneakers that he needed for work tucked in the pockets of this trench coat, and he didn't want to just leave it heaped over there with everybody else's wet stuff. He took a deep breath and tried to relax. "Well, I guess I'll just come back some other time then." He smiled and turned for the door.

"Wait a minute." The cop caught the potential suspect by the sleeve.

Marcus froze and fought hard the urge to remove the dude's hand from his person.

The official commanded, "Turn around," and he tugged to help Marcus comply. "Why are you in such a hurry to leave now?" The incident was becoming a spectacle.

Marcus couldn't think of an acceptable answer and the cop didn't wait. He released Marcus's sleeve while he recited something about Homeland Security, moved his hand to his sidearm, unsnapped the holster, and ordered the possible perp to slowly remove his trench coat.

Tíng had a vision of himself in flight, just bolting for the exit. He knew he would have ten cops after him by the time he got to the parking lot, but he also knew they still couldn't catch him. Eventually though, they would track him down. Marcus was on a half-dozen cameras by now and this little exhibition was attracting more and more attention, exactly the opposite of what he'd intended. As it stood, Tíng was not charged with a crime. If he fled, that would likely change.

Marcus sighed, tugged down the brim of his hat, unbuttoned his coat, and by the time he pulled it off, the cop was snorting. "I can see why you wanted to keep your coat on. Nice tights, buddy!"

Marcus kept his eyes forward and disregarded the catcalls that ensued. A few swine spouted homophobic insults, which he tried to ignore, lest he become angry and raze a human path to the exit. He asked flatly, "Can I keep the hat?"

The guard ran his wand around Marcus's Kangol from several different angles then said, "Yeah, I guess."

No point in leaving now, he was famous. Marcus retrieved his metallic objects from the bowl, and then hiked back down to the foyer to hang up his trench coat, hoping it would still be there upon his return. He snapped his key into his bill clip, tucked his phone into his sash, and bravely marched back into the compound.

Upon Marcus's return, the beefy cop smirked and directed him to a wall of reception windows, about half of which were shuttered, and the rest staffed with uniformed attendants. As the dancing duelist walked over and got in the shortest line, he heard a few more bursts of laughter and crude attempts at humor as he made his way to the window though inwardly, the jokers were awed by Tíng's physique.

Marcus stepped to the window as the done-up female officer on the other side finished her paperwork from the previous offender. Stimulated by the emerging brightness in her peripheral, she looked up, raised her penciled eyebrows, and smirked. Marcus could see her oppressive little mind working behind her bifocals. He braced himself.

"Oh my gawd, it's *The Flash!* We haven't seen you in a while, hun. You lookin' for work?" She said it loud and everybody within earshot, officials and detainees, shared a fresh hoot at Marcus's expense. She had to get a high five from the girl at the next window before she settled back into her chair.

Marcus said, "Uh, I have an appointment with a Detective Lamonte."

She looked him up and down and smacked her gum. "I was just foolin' with you, sweetie. I do love a man in tights. You want the third floor." She took his ID, swiped it, gave him a printed adhesive pass with his picture on it, and directed him to a group of elevators.

A directory on the third floor listed Detectives Lamonte and Martines as both occupying 343. *Okay.* Marcus followed the numbers down a long hallway and his presence only inspired a couple of doubletakes, not too bad, classier folks up here. So despite what had just happened downstairs, he was determined that this meeting, whatever it was about, would transpire in a positive and courteous manner.

343 was open so he knocked lightly on the jamb and stepped inside. Both detectives were at their desks on their computers and when they looked up, Jack and Rick thought they were the victims of a prank.

Marcus said, "I can see by your name plate you're the man I need to see." He smiled and stuck his hand out to Lamonte, who neither moved nor said anything. The detective appeared to be waiting for the punchline to a bad joke. Pointing to his adhesive pass, Marcus continued, "As you can see by my name tag, I'm—"

"I don't get it," Lamonte interrupted. "What the hell are you supposed to be, The Human Flame?"

"Human Flamer," Detective Rick Martines intoned, and Lamonte had to laugh.

Marcus's outstretched hand fell. "Right. I'm Marcus Washington." He jabbed his thumb once more at his printed adhesive pass. "You guys called me in here for some unknown reason."

Jack had been wondering if *Ting* was going to show up. "Really? You sounded a lot different on the phone. Look Detective Martines, it's Ting. But he don't *know* us, so to us it's Marcus Washington."

Ting had a vision of himself escaping again. There was a tall pine tree outside the window that he could easily shimmy down. These two goons would fall like dominoes. He shook off the idea.

"Shut the door, Ching," Lamonte ordered.

There were four bulky, uncomfortable steel chairs lined up along the wall beside the entrance. With no wasted movement, Marcus shut the heavy door and then snatched up a chair as he whirled around and placed it six feet closer to the cops' desks. He was seated within a couple of seconds. The abrupt display of graceful strength caused Lamonte to put his hand on his sidearm. Martines sat up straight in his reclining office chair, kicking his feet up off the floor as a counterweight, since his torso was much heavier than his legs.

The smile on Marcus's face was joyless. "Ching, Ting, Marcus, it's all the same to me. So you gentlemen have some questions for me?"

Lamonte was formulating some kind of warning when Martines started in, "Yeah, first of all, why the hell are you dressed up like that?"

Here we go. "Right. This is sort of, like, my uniform. I'm on my way in to work."

Jack was aghast. "You go to work dressed like that?"

"What, do you work at a gay bar or somethin'?" Rick added. The two partners shared a chuckle.

"I dance at a night club. Everybody's gotta make a buck, right? I ain't no 'Fortunate Son'."

Lamonte got the Creedence reference and regarded Marcus more seriously. "Right. So where exactly do you work?"

"Um, The Fallout Shelter."

"The Fallout Shelter over there off Montrose?" Martines asked.

"Yup, that's the one."

Jack glared at Rick. Then turned his attention back to Marcus. "So, did you work last night?"

"Yes," Tíng said cautiously.

Lamonte drew a horizontal line across his notepad, jotted something down and then continued. "So how long have you known Sean Dorsey?"

"Who?"

"Don't play dumb, *Thing.* We know you spoke to him last night."

"What are you talking about? You mean—" Marcus stopped. *Sean Dorsey.* He had a message from Sean and he'd been so flustered earlier that he hadn't even checked it yet. And Tíng didn't want to premier any unknown voicemails in front of these two axe-grinders.

Lamonte was studying Marcus's body language, looking for a tell, a tick.

The dancing duelist carefully began again. "Right, Sean. I'm pretty sure his last name *is* Dorsey. I was at work pretty late last night. I saw him there. We said what's up. That's about it."

"On the phone, dipshit, what did you two talk about on the phone?"

"The phone? Wait a minute, what did you call me?"

Jack shook his head. "Uh-uh, we ask the questions. Anyway it's all the same to you, remember, Ching?"

Ting bit his tongue. Detective Jack wanted him angry, wanted him to do something stupid, to confess to something. Marcus took a deep cleansing breath.

Lamonte frowned as he watched Ting relax and refocus. "We got your pal Sean's cell phone. You were the last one he called before we confiscated it."

"Confiscated it? Where *is* Sean? You guys got him locked up? Is he okay?"

"Why don't *you* tell *us* if he's okay? You know, the more you act stupid, the more I think you got somethin' to hide. So what time *exactly* did you leave work last night?"

"I don't know exactly, probably close to three? We were pretty busy."

The cops shared a knowing look. Jack jotted down a note.

Marcus didn't want to give these two any more of his personal data. Nor did he want to get Sean into more trouble than he already seemed to be in, but two things compelled Ting to cooperate: First, he had to know if Sean was alright. And second, he didn't do whatever it was they were trying to make him admit to.

Lamonte had just asked Marcus a question and was waiting for a response. "Hello, Chang, you in there? What, are you high or somethin'?"

Without looking down Marcus whipped his phone out of his sash and both cops flinched.

"Take it easy. It's just my phone. I *didn't* talk to Sean on it last night, but I got a late voice message notification I haven't checked yet. I miss a lot of calls on this thing for whatever reason." Marcus dialed his voicemail, put the phone on speaker and laid it on the edge of Jack's desk.

Rick frowned at the battered, outdated device and said, "Man, that's your problem. Why don't you upgrade to a—"

Jack shushed his partner.

The automated voice announced that there was one *new* message, which pretty well verified Marcus's story about not having listened to it yet. Sean's phone had been so low-tech that it didn't differentiate actual conversations from voicemails on the recent calls list. Lamonte took note; the call had been received at 2:37 a.m. "Ting, what's up man? I had to run down the street to pick something up, but—" There were traffic sounds, a horn. Sean sounded winded and a little frantic. "Damn! I think I might need some help, bro. Call me back." And that was it. The automated voice came back on and said there were no more messages.

"Play it again," Jack ordered. "What was he going to pick up? And what did he need help with?"

"I don't know. Maybe he was in some sort of a jam."

"Yeah, ya think? Most people call the police when they're in a jam."

"Not anybody that I know."

"Yeah, and *look at you.*"

Ting almost warned Jack to watch his mouth. The crew-cut detective probably lived for altercations, but this one would be quite different.

Lamonte produced a small digital recorder and placed it on the desk near the phone. Marcus noticed a green light on the device that indicated it had already been taping before it came out of Jack's shirt pocket. "Play it again."

This time when he played it, Marcus focused in on the message, trying to isolate and identify each individual sound, from the blaring car stereos and droning engines passing by in the background, to the unsettling words of his panicked friend. At one point, he thought he heard a deep voice shouting something unintelligible from a distance, buried within the automobile noise.

The detectives didn't register it. Rick was using a long frilly toothpick from a former club sandwich to dislodge something apparently stuck near his larynx. Jack was doodling the symbol for infinity on his notepad, but then he added nipples to it. When the message ended for the second time, Marcus reached down and pushed END.

Jack put down his pen and sighed. "I suppose you didn't speak to him again after that?"

"No. I already told you that. So, you guys have his phone. Do you have *him* too? Is he okay?"

"You just hush up 'til I tell you to speak." Jack glanced at his notes. "So how long have you two known each other?"

"Seriously? Probably about six months or so. *Is he okay?*"

"That can't be confirmed yet."

"Can't be confirmed? What the heck does—"

"We ask the questions, Tang! I'm not gonna say it again!" Jack waited a moment for Marcus to retaliate. "So why did he call *you* of all people? Y'all boyfriends or somethin'?"

Martines chuckled but played it off as a cough.

Marcus was looking out the window at the pine tree again, breathing deeply. "No. We already covered this. We're just friends. And like I said, we're not even that close. I'm pretty sure he's from out of town. He's only been a regular in the club for like six months or something."

Martines chimed in, "So where's he been stayin'?"

"How should I know? I think he stays here and there. He's a cute kid and he plays it kind of loose. I heard him mention The Lamp Post once. I doubt if he has trouble finding places to crash."

"Yeah, I bet." Jack scoffed. "So, The Lamp Post, that's a pretty classy hotel. Where's he get the bread to stay there? Accordin' to the IRS, he's got zero income."

Marcus thought he detected envy in Jack's voice. "I don't know. It's none of my business how people shake up their cash."

"So you buy drugs from this kid?" Martines interjected.

"What? No. When did we start talking about drugs?"

"You think we're stupid?" Jack spat. "I know there's tons of drug traffic in those freaky after-hours clubs. And I'm bettin' y'all are involved. Maybe he's a fresh junkie on the scene. Maybe he's a dealer. Maybe he sampled some bad shit, lost his mind, and jumped off that bridge. Or maybe you ran down there and threw him off in some kind of lover's quarrel. You look like a strong fella."

"Bridge? What bridge? Is Sean dead? Is that why we're playing this stupid game?" Marcus's hands and feet were buzzing. Challenging a cop was dangerous but he was sick of this. "This is bullcrap. Answer me or arrest me. Otherwise I'm outta here." He stood and picked up his phone.

Jack studied Marcus's eyes and said, "We fished your buddy Sean out of Buffalo Bayou this morning. Just got a positive on his ID. He took a dive off the Sabine Street Bridge and hit a log."

Marcus was stolid. He wasn't going to show emotion in front of these two. Tíng had some questions of his own for the Detectives, but he wouldn't get any answers here on their turf. For now he was just glad they appeared to be done with him. Jack ordered him not to leave town until this was settled, whatever that meant. He allowed Marcus to keep his phone and told him he'd better answer if they called it.

Tíng wasn't that far down the hall when Lamonte said to his partner, "He's guilty of bein' queer for sure, but I wouldn't peg him as a killer. We got no motive, no witness, no weapon. No crime. I'll prob'ly call this *Nelly* person, but I think Tang was our prime suspect based on the timeline."

"Yup," Martines said, disinterested, pecking at his desktop keyboard.

Still turned in his seat, looking at the empty doorway, Jack said, "I never seen a high-yella Chinese before, kinda ironic."

"Prob'ly got some o' that Creole blood," Rick theorized.

Fresh jeers bounced off like balloons as Tíng barged back through the heavily guarded lobby, trying to sort all this out in his head. His trench coat was heaped on the foyer floor and appeared to have been stepped on, but he was just glad it was still here. He picked it up and shook it off, self-absorbed, when a girl rushed up the steps and busted through the nearest entryway.

She paused on the black rubber doormat, half closed her umbrella and tossed it into the corner. Her strawberry blond bangs were damp and spiraled down past her light eyes, framing her cheeks and lips in thick, wavy strands.

Her gaze wandered from Marcus's head to his feet and then back again. Her grin was devious. He smiled back at her, but it faded when he saw his flaming image reflected in the glass door that swung shut behind her. She passed by him within inches, raised her eyebrows and said, "Wow. You goin' out to fight some crime, or what?"

Marcus blushed, his nervous system running a continuity check as he shrugged on his fouled trench coat. "I.... " He shook his head, trying to formulate a response but his interview with the detectives still ruled his thoughts. "I guess it's possible," he finally uttered.

She frowned and said, "Oh-kay." They eyed each other pensively for just a moment before she strode away into the lobby.

The dancing duelist faced his reflection in the exit door made of steel and heavy glass. He kicked the thing open and strode out into dreary daylight, details of his interrogation surfacing in his mind. *Sean wasn't suicidal.* The dude had been totally in control and having a good time when Marcus had seen him last night. And what about that creepy voice in the background of the voice-mail? The message warranted further scrutiny for sure.

Tíng moved to the tree at the edge of the police compound where he'd chained up his wheels. At least the rain was letting up. He shook the Frankenbike, dispersing hundreds of water droplets. Then he dried the seat off with his sleeve and rode the short distance to the Sabine Street Bridge.

蛉

Ten minutes later, Marcus hopped off the Frankenbike at the bottom of the levee on the north side of Sabine Street along Buffalo Bayou. He walked underneath, scanning the floating debris and looking along the banks. This was useless. The cops had probably gone over the place with a fine-toothed comb. Tíng's eyes wandered to the empty park bench beneath the live oak at the top of the levee, and it struck him: *Where's Farah been this whole time?*

Farah pretty much lived here. If anybody had seen what happened on the bridge that night, it would be her. Marcus extended his visual search, three-hundred-sixty degrees, up both levees and as far up and down the bayou as he could see, but she wasn't here. It would be dark soon and he started to worry a little. Hopefully she was okay.

Marcus picked up the Frankenbike and was about to ride away when a tag on the concrete across the bayou caught his attention. *Another one.* It appeared to be done in the same hand as the mural under the Waugh Street Bridge. It reminded him of something Jaime might have done, back when he could get around better.

VIENE SUS MADRE
OCEANA

Marcus didn't have his pen and pad so he took a picture of it with his phone. He stared at the mural a moment longer. Then he stashed his phone in his trench coat pocket and cruised to work in the failing light. It was a contest night, so Big Nelly would be coming in early too.

3

TRANSALVATION

The Fallout Shelter had been a rundown warehouse space for a decade and a half before a savvy local couple had realized its provincial potential within the current Montrose vibe. One a successful artist and the other a restauranteur, the partners had transformed the old building into an icon.

The structure sat under a grove of Mexican fan palms that had been planted when the place was built. The artist owner had painted the metal exterior drab green and dotted it with dozens of "radioactive" trefoils of various size and color. From a distance the array appeared to be a field of multicolored flowers. At the front entrance sat an inoperable WWII-era aircraft searchlight, engulfed by pink bougainvillea. The entire lot was ringed with honeysuckle, climbing over unchecked clumps of pittosporum and azalea. The place could be an embassy for some sassy banana republic.

Inside, evenly spaced across the floor, were twelve structural iron poles, one of which, near the center of the room, was chromed. Furniture was minimal and bolted down. The place was ninety-percent dance floor and the lighting was pretty much black or neon, except for what was rigged above the stages. The eleven non-chromed poles were padded up to a height of about six feet, with that coarse gray felt used to pad homemade speaker boxes, and painted in various bright colors to minimize collisions.

The two elevated stages sat side by side, almost touching, out on the slab floor. The larger stage was for feature acts, typically males dressed as females, lip-syncing to hit songs by pop divas. The smaller stage was closer to table-sized, and the solo chromed pole in the joint ran through its center. This chromed pole belonged to Tíng on most nights.

When Marcus had first started at The Shelter, he'd still been freshly mourning the death of his mother, who'd taught him dance in his youth. An insomniac in need of income, he had responded to an ad paying cash for a *skilled dancer / nights / nonstripping gig*. Tíng had gotten the call for an interview, given a solo performance, and the rest was history. Early on, his work attire had consisted mostly of athletic gear, combined with accessories borrowed from The Fallout Shelter's stockpile, mainly hats, hoods, or sunglasses to obscure his face.

The modest wage he earned on the books paid his minimalist bills, and the tips he collected from the plastic jug passed around his stage, he mostly stashed. Over time, Marcus learned to play to the crowd, investing in brilliant bodysuits, capes, boas, and sequins, and choreographing with feature acts on the big stage. But he was always masked in some way, not so much to shield his identity as to provide a barrier between the public and Tíng's sensitive psyche.

By default, Marcus had also become The Shelter's peacekeeper. More than once he'd earned extra C-notes by descending from his stage to remove perpetrators of thuggish behavior from the premises. Among longtime patrons of The Fallout Shelter, Tíng's proficiency in the martial arts was legendary. And now with Big Nelly on the scene as well, the club never had that kind of trouble anymore. Almost.

Nelson Riley made a pretty good Cher despite the extra couple hundred pounds and foot of height. He was the proprietor of a small but prestigious construction company by the light of day, but late nights, in The Fallout Shelter, he was Big Nelly. And tonight his cavernous lungs and boyish pipes would power through *Believe* and leave hardly a dry eye in the place. Few contestants actually sang. Most lip-synced and hoped their style and choreography would carry them. But when Nelly took the stage, the DJ knew to turn his mike on, turn the gain down, and let him resonate.

Tonight, Cher would have been proud. And on the chromed pole, Marcus did his best to incarnate Nelly's words with his body (as he did for all the acts). The dancing duelist ascended the twenty-foot shaft and spiraled back down with supernatural grace, attached, at times, by a single hand or foot as if magnetized, eliciting gasps from the crowded dance floor.

When the zero-sum contest was over and the little paper ballots were being tabulated in the office, everyone on the floor was ready to get live, and the DJ spun a remix of *Wolf Like Me*. Ting grabbed his tip jug and performed an aerial over the heads of a throng of admirers to exit his stage. Then he slipped away through the crowd.

At the north end of the club, the main bar was a wide semicircle, encompassing a semi-cylinder wall, decked with neon alcohol propaganda all the way up to the high ceiling. Marcus hopped behind the bar and vanished through a set of spring-loaded double doors emblazoned with EMPLOYEES ONLY. He passed through liquor storage into a small bathroom with a deadbolt lock. Opposite the toilet was a sturdy wooden ladder affixed to the wall and painted the same shade of invisible gray. Marcus climbed through a square hole of absent ceiling tiles and stepped up onto a carpeted plywood floor.

This island of semicircular attic contained racks of costumes and trunks of accessories, a sofa, a coffee table, a battered armoire, a coat rack, and a giant, curved wall-mirror covered with stickers from local shops and bands. Overhead, steel beams and conduits sprayed with cellulose insulation framed a short iron ladder that accessed the roof. Employees of The Fallout Shelter called this space the Panic Room. It was the place where Marcus changed costumes, stretched, meditated and clocked his tips. $187 cash plus his hourly wage was plenty for the night, so he decided to just leave his empty tip jug up here.

Ting traded his dance sneakers for his oxblood Doc Martens boots, which fit his feet like soft leather gloves. He grabbed his trench coat from the rack, shrugged it on and buttoned it up to his chin. Then he removed his mask and stuffed it into his coat pocket. Marcus popped on his wool Kangol, pulled down the brim and dropped back down the hole, leaving the Panic Room behind. He rendezvoused with Ian behind the bar, who gave him a couple of hundreds for his $187 in smaller bills. Marcus stuffed the C-notes deep into his coat pocket and headed toward Nelly's table.

妗

Bill Cox felt a bit like Alice walking around in The Fallout Shelter, this big loud colorful place where people fearlessly, even ferociously, expressed themselves. He'd done a lot of networking today and affirmed that there was plenty of work to do for a pious man in this sprawling human experiment God had created. But for now it was time to exult. The anonymity of the city washed over Bill like a cool baptism.

Marcus wasn't the only one in The Shelter who'd flagged Bill as a tourist. Nelly was also keeping an eye on the skinny hayseed wandering around with the perma-grin. As Bill passed near their table, Nelly intoned, "Check out the new Ken doll. Poor Barbie."

Marcus added, "Looks like the victim of a tragic tanning bed malfunction." Bill's skin was peeling in little patches here and there, making him appear splotchy under the black lights.

Having wandered back to the bar, the country clergyman was crunching the last piece of ice from his cup when one of his new friends offered to buy him another drink. Bill politely refused and when he shook his head, it felt kind of fuzzy. He frowned at the numbers on his digital watch, which were hard to decipher for some reason, and after several seconds he confirmed that holy cow it *was* after midnight.

Bill felt like he'd gone through a time warp. He couldn't believe he'd gotten so tipsy nursing two fruity drinks, but he thought it more comical than perilous. The bartender must think him a total lightweight. Ian had offered to call him a ride twice. He obviously assumed Bill had a car to drive, which would be dangerous. Luckily with the proximity of his new flat, Bill was on foot. He wanted to tell Ian bye and thanks again but the fellow was terribly busy.

Bill Cox walked out in the general direction which he thought he lived, cutting across the parking lot to save time and losing his course as he weaved through the rows of sleeping automobiles. Jeez, these folks stayed out late. The lot was fuller now than it had been when he'd gotten here. Finally, he reached an open area in the back and headed for a gap in the sprawling, vine-covered azaleas. But Bill never made it to the sidewalk.

A white van rolled up and parked along the curb. The passenger and driver hopped out, but left the motor running like they had a quick task to perform. The two gents had close-cropped, bleach-blond hair, pale complexions, and either they wore eye makeup or they were seriously hollow eyed. Side by side they marched through the gap in the hedge, forcing Bill back into the lot. He staggered to the side and rotated his torso to avoid a collision, but he tapped the larger man's arm, which was jutting out. Bill's hand was batted forcefully away before he could apologize.

"Did you just touch me, you homo?"

Bill gasped when he saw the big man had a *mouthful of pointed teeth*.

Both he and his friend were powerfully built. One was about Bill's height and the other even taller. And they were circling him now, like a pair of coyotes. The country boy could barely hear people talking beyond the parked cars at the entrance of the club. Maybe he should scream for help. If he could just work his way closer to those voices.

Bill swiveled left, trying to keep the smaller man in sight as he babbled, "I just moved here and I think I may have had too much to drink."

The goon was shaking his head. "Sshh, you done messed up, fag boy."

Oh God, more fangs. "Help me!" Bill shouted toward The Fallout Shelter, but the bigger man was on him. The skinny clergyman threw his hands up, but it was a feeble parry and a stiff sucker punch slammed Bill's own hand against the side of his head. Starbursts appeared in his vision, his knees buckled, and his ears rang as he went down, semi-conscious and oddly thankful that he was drifting away from the nightmare creature who'd just clobbered him.

The fanged menace was laughing at his fallen victim, and was about to give him the boots. But the creep froze abruptly and snapped to his left, his face contorting into a mask of confusion and revulsion.

The fiend cocked back and threw a wicked left hook meant to connect with a person, who had charged in to join the fray. Bedecked in dark red boots, colorful tights, and a matching eye mask, the flamboyant newcomer ducked the punch with ease, and transitioned into a leg sweep that flipped the assailant onto his head and shoulders. The monster popped off the ground like a spring. But before he could defend, the fabulous fighter put the finishing snap on a spinning front kick aimed at the goon's chest. The sound of boot compressing ribcage caused approaching spectators to wince and utter expletives. The receiver stumbled backward from the force of the blow, bounced off an SUV, and fell onto all fours, gasping through his pointed choppers.

The other creep pulled a knife from his boot, and the foggy-headed Brother Cox tried to shout a warning. Then a shadow swept over the downed clergyman, cast by giant Cher. She caught the shank-wielder from behind, below his armpits with her manicured meat hooks, spun her great torso, and flung the smaller man through the air. Bystanders shrieked and jumped out of the creep's flight path before he was finally grounded by a Jeep several yards away. The four-by-four's roll bar hummed from the impact, and the goon went down in a heap.

Tíng slapped hands with Big Nelly. "Word. Thanks." *Even though I was about to smoke that fool.*

A spotlight swept the formerly indoor mob as an HPD cruiser lit up in the boulevard and then chirped its siren twice as it whipped into the parking lot. The melee had become a spectacle, as was always the case, and now dozens of people were trying to hustle back inside the club. The patrol car stopped in a position blocking the driveway. Then two uniforms dismounted and strode toward the fleeing crowd.

The two thugs with the fangs recovered enough to scramble back to their vehicle. Through a gap in the hedge, Marcus saw them tear away in a big, white, work van with a FISH decal on the lower left rear door. Tíng removed his mask and grabbed his hat and coat off the roof of a nearby sedan.

The lump on Bill's head throbbed and the corner of his right eye was swollen, but at least his vision overall was clearing. Marcus materialized, unmasked and wearing his hat and coat, looked down at Brother Cox and asked him where he lived. Bill frowned. "Uh, I live, over that way?" He pointed toward Downtown.

The cops were barking commands and infiltrating the mob beyond the barricade of parked cars. Marcus and Nelly each took an arm, hauled Bill to his feet, and walked casually away from the flashing lights. The dancing duelist said, "We can't get you home if you don't know where you live. Can you call somebody?"

Bill felt for his new smartphone, but then left it in his pocket. "Uh, nobody that lives in Houston."

"At least you know what town you're in. Where are your keys?" Nelly asked.

Bill opened his mouth to answer but could only shake his head; giant Cher was a man.

Marcus pulled out Bill's meager set of keys. "Do you not have a car?"

"Uh, nope."

Ting extracted the dude's wallet and flipped it open. A photo ID was mounted in a clear plastic window. "William Lee Cox from Oyster Prairie, Texas."

Bill felt a bit like he was being mugged, but he knew the odd pair of gents who held him had just saved his bacon and were still trying to help him out. Plus they could easily tear him apart, so he just went along with it.

Nelly could see over the tops of the cars. He sighed and said that his ride was not a good option thanks to the mob, and the road-blocking police car. As they walked, Bill dragged his feet less and less. He asked, "Why can't I just walk over there and talk to the police?"

"I wouldn't if I were you," Nelly said. "Those two are a couple of hard-asses and they're not gonna leave here empty-handed. They're gonna bust somebody."

Marcus elucidated as they walked, "Fighting at a bar is a sure way to get arrested, especially if you're drunk. Fights in public places lead to mob mentality and riots. It makes cops edgy and pissed off when they see a rowdy crowd of people in a parking lot, especially at a place where alcohol is served. They're gonna want somebody's head. And you're the only guy out here with a big shiner, too wasted to walk straight, who doesn't know where he lives. Trust me, you do not want HPD to provide you with temporary lodging."

The cops were shining their lights out into the parked cars where a detained kid was pointing. Nelly ducked and Marcus sighed. They couldn't just hide this poor guy out here and hope for the best. And trying to smuggle him back inside past the cops was too risky. The side door was locked from the inside, and Marcus wasn't going to go bang on it. A cab would have trouble entering this parking lot right now, and it would draw more attention, plus where would they go? Nelly was looking around for a place to stash Bill like a piece of contraband.

Marcus said, "We need to just get him out of here. He won't survive Harris County drunk tank."

Nelly shrugged. "How?"

"Screw it. Let's just head for the bike rack. I'll take him out the back way, if you could just stand him up on my pegs. The show's over anyway."

Nelly scoffed. "Dude, what if he falls off?"

"Then I'll stash him in a dumpster or something." Marcus smirked.

"Wait, what?" Bill chimed in.

They strolled from the cover of the parked cars, and slipped behind the northwest corner of The Fallout Shelter. The bike rack held only one sinister flat-black cruiser with knobby tires and two sets of wheel pegs, front and rear. Bill was apprehensive. If he understood correctly, he was about to escape the police by riding tandem on a one-person bicycle, off into the night with this fellow in a trench coat with lustrous tights underneath. He was having some doubts.

"So where's the other guy then!" a voice echoed from around the corner. The police had seen an outdoor mob at an after-hours club and they wanted the instigators.

"I won't fall off. I can do this," Bill said, willing himself sober.

Nelly grabbed the yokel under the armpits and helped him onto the Frankenbike's rear pegs. Bill placed his hands on the shoulders of Marcus, who was already in riding position, stabilizing the bike. Tíng asked, "So who were those Nazi dirtbags anyway?"

Big Nelly shook his head. "Wannabee vampire weirdos? I've never seen 'em before. But I bet they don't come back here either." He pinched Bill on the cheek. "Now get going and take this little hayseed home." He adjusted his wig and sauntered away to befuddle the authorities.

"Hang on tight," Marcus said over his shoulder. Then he stepped into the pedals and nearly left Bill on his rump. The country boy bent his knees and dug his nails into Tíng's trench coat. They rode a low wheelie for several yards, until a gear clicked in the back axle and the front tire finally descended onto the concrete. They flew off the curb onto a dark street and broke left. Bill tried to look back for flashing lights but got vertigo and had to face forward again. Another clack in the axle sounded-off third gear. Bill didn't know where they were going, but they were going there fast.

The pair of troopers turned their heads to look in unison when Cher appeared from around the corner of the Fallout Shelter, only she was built like a pro lineman. She feigned that she had only just arrived. "Oh no. Have I missed the party?"

The Frankenbike rolled through a sleeping residential area and crossed some railroad tracks without meeting a single car. The rushing night air was rejuvenating, and Bill could judge by the skyline that they were traveling generally north. Marcus rode straight through a T-intersection and across a patch of manicured turf between two high-rises. They crossed a sidewalk on the other side then dropped off another curb. Bill choked down a scream as his feet nearly came off the pegs.

They sped across a wide, deserted parkway, and Marcus steered straight through a break in the opposite curb. The cruiser's tires fell into a well-cut trail descending at an angle through a patch of tall bloodweed, and at the bottom they met another sidewalk, nearly perpendicular to their course. Marcus leaned hard on the heavy bicycle, and the rear knobby chirped as it caught traction on the concrete.

When Bill opened his eyes, he could see the shimmering surface of a bayou down on their right. Considering their rate of acceleration, he wondered if someone might be chasing them after all. Another ping sounded, and their speed leveled off. The path climbed, fell, and veered from left to right. Bill thought about jumping off a couple times, but there's no way he could run this fast right now. Plus, he might collide with a tree or park bench or something. He leaned forward and said, "Uh, this should be good. You can just let me off anywhere."

"Do you know where you are?" Marcus asked over his shoulder. He didn't even seem out of breath.

"No, but I remember where I live now. I just moved here. I have an apartment." Bill was ecstatic that he could suddenly remember his new address.

"That's way off in the other direction. Just hang on a minute. You don't want to get off here in the middle of the night. We're almost to my place. If you want, you can catch a cab from there," Marcus called back.

Five minutes later they were in an old neighborhood with big trees that blocked out the skyline, so Bill lost his sense of direction. They rode into an alley paved with sun-bleached oyster shell, and choked with dark heaps of debris and sprawling vines. The passage was shadowed by trees, but the bright shell terrain gave off a pearly luminescence underfoot. Marcus steered under a massive oak to their right, and the Frankenbike finally came to a stop. The driver said hop off and Brother Bill said amen.

They passed through a tall gate that seemed to be wrought entirely of creepers, and into a big yard that was darker than the ambient night, shrouded by untrimmed trees and surrounded by a barrier of towering bamboo. Ting leaned the Frankenbike against the wall. Then he led Bill into his garage apartment through the side door, and turned on a hanging lamp with a red wicker shade. There were two wide garage doors, and room enough for three or four modern cars inside, but this wasn't a garage anymore. The slab was covered in hardwood, though it was a creaky, patchwork job. And the walls were hung with shafts of colorful cloth adorned with Asian symbols and paintings of cranes, tigers, and craggy landscapes. There was a low orange couch along the opposite wall.

The décor inspired Bill to say, "It's a dojo. I love it."

"Thanks." Marcus pointed to the couch. "You want to sit down? Call a cab or something?"

"Yes. Okay." Bill ambled over, plopped down, and fatigue sat in his lap. He touched the lump on the side of his head and realized his hand, which had also been punched, was sore too. He pulled out his phone without much resolve and struggled to make out the characters as they morphed on the touch screen. "Oof, I feel weird again. What do they put in those fruity red drinks? I been havin' trouble readin' things tonight."

Marcus was busy across the room in his kitchenette. He rummaged around in his little refrigerator, hung up his hat, and approached with an ice-gel pack. Bill flinched as his new friend pressed the thing to the side of his face, saying, "Hold this on there for a while." Bill took hold of it with his sore hand, chilling his hand and head at once. Marcus studied him a moment and said, "Your pupils look way too dilated. Did you leave your drink sitting around?"

"Sittin' around?"

"At the club, your drink, did you let it out of your sight, even for a little while?"

Bill was pensive. "Well, yeah. I mean I don't remember specifically but—"

"Then you might have been drugged. Maybe some dirtbag slipped you something when you weren't looking. Adrenaline snapped you out of it for a little while, but it's getting back on top of you. Never leave your drink sitting around. And if you do, dump it out. You're in Houston. It's a big city. You gotta use your head." Marcus sighed. "Seriously though, we haven't had any trouble like that in forever. Tonight was just weird."

Bill looked overwhelmed.

"Look, you're safe right now. Why don't you just quit while you're ahead and crash here tonight." Marcus could hardly believe he'd said it.

Bill gave up on his phone and sat back. "Okay, yeah, that's probably a good idea."

Marcus grabbed him by the arm and said, "Come on, you'll sleep better up here. There's a bathroom and stuff." He fairly dragged Bill up a stairway, and then down a short hallway into a room with wood-paneled veneer, plush old carpet, a dresser, and a futon. Bill sat down and Marcus handed him a chilled mug.

Bill puzzled over its manifestation. "What's this?"

"It's herbal tea. Try it. It'll settle your stomach and help you sleep."

"It smells kinda like a Christmas tree."

Marcus smiled and nodded.

The tea was pretty good, and it was cold. Bill realized how thirsty he was and slugged it down. Marcus took the mug, assured his guest he was totally safe here, and then headed back downstairs. Bill managed to kick off his shoes before he passed out.

4

CLINGY COUNTRY CLERGY

Jake Bontemps, barefoot as always, picked out a dozing Brahma cow with a ghastly set of horns and smacked her on the flank. Billy Cox didn't wait to see her reaction, and the two blood brothers dashed down the long, gentle slope toward the old railroad trestle over Switch Cane Creek. They laughed as the mama cow bellowed and snorted somewhere behind them. Billy had a fresh coppertop mushroom in his belly. Jake had two.

They tiptoed out to the middle of the long-retired bridge and lay down on their backs on the scrap plywood they'd nailed there a while ago. Not too far away, a pack of coyotes sang an unsettling song of capture and feast.

"How do you know when they're workin'?"

"Just give it a little while. You'll know."

So Billy waited, and after a while he started to yawn. Then he realized Jake was right. He did know. Because up above, the story of the universe was playing out, and at its culmination was the rise of humanity. In the night sky, Billy Cox saw age-old prejudices eroded away by education, pain that he would help to heal, and great love that he would discover. A cluster of multihued stars came together and formed a wizened, broad-shouldered caricature of William Cox, who would lead a saint's life on earth and then ascend to Heaven, met by a chorus of angels and God's fulfilling embrace.

But where's all this comin' from? Not from me. There has to be a source out there, somewhere, everywhere.

The wind shifted and got colder. The youngster blinked and his eyes opened onto muted daylight under an angry sky. Bill was all alone now; his best friend, Jake, had vanished. He sprang to his feet, and the desiccated plywood beneath him cracked under his weight. Tiptoeing over the rotting railroad ties, he left the old trestle behind. The manicured pasture from just before had changed also. It was long untended, overgrown and slick with fresh rain. The sun was fading in the late afternoon sky, masked by a growing black thunderhead.

Somehow Bill was older, and he tested his young man's legs, running flat-out toward home. He leaped over prickly pear and mounds of thorny rose hedge, bounding higher each time until finally faith kept him aloft. He pitched his hands upward and climbed like a crop duster, gaining on the black cloud that was smothering his sun. Rain struck his face harder as he climbed, the drops getting bigger, stinging his skin and blurring his vision.

Bill leveled off, averting his eyes from the pelting rain. Looking down, he saw the accident, far below, at the intersection of two state highways south of town. There was a jackknifed big rig and a small, familiar-looking sedan, badly damaged and sinking into a rice canal. Bill dove, plummeting toward the earth. With this newfound power he could save them. But he couldn't seem to lose any altitude. How had he gotten so high?

The thunderhead lanced out with white hot plasma tentacles that struck the would-be hero and stole his power to fly. Burned yet lucid, hailstones tumbling down around him, Bill heard a voice in the thunder echoing from the storm. It said, "The past and future do not exist. Only the now. And the now is a free fall."

Bill awoke clutching a mattress to keep his body from floating away. Soon he discovered that he was in that strange and worrisome place where one doesn't recognize one's surroundings. An afro-baseline pulsed through the floor and walls, accented by the sound of someone hammering on something? Bill yawned and the side of his face ached. He explored the area with his fingers and discovered it was puffy and tender. There was a damp spot on the mattress where a melted icepack sat. The strong aroma of grilled cheese made Bill wonder if the part of his brain that controlled his sense of smell might be damaged.

Brother Cox sat up. Then he stood slowly with a hand on the bed until his equilibrium adjusted. The pain in his head dulled, but also spread somewhat into the side of his neck. He shuffled to a window to get a look at his surroundings, but apparently this room was tucked up into the boughs of a giant tree. Oddly, the window screen was already removed and propped against the wall, so Bill lifted the pane and stuck his head out for a better view. He was on the second floor of a garage apartment at the back of a big lot in dire need of some pruning.

Bill shut the window, went into the quaint, dated bathroom, splashed some water on his face, and then gulped some down from his cupped hand. The urban greenhorn had a flashback of the big-city goons who'd assaulted him the night before, and it made him shiver. Between that and discovering a dead body, Bill had to ask himself if he was really cut out for city life.

The answer was yes. He squinted and winced in the mirror for a minute, and then decided the damage could have been a lot worse. Falling asleep on an icepack had done wonders for the swelling. He turned off the light and crept to the stairway.

Stopping at the bottom step, Bill stooped down behind the banister and peered into the big open garage. He saw two electric griddles on a worktable that was built onto the back wall. Many grilled cheeses were cooking on those griddles and he was relieved that his sense of smell was apparently intact. *Pusherman* faded out on the stereo system, and the dojo-garage went quiet, save the gently sizzling sandwiches.

The hammering sound returned with a fury, making Bill flinch. He scanned the spacious room and saw, across the patch-work hardwood flooring over near the big, metal, garage doors, his rescuer from the night before, barefoot and pummeling some kind of torture device on wheels.

Another song cued up on the stereo, and Desmond Dekker began to sing *Israelites*. An aged Caribbean melody flooded the room, underpinned by the unsettling sound of flesh and bone pounding against wood. The combat engine had three rows of curved limbs, which Bill could see were formerly hardwood table legs, mounted to a segmented central column that looked like three cut-out sections of a telephone pole. The thing had to have an internal shaft and bearings to account for each segment's indi-vidual spin. The base of the contraption appeared to have been part of a wide, steel office chair set on casters.

Bill was transfixed as his host punched and kicked the animate piece of furniture with surreal force and the thing spun to retaliate. Fists constantly changing shape, faintly whimpering with every strike, Marcus drove the rotating juggernaut around the rickety floor, which flexed under its weight. Desmond Dekker and the Aces chanted from the oversized speakers.

The combatants circled toward the watcher at the base of the stairs, drawing closer and closer, and Bill was frozen like a deer in the headlights. Marcus cried out, leaping up and blasting his lumbering foe with a high, spinning back-kick, his left heel connecting with what would be the thing's forehead. The wooden monster's rolling base slammed into the orange couch near the stairway, and the contraption toppled over, crashing into the wall and cracking some panel veneer. Bill covered his ears and shouted, "Jesus!"

Tíng's eyes swept to the source of the voice at the foot of his stairway.

Bill recovered quickly, smiled, and said, "Yikes, what did that poor coatrack ever do to you?"

Marcus's face thawed with recognition. "Oh, sorry, I was just working out. Did I wake you up?"

"No-no, it just took me a little while to *get* up and get moving, and actually remember where I was. You ever have one of those nights?" Bill asked hopefully.

"Not for quite some time, but I know what you're talking about." Marcus grabbed a remote and turned the music down. "Your face doesn't look too bad. Could've been a lot worse."

"Yeah, I'll be fine, thank you."

Marcus righted the twelve-limbed Diūqì Shìbīng (as his master had named it), and then shoved it away with his foot. Bill watched the sinister contraption rotate slowly as it rolled across the floor while Marcus walked to the deep sink at the end of his worktable. He quickly washed his hands. Then he grabbed a bamboo spatula and flipped several hot sandwiches from his pair of electric griddles onto a wooden cutting board.

"These are a little dark, but some people like 'em that way," he said under his breath. Tíng rubbed his twin, nonstick cooking surfaces with a stick of butter and covered them with new slices of bread.

Bill's curiosity was stronger than his desire to depart. "Um, what exactly happened last night, if you don't mind my asking?" he said as he walked closer. "I'm a little foggy on the details."

Marcus smirked. "Well, in your defense, I think somebody slipped a roofie or something into your drink. So you got more than just a little tipsy, and you felt like going for a walk through the city, after midnight. Then a couple of goons rolled you out in the parking lot at the club where I work."

"Rolled me for what, money?"

"Maybe they would've mugged you, but they didn't look like muggers to me. Probably just a couple of haters."

Bill nodded. "So what was up with their teeth?"

Marcus shrugged. "It looked like they filed 'em to a point to make themselves look scary. It's not unheard of."

"Right." Bill couldn't imagine. His stomach growled.

Marcus flipped the hot slices of bread, adding more butter to the cooktops under each slice. He grabbed a brick of cheese and carved off some generous slabs with his spatula, shingling them onto the bread. He was saying, "Anyway, I'm sure you know it by now, but it's worth repeating. H-town's a big city, brotha. It'll swallow you up. Drunk or sober, you can't just go walking around anywhere you want at night, or some places even during the day." He glanced at Bill. "Especially looking like a lost frat boy."

Bill chuckled. "Ouch. Okay. I'll remember that." He planned on giving the nightlife a rest for a while anyway. It struck him suddenly how indebted he was to this guy. He said, "I'm so rude. You pretty much saved my life and I haven't even properly introduced myself." He stuck his hand out. "My name is Bill, Bill Cox. And thank you so much for helping me last night."

Marcus shook Bill's hand. "I'm Marcus. Some people call me Tíng." Then he turned back to his worktable, adding lettuce and tomato slices to the cooking sandwiches, and then pressing them together with the spatula to make sure they stuck. He moved them to the cutting board next to the sink to cool, and then distributed more butter and bread across the griddles.

Bill watched with interest. "Did you say Ting, like T-I-N-G?"

Marcus didn't look away from the toasting bread. "Uh, yeah, it's actually one of my middle names, the one my mom gave me. She was Chinese."

"I love it. So you have more than one middle name?"

"Garvey is my other middle name, the first one. It's from my dad," he said, without looking up.

"Okay, wow, Marcus Garvey. Big shoes to fill."

"Indeed." Marcus left it at that.

After a minute Bill said, "So, I guess you like grilled cheeses, huh?"

"Uh, yeah, I do, but these aren't for me."

"You goin' to a luncheon or something?"

Marcus had to smile. "I guess you could say that."

"Oh-kay." Bill waited.

"It's just this thing I do sometimes. I make a bunch of sandwiches, then I ride out on my bike and visit with some folks and give 'em a sandwich if they want one." His attempt to be vague only piqued Bill's interest.

"You just ride up to random people and offer 'em a cheese sandwich?"

"Yeah, well, generally it's all these people I already know. People who sort of live on this route that I like to ride anyway."

"Oh, you mean sort of like Meals on Wheels or something?"

"Yeah, but I don't actually literally like go door to door. These people sort of live on like the *fringe* of society." Marcus was somewhat annoyed with himself for being so chatty, but he could tell Bill was a good guy.

"You mean like homeless people? You make sandwiches for homeless people and deliver 'em on your bike?"

"I mean, you could say that, but it's not like I'm on a mission or something. They're my friends, and I'm kind of an exercise freak. I've been riding my bike around here since I was a kid, and I used to wonder about all these people who were always on the corners and under the bridges. One day I started talking to them. Pretty soon I was packing sandwiches along on my bike rides for some of the older guys, so they wouldn't have to beg so much."

He gestured toward his griddles with the spatula. "Now I guess it's kind of gotten out of hand."

Marcus stuffed each of the cooled sandwiches from the cutting board into a baggy, along with a chewable vitamin wrapped in a brown paper napkin. He stacked them into an olive-green Tupperware container designed for transporting cakes. Then he moved the new batch of hot sandwiches from the griddles to the cutting board.

"No, that's awesome," Bill managed to say as he turned away, inspecting the décor again while blinking tears from his eyes. He made his way to a foggy window on the left-side garage door and asked over his shoulder, "So is it just you in this place?"

"Yeah, sort of. My mom paid the place off and left it to me when I was, like, nineteen I guess. Right before she passed away. My dad died a long time before that, before I even knew him. Now I just have to keep up with the taxes and insurance." Marcus was wiping up and putting things away.

"I'm sorry about your losses. It's strange. Both my parents are gone too."

Marcus looked at Bill. "That *is* kind of a coincidence, considering our age. What happened?"

"It was a bad car wreck." Bill left it at that.

"Oh. Dang, I'm sorry, man."

"Thanks. It was a long time ago too." Bill looked out the window. "I see this is a garage apartment like where I stay. Does somebody live in the house up front?"

Marcus hesitated. "Yeah, the main house is mine too. But I don't go in there much." A long moment passed and Bill was about to press when Marcus redirected. "So what's your story? I saw your ID last night. What are you doing up here in the big city? Besides trying to become a statistic?"

Bill thought briefly of the dead body he'd seen in the bayou and shivered. "Well, as you saw last night on my ID, I'm from

Oyster Prairie, which is a little town about an hour south of here, right on the coast. I don't know if you've heard of it."

"I've seen it on a map. And actually, it made me wonder, isn't a prairie oyster, like, a cow patty?"

"Well, yeah, I guess I've heard that. But it's Oyster Prairie not prairie oyster."

"So it's like, a prairie with a lot of oysters on it?"

"It was founded on a rich, coastal prairie, and Old Oyster Bayou runs through it on its way to the Gulf. That's how it got its name. Of course nowadays it's mostly farmland. And anyway I live here in Houston now."

"Why'd you move up here? Get away from the small-town drama?"

"Yeah, you could say that. It's not easy bein' gay in a small town. Especially a gay pastor." Bill glanced at Marcus and saw acceptance, and it felt good. He smiled a little and continued. "Like I said, my folks passed away a long time ago, and after that I moved in with my mom's parents. My dad's parents had already passed a few years earlier, one right after the other." Bill paused to regain his composure. "Anyway, I guess because of all the people dyin' around me, I became very interested in God's plan. And I ended up goin' to seminary school. Then I came back home and went to work at our church for, wow, I guess it's been about eight years now. But recently a lot of bad stuff's been happenin' down there. Even more than usual. Political stuff. Hateful stuff. And to top it off, the Church I'd been workin' at forever just burned down."

"Yikes. Did anybody get hurt?"

Bill looked away as he spoke. "Actually, my old boss, the Deacon, he got trapped inside and killed. I couldn't get him out."

"Holy crap. I'm sorry, man. Well, at least we know he went to Heaven, right?"

"I prayed for him." Bill left it at that.

Marcus took a more appraising look at his guest. "Crazy stuff. So you were right there, on the scene when it burned down? That explains your patchy tan." Tíng smirked. "*You* didn't burn the church down, did you?"

Bill gasped and squinted his eyes at Tíng. "No. I did not burn the church down." He was shaking his head as he wandered back to the sandwich prep area, seeking to change the sore subject. "So what else do you cook in here?"

"Just grilled cheese, man. You want one?" Marcus handed his new friend a sandwich off the cutting board and then started to wrap and pack up the rest.

"Mmm, very good," Bill mumbled. He finished chewing and added, "So does anybody ever help you deliver these sandwiches? You got an extra bike around here?"

"Uh, actually I do, but this is gonna take a while; I don't know how long I'll be gone."

"I got nowhere I'm s'posed to be today."

"I might ride fifteen or twenty miles."

"I bike and jog all the time. I think I'm up for it."

"I'm gonna go to some pretty unsavory places."

"Uh, for some reason I feel pretty safe with you around."

Marcus was shaking his head as he slipped into a nearby pair of socks and shoes. Then he stuffed two bottles of water, plus the big Tupperware of twenty-odd grilled cheese sandwiches into his big black backpack and zipped it up. "Alright, fine, you can come along." Tíng went out the side door they'd come through the night before and then came back in with the Frankenbike. He squeezed the tires and passed it to Bill, who vaguely remembered it from the night before. The mix-matched thing had dirt-bike tires, and a lot of iron in it judging by its weight. Brother Cox hoped he really was up for it.

Marcus walked past the far end of the worktable and opened a big storage closet with a sliding door. He rolled out a charcoalprimered, adult-sized tricycle, squeezed its tires, and then laid the backpack of grilled cheeses into the thing's rear cargo basket. Then he punched one of a pair of dimly glowing buttons on the wall. The right garage door startled Bill as it sprang to life and started to rise.

"Take off," Ting said. "Follow the path around to the right and wait at the gate. I'm right behind you."

Bill mounted the Frankenbike and set out.

5

CHINA MAN

With Marcus in the lead, they rolled out of the shell-paved alley onto a deserted, dead-end street. Bill was trying to get his bearings, but the surrounding trees still dominated the view. The country boy heard the din of automobile traffic, the city boy did not.

They passed right through the dead end and onto a dirt footpath that began where the pavement ended. Marcus turned left on the trail and led them east, riding alongside a broad deep ditch, across which were railroad tracks and an expansive, fenced-in industrial area. The path fed into a sidewalk along the west side of Yale Street and they took it south, picking up speed on the smoother terrain.

Nearing the I-10 overpass, Marcus noticed a new billboard sign along the freeway that struck him as weird. It was a huge headshot of an eerily handsome white dude fringed by the words *American Missionary–Coming to Texas.*

Tíng frowned. *What in the?* He shrugged it off and shouted over his shoulder that they were turning. Then he peeled off southwest onto a faint trail through waist-high weeds. Bill followed, his look of wonderment shifting to one of concern. The grass ended abruptly and they pedaled onto acrid dirt tainted with petroleum runoff and spackled with pigeon droppings. Tíng continued on and led them way out amid the massive pillars beneath the interstate where it crossed over Yale Street and White Oak Bayou.

As they neared the bayou's concrete bank, Bill saw a man sitting facing them and reading a newspaper, his back resting against the last pillar on this side of the bayou. The fellow had thick gray hair that connected seamlessly to a matted beard of equal fullness. What he wore wouldn't pass for rags, and he was barefoot. Beside the gent was a worn-out pair of high-top sneakers, a medium-sized cardboard box, and a discolored twin mattress topped with dirty blankets. The roar of the freeway overhead was all-consuming.

Marcus stopped about ten yards away, slipped off of the trike and extracted two grilled cheese sandwiches from the cargo basket. He walked toward the old timer and yelled, "Hey, Marty!" when he was halfway there.

Marty looked up, grinned, and then stiffly rose to his feet. He folded his paper and used it to dust himself off. Marcus handed him the sandwiches and Bill could barely hear Marty say thank you as he stashed the delicacies into his cardboard box. Marty straightened his back and shot a curious glance at Bill, still many yards away.

Marcus looked over his shoulder and shouted, "You wanna come meet a friend of mine?"

"Oh, yes of course, sorry." Bill walked the Frankenbike over since it didn't have a kickstand.

"Bro, you can lay the bike down."

"That's okay. There's lots of bird poop around here."

"Right. Well, Bill this is Marty. Marty, this is Bill."

Marty stuck a filthy hand out for shaking and Bill took it without hesitation. "Nice to meet you, sir!"

"A pleasure, yessir, a pleasure."

Marcus hollered, "You're looking good, man. You been doing okay?

"Yup, yup, I been doin' fine. You doin' okay, Tíng?" Marty looked from Marcus to Bill. "How d'you two know each other?"

"I'm good as always. Bill just moved to town. I met him at work. He's a man of the cloth, and he just wanted to tag along for a bike ride today, meet some new people."

"Alright, alright, glad to hear it. Bless you, brother." Marty's hands came together in prayer fashion.

"Thank you, and God be with you also," Bill replied.

Marty looked back at Marcus, about to say something, but the sandwich-bringer was looking elsewhere, his gaze locked on something way across the bayou. Tíng pointed. "How long has that been painted there, Marty?"

On the concrete bank opposite them was another painted mural that read:

EL CIELO
LLORA

"Hmm, I uh, I don't believe that was there yesterday," Marty replied pensively.

Marcus went into his pack and dug out his pad and pen. Then he copied it letter for letter.

"Maybe it was hoodlums, but it don't look like it," Marty added, scratching his beard.

Bill said, "All I know is *el* means *the*, but the other two words I'm not sure about."

Marcus glanced at him sideways. "Thanks for your help." He looked back across the bayou. "It looks weird. Doesn't even look like paint." Motion caught Tíng's eye, and he looked away upstream where a man was walking the opposite levee followed by a big red dog. They were just about to disappear around the bend when the canine stopped and looked back. Marcus wondered how far the dog could see.

"Uh, Ting, what're you lookin' at?" Bill asked.

Marcus pointed west toward the bayou's bend. "Marty, do you know who that is?"

"Who?" Marty shielded his eyes, though he stood in deep shade. "I can't see that far. What are we lookin' at?"

"A little guy in a straw hat with a big red dog," Marcus said as the pair vanished around the curve.

"Yup, I seen him pass by here a few times. We waved at each other, but he's always on the other side of the water. Always comin' from thataway." Marty gestured upstream. "Seems like a nice fella. Good-tempered dog too."

Bill said something but Marcus didn't respond, caught up in his own thoughts. It was time to get going. He needed to see Jaime, but he needed to see Teacher first. "Right on, well, we gotta run, Marty. We got a lot more sandwiches to deliver. Take care of yourself. I'll swing back through here soon. Take your vitamins."

"Okay, thanks Ting. Sometimes I don't know if I'd make it without you," the old man said with reverence as his young friend hopped up onto the big trike. The patron saint of grilled cheese.

"Right on. Take care of yourself," Marcus said as he started to pedal away.

Bill quickly shook Marty's hand again. "Nice to meet you, Marty. I'll be back soon too." Then he flung his long leg over the Frankenbike and set it in motion.

"Great, yup. God Bless. Come by anytime," Marty said, glad for the prospect of a new visitor.

Cutting across the desecrated dirt back toward Yale Street, Bill glanced over his shoulder and saw Marty stooped over coughing. Brother Cox's eyes were damp again when he caught up to Marcus at the sidewalk. "Oh my gosh, Ting! You think he's gonna be okay?"

Marcus glanced at him, "Okay compared to who? He lives under a freeway. He actually looks a lot better than he did a couple weeks ago. I thought he had pneumonia or something, but he looks like he'll pull through for now."

"For now?" There were people down on their luck in Oyster Prairie, but nobody lived under the bridges. Bill asked, "So how many homeless people you think there *are* in Houston?"

Marcus shrugged. "Probably more than there are *non*-homeless people in Prairie-Oyster. You should look it up."

"Oyster Prairie," Bill corrected, but his mind was elsewhere. He was trying to wrap his head around the concept of hundreds, maybe thousands, of people within cycling distance who *actually* needed his help. Even if only one at a time, how many lives could he touch? Then he realized Ting was leaving him behind. Bill picked up the pace and thumbed the Frankenbike into third gear.

Marcus hollered over his shoulder, "We're gonna go down and cross the bayou at Studewood, but first we gotta stop by the China Man." Ting needed to see Teacher. He visited his master less often these days and was disrespectfully overdue. He drove off the curb, cut across Yale, and cranked the primer-coated trike east on Fourth Street without looking back.

蜻蛉

The China Man was a convenience store, and inherently the China Man was the longtime nickname of the store's proprietor. Over the decades, Mother Nature had wreathed the China Man's peeling shiplap edifice into a floral basket of trumpet vine and bougainvillea, its metal roof a watercolor of oxidation. The China Man made his home in a small apartment built onto the back. A tall fence of reclaimed boards braced by soaring green bamboo enclosed the rear of the property. The front lot was gravel parking for a few cars, though it was currently (and often) empty. The

China Man's low wooden front porch was pushed up on one side by the roots of a ragged old tallow tree, its canopy still spinach green this mild, wet autumn.

Tíng skidded into the front lot, grinning and looking to see how far back his trailer was. Bill was just making the final turn, only a couple blocks back, not too bad. Marcus faced front and saw the China Man standing on his porch in silent repose. He was short, wiry, and well past middle-age with close-cropped, white-gray hair and a wispy goatee. He wore a simple gray shirt and pants that resembled hospital scrubs. High mileage sandals adorned his feet.

Tíng rode up to the steps and dismounted. "Hey, Master," he said as he strode onto the porch and they slapped hands.

Bill coasted in on the Frankenbike, panting and sweating, while the two men on the porch watched him. Marcus smirked while the China Man bore a look of mild disgust. Bill propped the bike against the porch and laboriously ascended the steps.

Marcus gave him a moment and said, "Uh, this is Bill. Bill, this is my, uh, the China Man."

Bill wasn't sure if he'd met the man or the business since CHINA MAN was emblazoned on the faded sign overhead. Either way he managed a "Hello, nice to meet you, sir," while trying to get his breathing in check.

The China Man spoke methodically, with words chosen like beads on an abacus. His tone rang of Master Bruce Lee, raspy with age, but still with that swagger that comes from knowing ten men couldn't subdue you. He nodded to Bill and said, "Welcome. Now come in and cool down, before you pass out on the porch." Then he turned for the door.

The China Man was stocked with a slim selection of standard convenience goods as well as many items one might find in a specialty shop in Old Chinatown. The décor reminded Bill of Tíng's dojo or vice versa. Brother Cox bought a half-liter of water, chugged some, and then promptly asked the proprietor where his restroom might be located. The China Man pointed Bill in the right direction, his expression neutral.

Marcus grabbed a ripe red pear from a basket at the end of the front counter and wiped it down with his shirt. Standing by the register, the China Man observed but said nothing. Marcus took a bite, chewed some, and then he let go, rambling through a synopsis of every major event that had occurred in his life since the last time he'd been in here.

He spoke about Sean's death, his mandatory meeting with the cops, and the fake vampires who had appeared at the club that night, which led into how he'd met Bill. And all the while, Marcus chomped on his pear. At the end of the tale, he seemed relieved but still slightly exasperated, and he added, "I don't know, lately it's like I just walked into another dimension or something." His purloined pear was gnawed down to a bare core, and he threw it into a nearby trash can without thinking. Then he winced.

The China Man looked at the defiled waste bin and said, "Talking with food in your mouth is regrettable, but throwing compost into my trash can is reprehensible, insolent pupil."

"Sorry, Teacher." Marcus went to pick it out.

Teacher? Bill was out of the restroom and feeling better, having refreshed himself in the sink. He began to peruse the back of the store, trying not to eavesdrop. But obviously the China Man was some sort of a mentor to Marcus. The clergyman grabbed a magazine off the magazine rack.

The little old master spoke. "And why is it so strange to find yourself in another dimension? Every moment in life brings a new array of dimensions, hinging on the outcomes of preceding possibilities. In the multiverse exists every dimension that can possibly be, every version of yourself, so some of them are sure to be strange indeed. But it is not like you are here and they are there. Everything is everywhere, and is happening now, all at once. Do you understand?"

To Bill, science was pretty much a jumble of numbers and theories, but even *he* knew enough to debunk that last part. He didn't mean to interrupt. The truth just had a way of tumbling out of his mouth sometimes. Looking up from his magazine, he said aloud, "I thought different things *couldn't* exist in the same place at the same time, you know, physically. So how can everything be everywhere all at once?"

Marcus had been nodding, mechanically agreeing with his Master's obscure theories as usual, but now he stopped and raised an eyebrow at Bill, who was beginning to wither under the China Man's gaze.

"Actually, different things *can* occupy the same space if they exist in *harmonic vibration*, but that is not what I am talking about. You see only one color in the enigmatic spectrum of being. And you view it through a pinhole."

Bill was pretty sure there was an insult or two tucked in there. "Uh, okay, sorry." He went back to his magazine.

Marcus was eyeballing the door.

The China Man continued, "Also Tíng, do not forget, your Saturn is coming back around. And who can know how profoundly this might affect you?"

Marcus nodded. "My Saturn's coming back around, right."

The China Man lowered his tone and said, "I am sorry about the death of your friend, Qīngtíng, but know this. Your losses and your burdens will grow with your strength and your honor. It is the way of things." Teacher's eyelids closed for a moment, as if he had a vision. Then they popped back open and he added, "And remember, authority corrupts without fail. Be very wary of officials you should encounter."

Teacher's eyes locked onto Marcus, who'd been staring at the door again. "So go now. You have unburdened yourself and I can see that you have some important place to be. But come back soon. Your training is not nearly complete. And remember what I have told you."

The English language had always felt unnatural to the China Man, affecting his pronunciation of R's and L's, a fact that Marcus shamelessly exploited from time to time.

"Right, what was that last part again, 'Be vely waly of the fishers.' Got it!"

"String bean, you know what I said! Now go, before you feel my *Iron Palm*." He prodded Marcus toward the door with his right hand, while his left open-palm hovered at his side like the gat of a gunfighter.

"You know Iron Monkey defeated the Iron Palm!" Marcus fairly sang as he slipped out the door.

"You are not Iron Monkey! Ha! And next time you pay for your ill-gotten fruit, disrespectful monkey boy!"

"See you soon, Teacher!" Marcus hollered from the front steps.

Bill hurried out, issuing apologies and goodbyes, but the China Man hardly noticed, tugging at his thin white beard and staring out the window at his full-grown pupil, who would be even stronger than Iron Monkey.

Marcus hopped onto the trike and pedaled across the gravel front lot at a pondering pace. Having finally spoken about Sean's death out loud again, the whole thing sounded even fishier. He still hadn't deleted the weird voicemail from his recently deceased friend, even though it felt like a brick he was carrying around.

Bill caught up about the time they hit the blacktop again and he asked, "Hey, you okay?"

"Huh? Oh, yeah, I'm fine." Marcus was picking up speed. He said, "Car," and Bill fell in single file as a gray sedan passed them. After a moment, the country boy asked if his leader wouldn't mind keeping a little slower pace for a while. Marcus smirked and said over his shoulder, "Yeah, sorry, I was kind of messing with you earlier."

They made a couple of turns and picked up the sidewalk going east along White Oak Boulevard. Marcus led them through White Oak Park where they dropped off a few more grilled cheeses. Then they popped back out onto Studemont and crossed the bridge over White Oak Bayou. Bill's heart pounded as cars whizzed by on his left, while on his right, a low guardrail was all that separated him from a forty-foot fall into dark, rushing water. Ahead, Marcus pedaled along without regard for the traffic. He stared down at the bayou as if looking for something, or someone. Bill gave thanks when they reached the other side.

Studemont turned into Montrose Boulevard and the leader picked up speed. They passed a couple miles of storefronts and apartment compounds that finally opened up to a leafy green panorama bordering Downtown in the east. They were in the basin of Buffalo Bayou again, and the ribbon of dark water and tall trees reminded Bill of home. They rode toward Allen Parkway, and the country boy's head was on a swivel as he took in the beauty of this lush little valley tucked into an urban canyon of concrete buildings and elevated roadways. Then a hulking, dark presence ahead in the distance drew Bill's attention forward.

At the upcoming intersection sat a giant black man in an Army field jacket, black slacks, and worn-out jogging shoes. Dreadlocks spilled over his shoulders and connected to his expansive black beard, interwoven with veins of silver. Like Marcus the fellow was astride a huge tricycle, though this one was even bigger and less repaired. From a distance, it appeared to Bill that there was a shopping cart parked behind the big man's conveyance, but as the clergyman drew nearer, he realized the cart was actually mounted to the trike, in place of the original rear cargo basket. The cart's front wheels had been removed so that the rear wheels of the tricycle bore the load. The cart's back wheels were still attached, though they were tattered and hardly touched the ground.

Marcus pulled up next to the big man, who was grinning with big, perfect teeth, and they slapped hands. "What's up, Leo?"

"Mah-cus, my lil' brotha." His voice was all bass.

Marcus introduced Bill, who hobbled up behind him on the Frankenbike. Bill felt like a child when he shook Leo's callused paw. "Nice to meet you, Leo."

"Hello." Leo hardly made eye contact.

"Bill's a man of God. And uh, well, he just wanted to come out for a ride with me today," Marcus said.

Leo nodded. "Y'all headed up to the village?"

"Yup, you wanna lead the way?"

Leo said, "I knew I smelled grilled cheese," as he turned away and started to pedal.

Bill noticed Leo had a stiff leg as the big man got his tricycle going. Then he saw movement in the smaller basket mounted to Leo's handlebars. A scruffy dog had been swaddled there among rags, but now the mutt stood in the basket and faced forward as if to help navigate. The rear cargo-basket shuddered along behind them, bearing a load of crushed cans, which vibrated harmonically.

They crossed Allen Parkway, then crossed again to the east side of Montrose Boulevard and followed the sidewalk several yards past a bus stop, where Leo pulled to the right and dismounted. He gripped the center of his handlebars with one hand and began to walk backward up the grassy, littered embankment on their right, his tricycle in tow.

Marcus pulled a cable lock from his pack and called Bill over to a stout little sycamore behind the bus stop. Ting locked the Frankenbike and his trike to the tree and took the pack of grilled cheeses from the cargo basket. Then he walked to the spot where Leo had started his climb, the head of a faint trail cutting up the high weedy slope, a slope that Leo was already halfway up, pulling his cargo-trike, canine passenger and all. Bill approached, with his jaw dropped, as he watched the big man advance up the hill. Marcus smiled at him and said, "Leo likes to keep his stuff together," before he turned and bounded up the path.

6

UPHILL DESCENT

The village was a several-acre arena of fenced-in weeds, in the shadow of a relatively low but stalwart old building. The blocky edifice sat on a mesa-like slab, with iron-girder bones wrapped in thick, white shale that had been ferried down from the hill country over a century ago. It had been built to last for ages.

The structure had initially been the hub of an inland shipping company, about the time Buffalo Bayou was first dredged. Since then, the huge lot had changed hands several times and been home to a half-dozen different commercial entities. With time, the place had become rundown. Currently, having been ignored by prosperity for more than a decade, the building had been dubbed "the shrine" by its most recent inhabitants.

Bill scrambled over the hilltop, breathless again; Ting seemed to have that effect on him. Marcus and Leo were waiting for him where the trail terminated at a tall hurricane fence, tangled with underbrush and topped with three sagging strands of rusted barb wire.

Marcus was grinning as the winded clergyman approached. "Bro, are you gonna make it?"

Leo turned and swept the corroded chain-link aside like a bead curtain. Then he ducked under the top rail, and dragged his cargo-trike through the fence. Somebody had cut the chain-link long ago to provide unauthorized access

Bill's head was on a swivel. He asked Marcus, "Who owns this place?"

The dancing duelist just shrugged. As he turned to go through the fence, Bill tugged on his shirtsleeve and added under his breath, "Hey, is Leo okay? Does he have a hurt leg?"

"He's fine. He hurt it a long time ago."

They entered the village from the north, on a path of trodden weeds over packed earth that had once been a limestone-rock driveway to the loading dock jutting from the back of the building. Surrounding the dock, a half-acre of concrete apron had crumbled into a grassy gray tundra as it succumbed, over time, to Mother Nature. The rest of the village had once been paved entirely with crushed oyster shell, dredged from the bayou decades ago. But now the shell was part of the topsoil, ground under the weeds and patches of St. Augustine and Bermuda grass that covered the lot. Several trails crisscrossed the village, and a few of them led curiously into the dense patch of ten-foot bloodweeds obscuring the east end of the property.

Along the border of the oyster-shell meadow and the concrete tundra stood a massive hump of cultivated earth covered in *tomato vines?* Yup, Bill was sure of it. From seedlings to mature seven-footers, there were dozens of plants on and around the heap of black dirt flecked with oyster shell. A couple of soiled gents stood next to the impressive garden, chatting alongside two five-gallon buckets filled with ripe tomatoes. The slighter fellow on the left was leaning on a shovel with two-thirds of a handle when he saw the new arrivals. He excused himself from the conversation and walked toward the dock to meet them.

The shrine's loading dock was an extension of its high,

concrete foundation, and ran the entire length of the east wall. Four big bay doors stood along that wall, covered in rust and flaking yellow paint. Three of the doors were corroded shut; the one farthest north, the one closest to the new arrivals, was open about a third of the way. The bay doors were shielded from direct rain by an extensive, heavily-oxidized steel awning. Beneath the awning, safe from crawling vermin and the sun, were many tranquil human beings. Bill counted at least twenty altogether. Nearby were all their possessions, stacked in sections against the wall. They were mostly older, and nearly all men. Some slept on pallets, some chatted in small groups, a couple read in solitary, but they all seemed at ease.

The largest group sat in a loose circle at the south end of the dock, centered around a dark-skinned man with hawkish features and long, stringy gray hair. The ringleader spoke slowly, animatedly, and whatever he was talking about, his little audience was listening.

Marcus shoved the pack of grilled cheeses into Bill's chest, snapping the newbie out of his reverie. Tíng said, "Here you go." Then he turned and bounded onto the dock, whereupon many of the inhabitants rose to greet him.

Leo parked his trike alongside the slab, and the little mutt clambered out of his front basket onto the dock. Then the big man turned and headed straight for Bill. Rubbing his paws together, he said, "Brotha Bill, whatcha got in that bag?"

Bill unzipped the wrong zipper twice, fumbled with some Velcro, and then just handed the whole thing to Leo saying, "Uh, here you go. Maybe you should do it." Without thinking he added, "Leo, is your leg hurt?"

Leo looked down. "Huh? Oh, naw—"

"Oh, fer the love o' Pat, no goddamn war stories today," said the fellow with the broken shovel as he walked up from behind Leo.

Leo broke out in a grin and patted the older, thin little white man on the back saying, "Here go Frank, carryin' that shovel like he been farmin'."

"Ain't you a fifth-generation cotton picker?" Frank replied. Then he stuck his dirty hand out to the newcomer and said, "Hello, sir. Frank Gaffigan."

Bill felt grit between their palms as they shook. "Hello, Frank. Bill Cox. Looks like you got a fine crop of tomatoes over there." He nodded toward the heap.

Frank shot Leo a smug look. "Why thank ya, Bill. They pretty much take care o' themselves though," he lied.

Leo chimed in, "He *Brotha* Bill. He a minista."

Frank took a good look at Bill, and then said, "Well nevertheless, any friend o' Marcus is a friend o' mine." He grinned and his few gray teeth looked like their days were numbered.

Bill said, "I've got lots of friends who are farmers back home, and everybody I know has a garden."

Leo unzipped the backpack, having nearly as much trouble as Bill, because the zippers were so small in his fingers. Then he offered the first sandwich to Bill, who declined saying he'd had one already. Frank slipped one into his baggy jeans pocket, and said he would have it in a minute.

Leo sat down on the dock and set the pack beside him. He grabbed his pantleg and lifted his stiff leg up onto the high slab. Then he muscled his way to his feet and hauled the grilled cheeses away to the others on the platform.

Bill felt ashamed that he'd failed at sandwich duty until Frank smacked him on the shoulder and said, "Don't go worryin' 'bout Leo. That's ol' Mississippi slave stock. Harder than a cold chisel. An' that wound in his leg's older than you are. We all got our scars don't we, boy-o? Come on. You wanna see what we got comin' out o' the ground over here?" As Frank walked the trail, he tugged a pint of dark liquor from his back pocket, took a pull, and then put it back. Bill bit his tongue. He didn't know these folks well enough to counsel 'em, yet.

When they got to the edge of the heap, Frank stuck his shovel in the ground, turned, and said, "What we did ya see, is we just started throwin' all our vegetable waste over here to start kind of a compost pile, ya know. Then I found me a spade and started turnin' the ground every so often. Stuff sprouted here and there but I just kept buryin' it, ya know, keepin' the raw dirt pitched to the middle. Then, a few springs back, I started cultivatin' the seedlin's around the edges ya see, whenever I saw one. An' over the past few years they got pretty thick, as you can bear witness. We can't eat nowhere near what we produce, so I let most of it just seed-out 'n' die ever' winter. It's a delight now to see the volunteers come up every spring and fall. Ya never know what yer gonna get."

"Are those cucumber vines too?"

"Yup." Frank started to walk again. "Mebbe somebody tossed some pickles out here with good seeds in 'em." He led Bill over to a reclaimed bucket, full of cucumbers.

"Oh my gosh, those are huge."

"My paw Keagan used to call those home-wreckers." The old farmer chuckled and grinned at Bill, who smiled and nodded uncomfortably.

Frank cleared his throat. "Anyway, we had a fine melon crop this year too."

"Watermelons?"

Frank nodded. "And cantaloupes, and some weird-lookin' cross-breeds, like cucumber-melons. They were pretty seedy, but sweet enough to eat for sure."

"It takes a lot of water to grow melons."

Frank grinned and pointed up at the shrine. About halfway up, a row of reclaimed, fifty-gallon drums was lined up on the old, iron fire escape. "We got water catchment, boy-o. Me and Leo even plumbed one o' the bathrooms inside with it. So folks can catch a cool shower when they need one."

Bill shook his head. "Oh my gosh." He turned and let his eyes wander across the urban garden. "So you grow all this stuff, and then you just let most of it rot?"

"Yessir. And go to seed, that's how Mother Nature grows her garden. Anyway, me an' a couple of the guys tried sellin' some tomatoes a few blocks down, but the cops come along and asked us where we got 'em from. Of course, we said we found 'em, but couldn't remember where. They made us dump 'em in the weeds, and that was the end of it."

"I don't understand. Why didn't you just tell 'em the truth?"

Frank snorted. "Cause they'd wanna come up here and have a look-see. Everybody knows never to bring the cops up here. We don't know who owns this place. We piss 'em off an' they'll boot us all outta here."

Frank led Bill to a wild onion patch he'd been cultivating, right next to some prickly, citrus saplings of yet unknown variety. The old farmer said, "I been savin' some money up for a tiller. There's a fella up on 'leventh Street sellin' a solid, old walk-behind Husqvarna for fifty bucks. It'll cut this black ground like butter. Fella said he'd hold it for me 'til winter. I'm gonna drag it up here one night. An' mebbe I'll put a real crop in here come spring. Or maybe not if we all get run-off before then." He laughed but without much humor.

"But that'd be a shame though, 'cause I never seen dirt like this before." Frank stooped down and clawed out a handful, showing it to Bill. "They dredged the Bayou to make these levees bigger and the channel deeper a long time ago. This black hump we're standin' on is ol' river bottom." Frank crumbled the dirt in his fingers. "An' look at all this busted-up oyster shell. These levees 'ould grow enough to feed half the city." Frank looked at the surrounding buildings as if to verify his estimation.

Bill asked, "So nobody knows who owns this property?"

Frank dusted off his hands. "Nope. Don't wanna know. I'm sure one day some official-type fellas will come in here an' kick us out. But ya live with what ya got for now. Nothin' lasts forever."

"Some things last forever," Bill mumbled, staring off at the bumper crop of volunteer tomatoes.

"Huh? Oh, well, if you say so."

Bill cleared his throat. "Frank, I know a little bit about nonprofits. Maybe I could help y'all get some kind of co-op goin' here or something."

Frank raised the bill of his cap. "Yeah, well that'd be nice I suppose. Like I said though, I'm gonna keep chippin' away at it. It's somethin' for us to do, ya know." He had his pint out and took a pull.

Bill nodded and forced a smile. "Idle hands do the Devil's work."

They walked to another dim trail and followed it single-file back toward the shrine. Frank was in the lead, still talking as he walked. But Bill was looking up, his eyes following the surrounding highrises until he'd halted completely and turned back to face east toward Downtown again. The sky was mostly cloudy but the cluster of glass towers was ablaze in bright sunlight with a complete rainbow arched above. Rain pattered the weeds, and Bill felt it tickling his exposed skin and tamping down his windswept hair. The noise of the city beneath the intensifying rain shower rang like a chorus, and Brother Cox wondered what an epiphany was supposed to feel like.

Frank croaked in the background, "Come on, preacher man! You're gettin' soaked!"

"Sorry!" Bill said, startled. He turned and jogged to catch up to the geezer, who was moving faster than he should be able to. The trail led to the south end of the dock, where they ascended a battered set of concrete steps.

The group of folks seated around the emaciated orator had grown. Marcus had joined their ranks, and Leo too, having worked his way down passing out grilled cheeses. The wind cast a mist across the dock and the ringleader rose with some difficulty saying, "Whoa, you guys wanna move inside?" The crowd mumbled concurrence and hustled as a loose unit toward the northernmost bay door. They slipped under, two or three at a time, and Frank and Bill brought up the rear. When Bill straightened his back on the inside, his jaw dropped.

The "shrine" was gutted from its extensive slab floor to the I-beams supporting the high ceiling. Two rows of windows ran along the west wall opposite the big bay doors. The upper-row windows were small, impossibly high and filthy, rendering smoky light that made the ceiling appear even higher. The lower windows were several yards tall and wide, with fractured glass panes inlaid with steel mesh that let the elements seep in but refused to fail completely. The exposed girders in the walls, which served as built-in shelving, were adorned with rows of multihued, empty booze bottles. Many shards in the big, leaky windows were prismatic, and they dappled the expansive concrete floor with iridescent light as the sun broke free in the western sky. Bill was prone to weeping and he nearly gave in.

"Ah there, ya see why we call it the shrine?" Frank patted Brother Bill on the shoulder. "We do what we can to keep the place up. There was a lot o' cheap wood furniture in the beginnin', but it got burned over the winters. An' Leo never stops pickin' up an' sortin' trash. It's his penance, I suppose." Only a few metal chairs, desks, and blackened steel drums remained.

Jaime, the emaciated ringleader who had been speaking to the group outside on the dock, took his position on a chair with his back to the wall amid stacks of tattered paperbacks and piles of periodicals. Everyone else gathered in a loose semicircle occupying the weathered office furniture or the floor.

Marcus recognized Farah in the crowd, wearing a shabby full-length dress and drooping wide-brimmed hat, her face seamed and brown. He had seen her outside before the rain had ushered everyone inside, but he had decided not to approach her. He was trying to remember how many times he'd seen her up here at the village before—not often, maybe once or twice. She sat down close on Jaime's right, avoiding eye contact.

The Sabine Street Bridge wasn't far upstream. Something was brewing here. As if on cue, Jaime looked up at Marcus and asked, "So, Ting, did you hear about that poor kid they pulled out of the bayou yesterday?"

Ting was ready. "Yeah, I heard about it."

"Man, it's a wonder anybody heard about it. It was just a blip in the news, 'troubled youth drowns' or some variation of that in a few different papers, and the cause was all speculation, no hard facts. Don't news people get that kind of information from the cops?" Marcus started to answer but Jaime held up a hand and cut him off when he noticed Bill and Frank approaching. "Oh, I'm sorry. Frank, who's your new friend?"

"He's Brother Bill. He's a deacon or somethin'. Come up here with Ting."

"Ah, a holy man, welcome."

Bill smiled and reached over several heads to shake Jaime's hand. "Thank you. I *was* a minister, but right now I'm kinda lookin' for work—"

Marcus cleared his throat. "So yeah Jaime, I actually knew that kid they pulled out of the bayou yesterday. His name was Sean. So what *hard facts* are you talking about? Are you saying you know more about it than the cops, and the news people?"

Farah glanced at Marcus, but then looked back down.

Bill's mouth had fallen open. He interjected, "Oh my God, Ting, was it right down there at Sabine Street? Because I was the one who discovered that body."

"What?"

"I was ridin' my bike and I saw him out there in the water, so I called the police and two detectives showed up and—"

"Did it look like a suicide?"

Bill's voice pitched higher. "I don't know, Ting. I didn't stick around and watch 'em fish him out. They asked me some questions and let me go."

Marcus frowned at Bill for a few seconds while the clergyman fidgeted.

Jaime cleared his throat and said, "Ting, we have reason to believe that your friend Sean didn't just dive in or fall in and drown, or any of that stuff they wrote about in the newspapers."

"News people are idiots. *I* went to see the cops and even *they* know the dude didn't just fall in and drown. They know he crashed into a log in the bayou, and that's what killed him because there was hardly any water in his lungs. They *do* think he dove off the bridge because he was suicidal or trippin' on something. But I knew the guy, late night. He was never out of control and he wouldn't just dive off a bridge."

Jaime looked surprised. "*You* went to see the cops? How'd that happen? Did they strongarm you to come in, or come pick you up?" He took a pull from a green jug of red wine.

"Some Detective Lamonte called me in. Because, as it turns out, I was the last one Sean called on his phone the night before last … right before he got killed."

Jaime raised his eyebrows. "Whoa. And what did Sean have to say that night?"

Marcus was already pulling his phone from his pack. "I missed the call because I was busy at work," he said with regret. "But I've still got the message." He played the voicemail. He tried to point out the menacing voice in the background, but again no one else seemed to hear it.

Jaime was thoughtful for a minute. Then he said, "So you

think maybe Sean needed your help because somebody was after him. And the cops think he was saying he needed help because he was suicidal on drugs, and you guys were lovers or something?"

"Something like that. So what do you know about it?"

"Well." He looked at Farah.

She took a deep breath and picked up her chin. She spoke softly, but everybody heard her. "I saw two big, mean fellers throw that boy off the bridge."

There was chatter in the assembly. Bill opened his mouth but covered it with his hand.

Marcus knew Farah was fragile, sitting there staring down at her own worn-out shoes. He'd hate to guess at her age. So he gave her a moment, but then pressed on. "He was alive when they threw him off?"

She looked up at him, wiping her eyes with her sleeve and said, "Yessir."

CHAPTER

7

THE GROWING TALE OF SEAN

"It was pretty weather out, an' I was 'sleep under that big crepe myrtle over by the start of the Frisbee golf game. Norm'ly I don't hear the cars in the middle of the night, but this pickup come a-skiddin' onto the bridge, with hooligans hollerin' out the winders, an' it startled me to wake. I looked over there an' saw a boy in a pink coat was a-runnin' from that pickup truck, an' he looked scared an' tired." Farah was working hard not to cry.

Jaime put his hand on her shoulder. "It's okay. There's nothing you could've done. Tell Ting what you saw."

She straightened her back and continued. "Them two devils, they stopped their pickup and jumped out. They was fast an' they caught the little fella 'bout halfway 'cross the bridge. They was so big he looked like a child when they grabbed him. They was laughin' and—" Farah stared straight ahead. "Even from where I was, I could see fangs in their mouths, like they was demons."

Fringe people squirmed.

Ting frowned. "Fangs."

Farah glanced up at him and nodded. "An' when they threw him off the bridge, I couldn't do nothin' but close my eyes. He hollered and then I heard him hit that pile o' trash hard, an' I knew—" She took a halting breath. "An' when I opened my eyes, the one devil was already back in the pickup hollerin' they had to go. His teeth made him hiss like a snake. But that other one, before he got in the truck, I know he saw me. He looked right at me, a-grinnin' an' shakin' his head. He had black eyes and ragged teeth like a possum. I wanted to shut my eyes but I was all froze-up. Then the one in the pickup pulled 'long next to him and he got in. They pulled a U-turn an' then burnt off back toward town.

"I could see that boy's body layin' down there in the middle of the bayou, an' he never moved. I closed my eyes and laid there for a minute thinkin' them devils might come back. Then I sneaked up here t' the shrine. Mebbe they know me now. I can't be sure. So I can't go nowhere, for who knows how long."

Sean was murdered. Damn it. Marcus breathed deeply through his nose, unclenched his jaw, and asked aloud, "Anybody else seen any of these wannabe vampires around?"

A lithe, thick-bearded man cleared his throat, stood, and removed his dirty cap. "Yessir, I have. I seen 'em pull into one of them little parkin' lots along Memorial one night." He gestured vaguely north. "They was drivin' real slow, in a white pickup truck too."

Marcus nodded. "You remember anything else about the truck?"

The gent shook his head. "Was white, maybe a Ford; ain't sure. Had dark winders."

"Dark windows." Marcus nodded. "Anything else? Did you see the word 'fish' or a company name or logo or anything like that?"

"Don't think so. I figured they was up to no good though, barely movin' like they was. Maybe lookin' for somebody to hurt.

It was real late, dark an' cloudy out, and I was in among the trees. So I just stood stock still 'til they passed on by."

Good thinking, Marcus thought. The weedy gent could pass for a sapling in the dark. "Okay, thanks. Jerry, right?"

"Yessir. And thank you as always for the sandwiches."

"Right on. Anybody else?"

Nobody spoke up, but there was mumbling.

Marcus began to pace the edge of the crowd.

Jaime asked, "What's on your mind, Holmes?"

Marcus jerked his thumb toward Brother Cox saying, "Bill got jumped outside The Fallout Shelter by a couple of these same goons, except one was quite a bit shorter than the other. But their teeth were unmistakable. Farah, you didn't say whether one of them was shorter than the other, did you?"

"Nope, they was about the same height. I couldn't tell 'em apart 'cept by their clothes."

Marcus looked at Jaime. "The punks that jumped Bill definitely weren't the same height, but otherwise they sound just like these two murderers on the bridge, bleached hair, fangs, and all. And they weren't in a pickup truck, but they took off in a big white van with dark windows, and it had the little black "FISH" decal on the back. You know what I mean?"

"Like for a vehicle hauling seafood, commercially," Jaime said.

"Yeah. And as far as I can tell, Sean had just left The Fallout Shelter that night right before *he* was attacked. On the voicemail he said he had to go pick something up. So maybe he was headed for one of those lofts off Sabine Street or something, and those punks chased him and caught him on the bridge. It's not that far from The Fallout Shelter, especially for a fit kid like Sean."

"It's not that far from *here* either, bro," Jaime pointed out.

Marcus took a deep breath. "Yeah. There's no way this is all just a coincidence."

"So you think we're being terrorized by a clan of undead seafood vendors?"

Marcus considered it and said, "Not exactly. They're definitely mortal men. Me and Big Nelly tested 'em on that point."

"I bet you did." Jaime was well aware of Ting's skill as a pugilist.

Bill spoke up. "So maybe we should get together everything we know now and go back to the police."

Marcus shot him a sideways glance.

Jaime said, "Believe me, Bill. The cops have no interest in reopening this little can of worms. And anyway, testimony from street people is taken pretty lightly in court. Plus, we're too vulnerable to depend on their protection."

"Too vulnerable for their protection? That doesn't even make sense."

"We just don't trust 'em."

Farah piped up, "I ain't talkin' to no po-lice, an' I ain't goin' nowhere near no po-lice station."

Bill kept on. "So what, these murderers just keep terrorizin' everybody? What if they kill somebody else?" He was speaking to anyone who would listen.

Frank looked up from paring his nails with a rusty pocketknife and said, "People die all the time, boyo. An' if Farah don't wanna talk to the goddamn cops she don't hafta."

"Sorry," Bill said, a little shocked.

After a moment Frank replied, "I'm sorry too, dammit. This is just upsettin', ya know?"

Marcus said, "I just don't understand their motive. Is it hate, pure and simple?"

Some shook their heads, some nodded, and some shrugged.

Jaime grabbed part of a newspaper off one of the stacks beside him, folded it to a particular section, and then extended it to Marcus. "Bro, maybe we could use a little help from somebody else, besides the cops, but in the real world too, you know?"

"Huh?"

Jaime shook the paper. "Not all news people are idiots, Ting. In fact, we really need the ones who aren't." He flung the paper at Marcus.

It was a weekly periodical he knew well. *The Houston Rag* was free, and most people read it to see what venue whose band was playing and when. Jaime had it folded to the section in back where *The Rag* covered some actual news, even if only a couple hundred words per topic. Jaime had circled a few paragraphs near the bottom of the page. "You see it?" he asked. "Down there in the corner?"

Marcus nodded. "'Slipped or Slain' by AKK?"

"Her real name is listed in the front, under staff. It's Amber," Jaime said.

Marcus shrugged, sighed, and scanned the article. It was about Sean. But unlike the recycled blurbs in the mainstream papers, this little piece questioned the authorities' version of the incident. And it contained some additional info that this AKK person had to have gleaned for herself somehow, maybe squeezed it out of the cops.

Jaime said, "The number to the paper and all the extensions are on the inside cover. I think hers is three-zero-two. You know, if you wanted to call her."

"I don't know what good that would do, Jaime. Nobody that matters reads this paper."

"Everybody matters, Ting. Or else nobody does."

"Okay, well apparently some matter less than others." Marcus sighed. "Give me a little time to wrap my head around all this. I'll work it out. In the meantime though, all you guys should be more careful. Try not to get caught out alone, especially at night. And if you see any big, pasty-looking goons around, get out of sight as fast as you can. Then be sure to tell me about it. And Farah, like you said, you should definitely hole up here for a while. Me and the guys will make sure you have plenty of groceries."

"I ain't goin' nowhere," she assured him.

"An' I'll be around," Frank said, glancing at Farah.

"I'll be checkin' on folks too," Leo added.

Marcus pointed at his towering friend and said, "Thanks, Leo." Everybody here was a rag doll compared to Leo.

Bill had more to say but kept quiet. He'd offered his advice. It had been rejected. Plus, he had to admit, he'd seen a new side of the police lately. Apparently not all cops were heroes, as he'd been led to believe in his youth.

Jaime grunted as he got to his feet, saying, "You should talk to her though, Ting. See what she has to say. We could use some fresh air around here, and I bet this AKK would love to know what we know."

Marcus rolled up the paper. "Yeah, I'm sure she would, but that kind of information is dangerous too, Jaime. It's the kind that can get people hurt. Or killed. These guys seem pretty organized. She might stir up a yellow-jacket nest she's not ready for."

Jaime nodded. "Well, you know how passive we are, man. We're usually not taken too seriously in the eyes of the law. But the truth, when you put it out in the light for everybody to see, it's even stronger than the law. Anyway, the ball's in your court. Sean was your friend. We never met him. Around here our main interest is Farah. She's really scared. And if those dudes come looking for her and find this place." Jaime shook his head. "I'm just saying, the yellow jackets are already flying, bro. They're already stinging."

Marcus just nodded, breathing deeply through his nose.

Thunder rolled in the east, but for now the rain shower had passed. Fringe folks ambled from the shifting, prismatic light inside the shrine back out onto the deck to shake water from their possessions. Jaime was among them, but he didn't walk as far. He hunched out from under the bay door and plopped into a battered lawn chair against the wall where the rain hadn't reached. He had his jug and took a swig.

Brother Bill emerged from the shrine at that moment, and by the look on his face he was about to say something about Jaime's alcoholism. Marcus materialized with his notepad in hand and cleared his throat. He would have to tell Bill that Jaime had lost his wife and daughter in a home invasion years back, while he'd been out of town for work. That's why he'd drunk away his tenure at U of H, and why he still couldn't climb out of the bottle.

Bill moved out of Tíng's way so Jaime could see the murals copied on the pad. Marcus said, "Dude, I almost forgot to ask. Have you been sneaking around painting this weird Spanish graffiti along the bayous?"

"Huh? Oh no, that's not me bro, but I heard about it, and I was actually just thinking about that. A couple of the *Mejicanos* that hang out around White Oak and Heights Boulevard came through here the other day. They told me there's this strange new cat living down on the bayou there. He's from the mountains down southwest, like maybe Michoacán, and the guys over there around White Oak have been calling him Panterito. Anyway, they say he's the one who's been doing it, the weird paintings."

Marcus handed him the pad. "Right. Well, these are the ones that I've seen. I copied them down so you could take a look."

"Cool." Jaime stared at the page a moment, then flipped to the next. It was blank so he flipped back. Marcus had all three murals transcribed and well-spaced on the first page, including the one he'd photographed with his phone.

Bill tried not to appear antsy.

"You must have read them like ten times by now," Marcus said after a minute.

"Huh, oh yeah this is interesting stuff, man." He looked up at Marcus.

Tíng's impatience was budding. "Dude, my Spanish sucks. What do they mean?"

"Oh right, sorry. Well, this first one says '*ojos del mundo y sol,*' which means like 'eyes of the world and sun,' or maybe 'eyes of the earth and sun.'"

"What about the next one?"

"Ok, the next one says '*viene sus madre oceana,*' which simply means 'your mother ocean comes,' or like 'your mother ocean is coming,' you know?"

"Right. And the last one?"

"The last one says '*El cielo llora.*' That means 'the sky cries,' or like 'the sky is crying,' in other words."

"That's a Stevie Ray Vaughn rip-off. So what, is this guy like a prophet or a poet or something?" Marcus glanced at Bill who shrugged.

Jaime took a sip and swirled his jug, frowning at its near-emptiness. "More of a mystic, I think. They say he's *Indio,* like he's got a lot of native blood. He has very dark skin and strange tattoos." Jaime looked at Bill. "They also say he can vanish into thin air."

"What, are you serious?" Bill asked.

Marcus shook his head. "Does he have a dog?"

Jaime was nodding. "Yeah, a big red dog that's always with him. So you've seen him."

"Can the dog vanish too?" Bill couldn't resist.

"Yes," Jaime said, straight-faced. "They also say that he's crazy, that he eats only grasses and mushrooms and things that he finds along the water. They say he lives under a tree somewhere upstream along White Oak. I'd actually like to go there and meet him some time."

Marcus knew Jaime had hardly left the village in years. "I'm pretty sure we saw him and his dog on White Oak Bayou. We were up under I-10 and they were walking away from us, upstream like you said. We were a long way off though. So they think *he's* the one painting these stamps under the bridges."

Jaime nodded. "The *Mejicanos* that live up that way say it

must be him. And if half the things they say about him are true, then it makes the most sense."

"I wish I spoke Spanish. I'd go up there and chat with him myself," Marcus said.

"I'll go with you," Bill said.

"I'm not gonna go because I don't speak Spanish, and neither do you so what good would it do?"

"Maybe just to take him a sandwich," Bill said.

"This guy doesn't seem like the grilled-cheese type. Anyway, the main purpose for going up there would be to talk to him, and we wouldn't be able to."

Jaime nodded. "*Palabra.*"

Bill dropped it.

Marcus said, "Jaime, if you do end up somehow getting to visit with this guy, I'd like to hear the rest of his story. And if you do go looking for him, be sure to take Leo with you. That's a long way."

By the angle of the jug, Jaime took his last drink then said, "I think everybody wants to know his story. And it's probably too far for me to walk anyway. Leo would have to take *me* with *him*." Jaime squinted and looked past Marcus, out at their immense friend standing near the edge of the heap, talking with Frank.

"Right, that's what I meant." Marcus followed Jaime's gaze, but then looked even farther, past Leo, way out east to the downtown skyline with its backdrop of dark clouds. It felt later than it was, and Tíng announced that he'd better get going. He collected his pad from Jaime. They slapped hands and half hugged.

"Later, bro."

"Right on."

Bill shook hands with Jaime. "Nice to meet you. God bless. Y'all take care and I hope to see you again soon."

"You're always welcome here Bill, as is anyone else who comes in peace," Jaime said.

"Thanks, thank you so much. I will be back."

Marcus was out by the tomatoes already, slapping hands with Leo and Frank.

Hurrying to catch up, Bill turned back after he hopped down from the dock, and saw Jaime on his feet, stooping to give his sandwich to an old-timer whom Bill had mistaken for a heap of linens lying along the wall. Brother Cox vowed to be more proactive the next time he visited.

蛉

The route they took back was straighter so Bill could exploit his extra gears. He only lost sight of Marcus once towards the end. The vine-covered gate was ajar when the holy roller rolled into the alley. He walked the Frankenbike through and saw Marcus standing at the side entrance to the garage-dojo, thumbing through a newspaper.

Tíng looked up and said, "Sorry dude, I have some other stuff to take care of. Thanks for helping me out today. You got all your stuff?"

"Uh, yeah, I think so." Bill leaned the Frankenbike against the garage and inventoried his pockets. He was still breathing hard from the ride.

"You still have that Yellow Cab business card in your wallet right, from last night? Or there's a bus stop right back over on Yale. As you know, I don't have a car."

Bill had out his wallet and phone. "Yeah, no, I don't either. I'll be fine. I got some networkin' and stuff to do too. But maybe you could call me if you needed help with sandwiches or somethin'. Or anything for that matter, I mean you did save my life last night."

"Right. Let's not blow it out of proportion. I doubt if they would've actually killed you." They both thought about Sean but said nothing. "Anyway like I said, it's my unofficial job to sort of help keep the peace around there, so it's not that big a deal."

"To you maybe. Anyway, could I give you my number in case you wanna ride again? I've got my own bike and I know where you live now."

"Uh, yeah, but my phone's about dead. It's in there on the charger."

"That's alright, you can just tell me your number and I'll call and leave you a message. Then you can just save my number, you know what I mean?"

"Yeah, I know what you mean. I'm just not used to giving my phone number out to people, you know?"

Bill nodded. "Right, okay, I just thought we, uh. Well, I had a good time today. I guess I'll just—"

Marcus gave Bill his number.

Bill tried to suppress a smile as he keyed it in and saved it, and not a moment later, the blond hayseed received a call. His ringtone was some twangy country-diva pop song and Marcus felt instant regret. Bill screened the number and said, "Oh, sorry, I have to take this."

Tíng smiled, nodded, and disappeared into the dojo. He leaned on the door and savored his solitude for a moment. Then he corrected his posture and breathed with purpose. As the negative energy left him, he thought of her again, the girl on the steps in the rain at the police compound. *Ridiculous.* He turned his attention across the dojo to the Diūqì Shìbīng; it trembled imperceptibly.

Amber Klara Karakyavik, AKK, the girl on the steps in the rain at the police compound, was on one of her phones talking to her friend Ryan Dylan, whom she often referred to as "bug nut" but he didn't mind the label. He was an entomologist at The

Bayou City Conservancy, a sprawling urban oasis overflowing with indigenous flora, birds, and critters near Reliant Park on the southeast side of town.

Ryan was talking Amber's ear off about butterflies again. Monarchs had infiltrated South Texas and many of them should be fluttering through town by now on their way to Mexico for the winter, but they weren't. The count was so low thus far that he considered it to be negligible. Ryan sounded weepy as he spoke. "Is H-town so foul and devoid of flora now that they're just totally flying around us? Has our city just become one big, reeking refinery?"

Amber knew he didn't mean it. Ryan loved Houston, but he loved nature even more. And she loved him, so she soothed him and promised she would write something emotive for him, and she would make sure it got reprinted in the Houston Chronicle. AKK had helped Ryan author a puff piece about butterfly counting last season, but this one would be more of a *save the environment* bit with some teeth. She told him to sketch her an outline with the pertinent data, and she'd fill in the compelling voice. He said he had just emailed it to her.

"M'kay."

"Love ya."

"G'bye."

"Smooches."

Ugh, more on my plate. Amber wanted to power down and completely recharge her multitude of data-receiving and transmitting devices, especially the three-pound one inside her skull, but that wasn't going to happen any time soon. It had taken everything she'd had yesterday to get the investigative article on Sean Dorsey done in time to print, and now she was behind on her obligatory puff pieces. She shoved her keyboard forward and rested her head on the edge of her cluttered desk for just a minute.

And here we go again. Amber started thinking about him,

the circus performer or superhero or whatever he was, in the foyer at the police station. She'd only met him for a moment, and his physique and attire had been otherworldly for sure, but there was something in his eyes, something more than just a story. She wondered subconsciously if he'd been thinking about her too. *Ridiculous.*

8

REBEL ASIAN

There was no contest on the big stage at The Fallout Shelter this evening, so Nelly was at ease, though still dressed to kill. A dime-sized, faux beauty mark accented her cinder-block jaw and platinum blond wig, which could house a clutch of eaglets. Marcus wondered what his friend had paid for her custom size-84 gown. The dancing duelist sat at Nelly's table in his Kangol and trench coat thinking it was hardly busy enough for him to be here tonight. The two friends were unusually quiet and brooding.

Marcus had just revealed the whole story surrounding Sean's death. He played the voicemail, trying to point out the creepy voice in the background, and then gave Farah's account of what she had seen transpire on the Sabine Street Bridge that night.

Nelly's eyes were still moist. The corner of the heavy wooden table where she sat, was cracked and nearly broken off, where her fist had come down on it. She had been much closer to Sean than Marcus had been. When Nelly threw a tantrum, there was something about her heavy hands that caused things to disintegrate.

Apparently a new breed of fanged hooligan was terrorizing the area, targeting the meek and-or gay for some ungodly reason.

It was working to the thugs' favor that their victims were the type to fear and mistrust the cops. Being one of only a few contacts saved in Sean's burner phone, Nelly had gotten a call from the police just like Marcus. But as a college-educated white businessman with a lawyer on retainer, Nelson had answered a couple of their questions, and then referred them to his attorney. Going back to the cops with this new information might help, but they couldn't drag an old homeless lady up to the police station if she wasn't willing to go.

Nelly finished her cocktail in one gulp and said, "You know, if you're ever in trouble, you call me, right Ting?"

Marcus nodded. He was scanning the modest crowd of angels, devils, and ghouls. Halloween was still a few days away, but working at The Fallout Shelter was always somewhat of a masquerade.

Nelly added, "If I'd known all this crap was going down, I would have stomped on that snaggle-toothed punk out there in the parking lot and smushed him. I freakin' hate haters."

Marcus spoke up. "And it's not like they're just skinheads out stalking the Montrose again, you know. It's weird. Nobody else has seen them around." He had called half a dozen other predominantly gay clubs, and they hadn't had any trouble other than usual. Certainly none of them had seen or heard of any fanged militants lurking around. Likewise, the fringe folks said their run-ins with the goons had been solely concentrated in this area.

It occurred to Marcus that The Fallout Shelter was considerably the farthest north and west establishment of its type inside this part of the loop. It technically might not even be in the Montrose District. It was in a gray area, on the fringe. He said, "It seems like they're kind of lurking between here and the Heights, sticking close to the bayou, but why?"

Nelly thought about it for a moment then said, "Down along the bayou's a good place to hide."

"Yeah. But I've never seen 'em down there below the levees, where I ride."

"Right." Nelly knew Ting travelled the sub-street-level trails constantly. "Maybe I-Forty-Five is their escape route and they stay close to it. What was her name? Farah? She said they sped back toward the freeway that night, right?"

"Yeah, but I'm not a hundred percent sure they got on."

Nelly sighed. "I'm just grabbing at straws."

Marcus sat up straight in his barstool. "What worries me most is the little *village* that I told you about, you know where Jaime and all of them sort of *live*?"

"Yeah."

"It's like right there at Montrose and Allen Parkway, right on the bayou and right near the freeway. It's perfect. If those dirt-bags follow one of the guys up that hill looking to terrorize some homeless people, they'll find a whole village of them, and they'd be trapped up there. None of them have phones, or any hope that the cops might show up and help."

Nelly shook her head, her painted lips pressed in a hard line.

After a long silence Marcus sighed and said, "I think I'm gonna go back on for a little while." He finished his Roy Rogers and bolted back through the double doors to the panic room. When he reappeared minutes later, sans hat and coat, he was clad in a black body suit with a full-face hood overlaid with a silver-white skeleton whose bones appeared holographic under The Fallout Shelter's black lighting. Onlookers gasped when Tíng bounded onto his stage. He caught the pole at an impossible height, scaled it up to the high ceiling, and then spiraled down, hanging by the backs of his knees. The DJ slipped into a psychedelic medley featuring Empire of the Sun, Tíng's body synced with the music, and onlookers were transfixed.

The chromed pole was a second home to Marcus, so despite his level of exertion, his mind was free to wander. Swinging by a single skeletal hand, he envisioned a pair of toothy goons laughing on a bridge, the two who had T-rolled Bill. But he knew that wasn't right. Farah had said those two were the same size. So there were more of them somewhere. Then a vision of a girl captured his mind's eye, with strawberry blond hair and earth-colored eyes—the girl on the steps at the police station.

Tíng's eyes opened upon the overhead lights rotating high above. He had dismounted the pole and was locked into a stream-lined whirling pirouette. Sheathed in gray light, the dancing duelist could be the prey of some giant spider, spinning in silk on the wind. Regardless of skill level, every dancer on the floor stopped and stared. The DJ timed the end of Marcus's spin with a harsh record-scratching sound bite and someone in the crowd shouted, "Yee haw!"

Tíng homed in on the source of the yell and saw Bill standing there with some tall, handsome redneck dude. Of course, what Marcus assumed to be a cowboy getup was Jake Bontemps's standard attire. Bill's bestie from down in Oyster Prairie had come up to party in the city on a wild hare.

There were catcalls and applause as Marcus came down and moved quickly through the crowd. Some touched him as he passed, but not disrespectfully. Anyway, he was used to it. He disappeared behind the bar again, and took his time changing so anyone hawking him would hopefully lose interest. His heart wasn't in it tonight.

When Marcus finally came back down from the panic room in his hat and coat, Bill and his hillbilly friend were seated over at Nelly's table; by the look on Nelly's face, Brother Cox was arduously thanking her for helping him the other night out in the parking lot. Marcus approached reluctantly and when Nelly saw him coming, she stood abruptly, causing Bill and Jake to flinch. Over the tops of her new friends' heads, Nelly said, "Dude, just take off. There's plenty of wannabes in the crowd tonight. They'll fight over your stage after they realize you're gone."

Bill was elated to see Marcus and was contemplating a hug, so Marcus put his hand way out for slapping and said, "What's up, dude?"

Brother Cox introduced Marcus to Jake, and would have gone on about Tíng's heroism except that Nelly barged back in. "And don't worry about us Ting, we'll be fine. 'cause if those little Billy Idol clones roll up in here, I will smack their pointy little teeth out." She snapped her fingers three times in an S-formation, and Jake seemed dangerously on the verge of laughter. Big Nelly stooped down to the lanky rice farmer and said, "And honey, you know I'm technically a man and I'm pretty sure you're straight, so you better *quit* ogling me. Skinny shit-kickers ain't my type."

Jake smirked, most of his blood in his cheeks. "Yes ma'am," he uttered, hoping it was the right thing to say.

Nelly slugged a fresh cocktail, adjusted her gown, and was not surprised when she looked up and Ting was gone.

蜻蛉

Marcus took an indirect route, so he could cruise part of Montrose Boulevard and observe its traffic. A couple of white trucks rolled by, but they weren't occupied by pasty-faced goons. Focused on passing vehicles, Marcus didn't notice the Econoline Van that was pacing him from a block behind, keeping its distance.

Deciding he was wasting his time, Tíng broke west and accelerated down a secluded lane. He would enter the village unseen from the south. When the Econoline reached the same turnoff, the skinny sumbitch on the bike was nowhere to be seen. The driver and passenger squabbled as the van searched in a hurried pattern, block by block, working its way west, the last direction its quarry had been headed.

It was too late for a visit, so Marcus crept toward the shrine on a little-used trail that connected to an alley at the southeast corner of the lot. He saw many peaceful human forms sleeping on the loading dock, and could even hear some snoring. He slinked back to the Frankenbike, and took the alley north.

The goons in the van were stoked when they saw Marcus emerge from out of nowhere onto Allen Parkway heading northwest just a couple hundred yards ahead. But they cursed when their prey crossed the wide thoroughfare diagonally and hopped the opposing curb, vanishing over the rim of the steep levee at a breakneck pace. They sped up and crossed Buffalo Bayou at the Waugh Street bridge.

Tíng crossed the water on a pedestrian bridge, and then weaved his way to I-10 and picked up the frontage road so he could cruise by the China Man from the south. The store was obviously closed so Marcus blew on by.

Teacher heard the Frankenbike whiz past as he unlocked the gate to his backyard. He had a garbage can bungeed to a dolly in tow. The little master pulled the can out into the front lot, craning his head up the street, in the direction Marcus had just ridden. He almost yelled something after his disrespectful student, but it was too late. Tíng was riding fast and already out of sight.

A tailpipe belched off to the China Man's left. A white van lurched into a dark corner of his parking lot and ground to a halt. The headlights went out, but the engine was left idling. The driver door popped open, and a bear of a man with a white-blond buzz cut got out and leisurely stretched where he stood. Another fellow who could be his slighter twin hopped out and walked around from the passenger side. Then the pair of them approached the China Man in step. Both wore roughneck attire and heavy boots that crunched the gravel under their feet. They grinned to show their fangs.

The little old man looked over his shoulder at the closed and latched gate to his high-fenced backyard, twenty paces away. He sighed, and when he turned back, he was already standing in the two men's shadows. The driver of the van smiled as he reached into a cargo pocket and installed a set of steel-knuckles that he'd welded-up himself at the shop.

Marcus turned south when he hit Yale and got off the road under the I-10 overpass, so he could see Marty's camp. But as he searched the darkness under the pillars, a moving light caught his eye. The glow was from far upstream, and moving away along the opposite side of the water until it finally disappeared. Tíng pedaled the Frankenbike down the sidewalk to the Yale Bridge over White Oak Bayou so he could see farther around the bend. Nothing. But as his eyes adjusted to the dark, he thought he saw the flickering light of a flame. *Somebody's campfire?*

Tíng was tempted to stash his bike and run up the bayou to investigate, but it would be a risky venture. At this hour, it was best to stay on the concrete, and there was no paved jogging lane on that stretch of the waterway, only rough foot paths cut through tall weeds, and a crumbling old railroad trestle. A thug could be the least dangerous thing one might encounter down on those trails, especially with this mild, wet weather.

More than once Marcus had looked down from this bridge and seen a water moccasin as thick as his arm basking among the driftwood below the trestle. Plus, there were possums, raccoons, skunks, coyotes, stray dogs, and who knows what else creeping along the water below the city at night. Leo attested to having once seen a panther at daybreak, running out of town along White Oak Bayou with somebody's lost pooch, collar and all, dangling from its mouth. The city supported an array of predators.

Marcus studied the darkness around the bend, but the light was gone. So he turned the Frankenbike around and rode home to meditate, and hopefully eventually to sleep.

蛤令

The China Man said with a smile, "I am so sorry gentlemen, I am closed for the evening."

The pair of brutes laughed their best, toothy, mock-Asian laughs. They'd been looking for somebody else and lost him; now this foreigner would have to sate some of their anger. The driver of the van said, "You shoulda left yer shit and ran for that gate when you had the chance, gook."

The diminutive shopkeeper undid the stretched-out bungee cord and calmly slid the trash can off his little blue dolly. He looked up, studied their apparently filed teeth for a moment, and said, "I don't run from suckas like you two." He beamed at them with his own square, yellowish choppers.

The driver understood well enough to know he'd been insulted, and at that moment things happened quickly. "You little muther—" The man-monster strode forward, raising his big right hand, which bore a four-finger-ring with a row of ball bearings welded onto the knuckles. The brute was enraged, but he tried to focus. *Just a body shot, don't kill him; just wanna hear him cry.* But the little bastard didn't retreat, didn't flinch.

Instead the China Man dropped his shoulders and thrust his little blue dolly toward his attacker's shins with unpredictable swiftness and force. The dolly was old but solid, and its welded angle-iron frame would not yield to flesh and bone.

The van driver aborted his assault and threw all efforts into avoiding the dolly. He skipped backward and flung his hands forward as a counterweight, and the inelegant maneuver combined with his high heavy boots saved him from severe shin-bone trauma. Still, the dolly ramped off his toes and wracked both tibias good, blowing out his footing completely. The China Man pulled the dolly back to his side with a bungee cord still attached to the handle. For a split second the driver was relieved that the dolly was gone, but then his chin and elbows hit the gravel and his bootheels swung up behind his head.

The van's passenger was shocked by the violent shift in odds that had taken about two seconds, so as the dolly turned his way, he didn't take any chances. He held his distance and reached into his left boot, where he kept sheathed the remains of an ancient oyster-shucker. The shank was black iron, honed razor-sharp on both edges with a delicate point, mounted to a slim handle of polished antler. As the passenger grabbed for his antique throwing knife, the China Man shouted, "Yoh!" and stepped into it this time.

The dolly barely touched the ground as it closed the distance between them in a heartbeat. The passenger was too slow, so he left the shank in its sheath and used both hands to block the blue dolly. He turned his head as it pushed beneath his palms, collided with his steel toes, and ricocheted up into his bent knees.

The hooligan shouted expletives as he fell forward, and shooting pain nearly seized his faculties. He snarled and clawed for the dolly as it zipped back to its master. The little gook was laughing at him. The passenger shifted to a three-point stance and made another grab for his blade; then he cowed and left it in place again as the dolly flew at him like a spear. The goon tried to tumble out of the flying bludgeon's path and almost made it, but the corner of it clipped his left humerus (and it wasn't funny). Neuromuscular fire burned from his elbow to his fingertips as the van's passenger cradled his arm and rolled in the gravel.

The van's driver was up from his stunning nosedive into the parking lot. He spat out some blood and charged, intent on leaping over the dolly this time and grabbing the little—but he slipped on some loose gravel, and was in no position to jump when the dolly came for him again. In a desperate move, the brute dropped his shoulder and punched the iron dolly with his homemade steel knuckles. The China Man offered a look of tacit approval when the dolly stopped cold with a resounding clang. But the lad's wrist hadn't endured the impact, and was bent at a sharp angle. The goon was rolling in the gravel again.

The bungee jerked and the dolly retreated with a scuff on its paint. The old man caught the lever on wheels, pivoted to conserve inertia, and fired it at the van's passenger. On his knees, the goon pulled his blade and threw. But the damned dolly was right in his line of sight, and he threw too high. He tried to spin away, but the dolly struck his shoulder and at that same moment, the China Man snatched the thrown shank from the air as it passed over his head. Teacher inspected the treacherous weapon. Then he snapped the blade off under his shoe, and stuffed both pieces of the ruined knife into his trash can.

The passenger was dazed, but he managed to laugh when he saw the broken bungee cord dangling from the dolly's handle. The thing was his now, if he could just hold on to it or something while his partner attacked from the flank, but he didn't move. He froze instead, because the little old man said something in Chinese-talk, employing the universal index-finger sign for "Come here." The dolly smartly rolled back to its master once again as if it were a natural occurrence. As Teacher slid the trash can back onto the dolly, he winked at the dazed hooligan.

The van's driver was on his feet again, but the China Man ignored him. The injured brute was stumbling back toward the vehicle, and promptly the passenger hobbled after his ride. As the van spun out and screeched onto the street, the little old man shouted after it, "First lesson is free! Next time you pay!"

Fortunately, the Econoline had an automatic transmission since the driver only had one serviceable hand with which to drive. Both thugs had injuries that would require some medical care and explaining at work. They drove south, taking bumps to manage their pain while they concocted a story that involved being jumped by several large black dudes. They would never again discuss what had actually happened, each one fearing that he might be cracking up.

The goons forgot about the dead-drunk old hobo they'd thrown into the back of the van until the next morning, when he emerged inside the Third Coast Harvest boatyard. The bum's name was Marty but that didn't matter much.

9

AKK

Jake Bontemps awoke at daybreak curled up on a rug in the fetal position in Brother Bill's kitchenette. The lanky farmer scrambled to his feet and his head sloshed like a half-empty diesel can. And he had the breath to match. Searching for his hat, he spied a can of Lone Star still attached to five empty plastic rings. Jake vaguely recalled having asked the cabby to stop for the sixer after he and Bill had left the club last night.

Sweet. Bontemps cracked the lukewarm survivor and drank it where he stood. His knotted back started to loosen, the room seemed to get brighter, and he spied his hat sitting on the drain board by the sink. Jake donned his straw brim, crushed the empty beer can, and grinned as he tossed it into the recycling bin. There were no such receptacles in Oyster Prairie.

The door to Bill's tiny bedroom was half-open. Jake cleared his throat as he peered in, but his friend didn't move. Bill was snoring softly in the position which he'd fallen onto his single bed a few hours prior.

It was cool and drizzling when Jake locked Bill's door from the inside, stepped out, and shut it. Then he turned and stood on the landing at the top of the wooden stairway, barefoot as usual. He figured the cabby from the night before was probably wearing his boots right about now. They were like new. Jake breathed in through his nose and took a long look at the buildings in the hanging gray mist. Bontemps had farmed his whole young life, been born into it, but he loved this city, and he'd be back real soon. But right now, he had to drive south and check the fields. Second harvest was coming, if it ever stopped raining.

蛉

Marcus spent the morning sparring with the Diūqì Shìbīng, cooking, and watching the sky get lighter through his garage-dojo windows. His phone rang and he answered it reluctantly: Bill was up and apparently bored. After rambling about how the weather was supposed to get nicer throughout the day for almost a minute, he asked if Ting was planning on going for a ride today.

"Uh, probably." Tíng winced. He wasn't a good liar.

"Alright, cool, so do you need some help, carryin' sandwiches or anything?"

There was a moment of silence before Marcus replied, "No, not really, I think I got it under control."

"How 'bout just some company then?" Another brief silence. "I'm already in the alley behind your house. Sorry." Bill admitted before it got any more awkward.

Marcus sighed. "Well then I guess I better let you in before you get T-rolled again." He hung up. The morning's drizzle had broken up into patchy sun, so he hit the glowing button on the wall that raised the south garage door. Tíng almost cracked wise about the squeaky grown-man-Huffy his new friend rolled through the gate, but instead he just slapped hands and welcomed Bill inside. The country clergyman insisted on carrying the cumbersome sandwiches this time, thus decreasing his dispens-ability. So Brother Cox slung the pack of sexy grilled cheeses on his back, and Marcus took the Frankenbike.

Under the I-10 Bridge at White Oak Bayou, they rode around the perimeter calling Marty's name. Then they circled back to the old mattress and the cardboard box with a few dollar bills and a tall can of Schlitz inside, among scant other things. Marcus said, "Man, I rode by here last night. But it was dark and I didn't actu-ally come over here and check on him." He knew Marty carried his box with him if he relocated for any length of time. The old-timer wouldn't have gone too far and left all his loot here. Finally, Tíng pulled a grilled cheese from the pack on Bill's back and set it beside Marty's box. "If he's not back in half an hour, the rats'll have carried away his sandwich. Maybe he just got caught by the rain and slept somewhere else. He'll probably be back soon."

Bill just nodded.

Marcus's head was on a swivel as they were leaving, and he noticed a busted pint of liquor beside a pillar about halfway between Marty's mattress and Yale Street. He hopped off the Frankenbike, picked up the bottle and saw that the neck was broken off, but there were still a couple fingers worth of booze in it. Bill stood beside him, straddling the Huffy. Marcus frowned and said, "It's hard to accidentally break a whiskey bottle; even if Marty had done this intentionally, he'd have found a way to finish the contents."

As Tíng pondered this, he looked down and noticed some prints and peculiar designs in the dirt, accented by white flecks of pigeon poop; otherwise they might have gone unnoticed. "Dude, it looks like something was being dragged here, or maybe somebody." Marcus followed two large sets of boot prints with an unbroken trail between them, away toward Yale to where the pattern ended at a patch of weeds just before the sidewalk. Bill followed, studying the patterns in the poop.

"I see what you're sayin' Ting, but who would wanna drag Marty away? I mean, would the cops walk out here and arrest him for bein' drunk or somethin'?"

Marcus considered it, scanning the area for more clues. "No, not under normal circumstances. But who else would've done it? A couple of psychopaths? Organ thieves?"

"Ting, I'm no doctor, but I can't imagine anybody wantin' those organs. Maybe an ambulance picked him up?"

"Paramedics?" Marcus shook his head. "They wouldn't drag him. They'd put him on a stretcher."

"That's true."

Ting sighed. "Well, H-town's a big city, and sleeping outside is pretty risky unto itself, you know?" He held the broken bottle close to his face. "I don't see any blood or anything. I guess that's a plus." He poured the whiskey on the ground, and then threw the bottle away off into the bayou where the current and the concrete would turn it back into sand. "Alright, let's go."

Bill asked, "Are we gonna stop by the China Man again?"

"No, let's just head straight to the village and see if every-body's okay. You want me to carry the sandwiches?"

"Nope, I got 'em."

Ting mounted up and tore off toward the street. He glanced over his shoulder to make sure Bill was on the move, and then he plunged the Frankenbike off the curb. He flew down Yale, changing pace only to catch the light at Washington Avenue. Brother Cox breathed and cranked the Huffy's clicking sprockets, trying to keep up with Ting, but wondering if even Lance Armstrong could do it.

Thirteen minutes later Bill jogged up to the village alone. He dropped his bike at the top of the trail and gasped a three-word prayer. Then he walked, hands clasped over his head, to the circle of fringe people gathered around Ting and Jaime under the awning at the far end of the dock. By the time he topped the steps, Brother Cox had regained most of his wind and his composure.

Then proudly yet discreetly, he unloaded the backpack of grilled cheeses into many grateful hands.

Marcus was busy explaining the circumstances surrounding Marty's disappearance to the group. He told them about the abandoned cardboard box of valuables, the broken whiskey bottle, and the designs in the dirt. Tíng couldn't see why the cops would have any interest in Marty, but if they had arrested him, it would take a couple days for him to be processed. And without a last name to give, there was no point in even checking yet.

None present believed the cops had picked Marty up. Most of the fringe people knew him or at least knew of him, the jovial old hermit who lived under I-10 at Yale, and (when he was out of sauce) got water from the public fountain at the south end of the Paul Carr Jogging Trail on Heights Boulevard.

Jaime said what everyone was thinking, "I'd hate to guess at the reason for kidnapping someone who's not worth any ransom. I can't help but wonder if it was our pointy tooth friends again. I'm afraid that something wicked has descended upon us." Fringe folks mumbled, revisiting recent occurrences that verified their leader's dark projection. Jaime cleared his throat, looked at Marcus and asked, "So bro, have you called Amber yet?"

"Huh?"

"AKK. That Reporter. The girl, man are you gonna call her or what? Do you still have her work number? I gave it to you. It's in that copy of *The Rag* I gave you. I bet she could help us. I have another copy if you—"

"Ok, yeah, fine. I'll call her. Take it easy." Marcus went in his pack and found the torn-out section of newspaper he'd kept. It *did* make sense when he thought about it. Something had to be done. Tíng couldn't patrol for goons twenty-four-seven, and he didn't want to just wait for the next bad thing to happen. Jaime read half a dozen periodicals a day, and if he believed this "reporter" could help their cause and work below the cops' radar, then Marcus figured he should give it a try. He wandered several paces away from the group as he dialed the number. It rang too many times. Then a canned voice came on and offered several mailbox options. He opted AKK's.

Her outgoing message was combative to say the least. "Hello. This is not the complaint department. So if you don't like something I've written about your sheisty company, then please hang up and contact my editor; but you'd better double-check your facts, because you can rest assured that I have. Don't make me drag your slimy butt out into the light, or countersue *your* corrupt ass for wrongful prosecution and civil rights violations. I know karate, and I also carry a licensed concealed weapon." Her voice softened at the end, but it was still laced with irony. "All other parties, if you'd still like to leave a message for AKK, please do so after this brief musical selection." A scorching guitar riff opened into a live rendition of *The Idiots Have Taken Over.*

Apparently, it was the entire track. Marcus almost hung up, but Jaime was sitting over there watching him, so he figured he might as well go through with it and put this to bed. This AKK person obviously had some serious reasons to screen her calls. He had to admit he liked her style.

When the beep finally came, Tíng wasn't ready. "Uh, hi. This is Marcus Garv-uh Washington, and I uh, have some—" The computer voice cut him off, informing him that the voice mailbox was full, and his four-minute call was dumped unceremoniously. "Aw, what the?" Marcus frowned at his insubordinate phone, but he was really angry at himself. What was he doing throwing his real name around?

Bill looked on, though he tried to appear involved in another discussion.

Jaime was overt. He took a swig from his bottle, and fairly hollered, "Dude, what happened?"

Marcus sighed. "Nothing, that's what happened. I get the

feeling this AKK person has made some enemies. Her work voicemail is a joke. There's no room on it for a message. I didn't even get to leave my number. So we can forget about hearing back from her."

"She prob'ly has caller ID," said Bill. Then he zipped it when Ting glared at him.

"I'm sure she does, but that voice mailbox is set up to discourage people from reaching her. She probably doesn't even check it. It's full."

Jaime said, "Hmm. Well, maybe we can try again later."

"Yeah, maybe." Marcus was putting his phone back into his pack when it rang. He checked the number, and then he looked at Jaime to verify that the dude was smiling. Bill was looking away.

"Hello?"

"Yeah, hi. Is this Marcus Garv-uh Washington?"

Marcus flexed his jaw. "Yeah. This is Marcus."

"Great. So, I usually don't check for messages in this mailbox. That NOFX song has been an effective deterrent, but apparently I need to choose a slightly longer track."

Ting started to say something, but AKK was on a roll.

"I also keep the ringer to this line turned off, but I was sitting here when the notification popped up, and I thought, 'Well at least this person isn't incapable of listening to some punk rock,' so I had to check it out. And wow, it's not every day that I get a call from someone with such a quasi-historical, trans-cultural pseudonym. So what's on your mind, Marcus?"

Instinct was telling him not to talk about this mess with anybody he didn't know, especially some ball buster like this "journalist" on the other end of the line, but this wasn't *for* him. It was for the fringe folks, and for Sean. Marcus took a deep breath and began, "Okay, so there's this certain article you wrote—"

"Here we go. I've written a few thousand articles? So if I hurt your feelings in this particular one, or you think I slandered your slimy little company or something, feel free to contact my boss. But he'll probably tell you to kiss your own ass and read the *Chronicle*—"

"Uh, excuse me, can I finish? Look, I'm sorry to be so vague, but I have some important information concerning a recently deceased friend of mine named Sean. I'd like to share what I've got. And we really shouldn't talk about it over the phone." He let her ponder that for a minute.

Amber had made more than a few enemies with her keyboard. She wasn't sure why she agreed—something in his voice maybe. "Alright, but it's gotta be in a super-public place. And I carry a Taser, and pepper spray, *and* I know kung fu."

Marcus had to laugh. "Yikes. Sounds like fun. I'm totally harmless. You name the place." Amber said she needed to call him back on another line and hung up.

Ten seconds later she rang him from a private number and explained that *The Rag* had been running ads for this music festival, and she was doing a write-up on it. Admission was reasonable, and it was a benefit for war-ravaged women and children in central Africa. Amber implied that Marcus should buy a ticket if he wanted to meet her. She would feel safer there with a thousand other people around, including security guards and cops. He agreed and she fired off the details.

"I'll be way at the back of the crowd, near the sound guy, in front of the main stage from four to five p.m. for sure. That's when Michael Franti's coming on, and he's who I kinda want to focus on."

"Okay, how will I recognize you?"

"I'm a white girl, five-eight, shabby blond hair, and I'll be the only one taking notes on a clipboard. How will I know you?"

"Uh, I'm kind of brown-ish, about six feet. I'll be wearing a hat."

She grinned. "Good enough. Why don't you just come find me? I'll look for you between four and five, okay? I gotta go. Ciao, Marcus Garv-uh Washington."

"Uh, okay. Sounds good," Marcus said to an empty line.

"Sweet," Jaime said from several yards away. "Sounds like you two are gonna meet up."

"Huh? Yeah, we're gonna meet at the concert down in Buffalo Bayou Park this afternoon. She has to do a write-up on it," Marcus replied, as if he still might not go.

"Cool," added Bill.

"Right," said Tíng with a humorless smile.

10

DANCING DUELIST

A fresh, fiery mosaic of autumn leaves covered the muddy ground in Buffalo Bayou Park. The afternoon was pearly blue and cool, and a cheerful mob of music lovers had gathered along the water at the toes of Downtown.

Michael Franti and Spearhead had gotten started early and were taking their first break. Amber looked at her watch—4:15. This Marcus guy said he would come find her between four and five. In her peripheral, a person was standing still, not walking or talking, just looking. She turned to face him.

He pointed at her and said, "Amber?" He was too far away to hear amid the throng, but he enunciated so she could read his lips.

She pointed back with her pen, holding her clipboard to her chest and mouthed, "Marcus."

Unshaven for a couple days, he wore dark shades and a thrift shop ball cap. His flannel shirt and jeans were a size too big. Ting was on display enough at work. He recognized her at once, and couldn't believe the odds. *The girl from the front steps at the police compound.* It wasn't just the hair and the clipboard, but the cheeks, the mouth, the aura. It was her. Marcus considered that, as a journalist, she'd probably been in there to interview the cops plenty of times. Still, this was a wicked coincidence. Tíng felt like he was wearing concrete shoes as he plodded toward her, trying not to slip on the muddy levee.

She thought he moved like a big cat blended among sheep. Something like fear flickered in her midsection, but she shook it off.

As he drew closer, he noted the concerned set of her jaw. She didn't recognize him. Or worse, maybe she did. He toned down his fierce smile, pulled down his shades, and stopped well outside her personal space.

Seeing his eyes, Amber thought this could be the love child of Michelle Yeoh and Lenny Kravitz. She pulled down her sunglasses too, and the sky picked out the blues in her earth-colored eyes while the fallen leaves ignited the amber. Some would call her skinny, but she had some muscle in the right places. Luckily, as Marcus stared, Amber's look of concern melted into a grin of recognition. She tucked her pen behind her ear and stuck her hand out. "Hi, I'm Amber."

"Hi. Marcus." He was surprised by her grip.

"Not out fighting crime today?"

"Huh? Oh right, I uh—"

"I hardly recognize you in your street clothes. Or should I say, as your mild-mannered alter ego?"

She's quick. Marcus fixed his sunglasses and glanced down at what he was wearing. "Right. I'm not actually a crime fighter," he said with no conviction. "That was just sort of a uniform I wear to work sometimes."

"That's a shame. It was pretty heroic just walking *into* that place dressed like that. I was very impressed."

He cleared his throat. "Right, and speaking of that day and that place, that's kind of what I need to talk to you about." A guitar rang and the crowd responded. Amber looked from Marcus to the stage to her clipboard. He began to doubt the wisdom of his situation once again and said, "Look, if you have work to do right now, we can try this some other time or something."

"No no, we're good. Spearhead got started early and I think I already have enough here for a good write-up." She glanced at her clipboard again, and so did he. The front page of the attached legal pad was blanketed with text organized into a sort of flowchart with circles, boxes, and arrows. She clipped her pen to the board and stuffed it all into her pack. "Yeah, I have enough for now." The music began to play in earnest, so she pulled on his shoulder and got close to his ear so she wouldn't have to shout. "You wanna take a walk?"

He said, "Yeah, let's go," a bit too anxiously, and motioned for her to lead the way. They left the crowd for the bayou, and the sound diminished as they passed behind the giant speakers flanking the stage. With plenty of room now, Marcus came up beside her.

Before he could speak she asked, "So where did you say you worked?"

"Uh, you know that club, The Fallout Shelter?"

"Uh-huh."

"That's where I work. I uh, I'm kind of a dancer there."

"Oh, wow, awesome, that explains a lot." She'd driven by it plenty, and been inside once or twice with friends. She tried not to speculate on Marcus's sexuality but couldn't help it.

He thought he saw her blush a little. "Yeah, well, it's just a gig, you know."

She cleared her throat. "No, no, that's awesome. That's gotta be a tough job. It obviously keeps you in shape." *That just came out.*

"Yeah, I guess so. But anyway, I know you're a writer for *The Rag*, obviously. And like I was saying, the reason I called is because I was a friend of Sean Dorsey."

"Uh-huh."

"You know, that kid that got killed a couple days ago, off the Sabine Street Bridge, like right over there?" Marcus pointed. "I read that article you wrote about it, in *The Rag.*"

She nodded but didn't overtly respond. She'd guided them to the merchandise section, where they merged with dozens of others amid booths selling everything from henna tattoos to sausage on a stick. They were in serious mud now, churned up by the drove of pedestrians. Some vendors had begun to throw flattened cardboard boxes on the ground to improve the footing.

Amber got in line at a booth, looked left and right, and then asked in a lower tone, "Sean Dorsey was *killed* you say, as in the m-word? You know more about it than the cops do, or are you saying they're lying?"

At the word "cops" Marcus glanced around, half expecting to see one.

She did the same. "What, are they after you or something? *You* didn't kill him, did you?"

"No, of course not, he was my friend, and no they're not after me, not right now, I don't think." Though he didn't want to test that theory. *This was a bad idea.*

She saw the uncertainty on his face, and was about to respond when a liberally pierced cashier asked for an order from behind her. Amber held up her finger, said, "One second," and turned to face the counter. Tíng eyed the crowd from behind his shades while Amber bought two big plastic cups of beer. She turned back around, handed him one, and said, "Here you go. Sorry, I assumed you would drink one."

"Uh, yeah, okay, thanks." He accepted the beverage and sipped the top off of it. It was hoppy, light, and cold.

"How is it?" She bumped into him lightly.

"Good."

She guided them back into the herd of paupers and jokers

with hair colored black to blond, pink to green or shaved off, pierced and tatted skin, swatches of every conceivable pigmentation. Tíng felt almost normal here. He looked at the skyline and breathed the city air in a fresh season. This felt good after all, this taking action. Plus—

"So where were we?" Amber was finally ready to get back to Sean when a situation arose. Everyone within a thirty-foot radius turned their attention toward the source of a booming, gravelly voice. Near the end of the line, at the very next booth, was a big white dude in an olive-drab canvas jacket and utility trousers. He had a dark shock of oily locks that shook as he cursed and threatened a much smaller man in front of him, prodding him in the chest. The aggressor was a monster. Marcus guessed him to be six-four in his muddy jungle boots, and had to assume the guy had some military training based on his apparel. Homeboy wasn't thin either—rotund and thick-limbed, chewing a stubby cigar, and sloshing a cup of beer while he accosted his victim with his free hand.

Everybody backed away from the altercation, but one person moved closer. Amber shouted, "Hey, buddy! Keep your hands to yourself! Who do you think you are!" Folks gave her lots of space lest they be associated with her, and as Amber stepped forward, the beastly man turned his attention to her.

"Who the hell are you? I'll choke you out, you little bitch!"

Marcus noted the unbuttoned, canvas coat was definitely DOD issue. The guy looked sleep-deprived, and his hollow eyes exuded rage. He hardly noticed Tíng at all, until the skinny little black-Chinese-looking muther caught the loudmouth girl by her backpack, cutting short her tirade, and stopping her from getting any closer. Amber had drawn the big fellow's ire, and Marcus was afraid he might actually put his hands on her. The brute's initial victim slipped out of line and gratefully fled.

Amber felt herself backsliding in the mud as Tíng pulled her by the backpack and stepped around in front of her. He held his left palm out at shoulder height and said, "Come on, dude. Why don't you calm down and quit while you're ahead?"

"Aw, what are you, her little queer boyfriend?" It was a rhetorical question, subterfuge while he stepped within striking distance. Then he lunged and went to shove Marcus in the chest with his big right hand, hard enough to put the shrimp on his butt. The attack was so telegraphed that Tíng initially thought it was a decoy. He countered with a forceful parry, batting the big man's hand away and knocking him off balance. But the goon used his inertia to swipe for Marcus's face with his other hand.

Tíng watched the paw with long dirty nails whistle over his head, and a flurry of counterattacks ran through his combat mind as the giant stumbled, flailed and swore, snatching and grabbing at the shrimp, who feigned and dodged but did not fight back. Marcus moved away from Amber and stayed just out of reach as his flailing attacker finally went down on the slick terrain, a victim of his own momentum.

The dozen or so people who had scrambled to get out of the way at the onset of the scuffle now lingered to witness its outcome. Tíng was so nonchalant about the situation that it was difficult for them to worry about him anymore.

Unhurt, the brute clambered back to his feet, muddy and furious, his beer and cigar abandoned in the sodden turf. Marcus tried to explain again that this wasn't necessary, but the fellow couldn't hear over his own murderous ranting. Then he charged, as best he could without falling down again.

The last thing Tíng wanted to do was hurt a troubled vet, but this was getting irksome. Guys in uniforms would be coming soon, and he had to put a stop to it. He frowned as his left hand drifted up again, hovering just below shoulder level, fingers fashioned this time as if holding a piece of chalk—*The Serpent's Head*.

The big man reached for Marcus's extended arm in an attempt

to snare him and pull him in close, but something almost too fast to see intercepted the assault. There was an audible hiss, and a sound like that of a ruler slapping one's palm. Tíng's Snake-Style Fist struck his foe's hand at the base of the thumb, The Serpent's Head recoiled, and the big man cried out as his arm was locked straight and twisted outward. He rolled sideways into the mud to prevent his elbow from being wrenched, or his wrist broken, or both. He hit the ground still ensnared, and flipped onto his stomach to relieve the torque on his arm. When Tíng released him, the pain diminished but the fog in the big guy's mind was slower to clear. *What the hell just happened?*

Marcus was just trying to keep this quiet, reassuring the crowd and scanning the area for enforcers. And as the monster lay there, his rage was supplanted by a harsh realization: He was severely outmatched. The brute's arm wasn't broken, but it wouldn't do him any good in this fight. He sat up, covered in mud, and noticed that he'd gone down right next to his extinguished cigar and his beer which was now just a crushed plastic cup.

Marcus patted a clean spot on the big fellow's shoulder saying, "Uh, sorry about that, dude, but it's time for me to go." Tíng handed the man *his* beer, which was still in his right hand, and still practically full. The dancing duelist hastily returned to Amber, shrugging and saying, "Woops, sorry about that." She answered with a vacant nod as he took her by the arm and skated her away on the muck.

Amber slugged her beer on the move and tossed the cup into a bin as they passed by. A hundred paces out, weaving through the crowd, she said, "I thought you said you were a dancer."

Marcus glanced back at her. "Dance and martial arts have a lot of similarities. Didn't you say you knew kung fu, on the phone?"

She laughed, then breathed deeply for the first time in a few minutes. "Okay, I was lying about the kung fu thing, but I do carry pepper spray." She added, "I like kung fu movies."

"Sweet. I do too."

Marcus led them back toward the stages near the gate where he'd entered the festival. He guided Amber out of traffic and partly up the levee for an elevated perspective; when he turned and faced her, it took him a moment to remember why he'd stopped. He looked over her head and saw the big muddy guy being interrogated by two uniformed officers, and it appeared to be making the matter worse. One cop was inspecting the guy's ID, and there was no way Tíng was giving them his. Amber turned to get a look just as the pair of lawmen decided to eject the offender. They started herding him toward the gate, toward Marcus's and her position.

Marcus said, "Uh, I think I need to get outta here. So, you wanna maybe go finish our discussion somewhere else?"

"Uh, yeah, okay. Where do you want to go?"

"Well, I rode my bike and I really don't want to leave it here so, I could meet you somewhere or—"

"You rode your bike? So you probably live close by. How about you take your bike home and I can just meet you there, unless there's somebody else there and it's not cool or something."

"Uh, no, yeah. I live alone. So you feel safe coming to my place?" He smiled. The sun backlit his shades so she could see his eyes through the lenses.

"I do, for some reason." She squeezed his forearm, smooth skin over cords of relaxed muscle. "You're not a serial killer, are you?"

"Well, I *eat* lots of cereal, so technically, you could say."

She shook her head and shoved him into motion.

Hustling to her car, Amber had a creeping suspicion about the directions he'd just given her. She had lived in The Heights for a stint, so she knew the area pretty well, and the street intersection he'd just described sounded nonexistent. The neighborhood didn't run that far south, did it? Was he trying to ditch her?

But why would he do that? And what the hell am I doing going to his place anyway? And why did I start drinking beer this early in the day?

Ting moved like the shadow of a hawk to the bike rack out front, scanning for uniformed personnel along the way. If they wanted to detain him right now, they'd better break out the helicopters.

11

CAUGHT IN AMBER

Marcus stood with his arms folded, grinning, as Amber rolled up in her aging, unwashed Hybrid emblazoned with bumper stickers touting to save the world in forty different ways. He signaled for her to just pull into the alley, and she imagined driving into a giant wreath, the place was so choked with vines and unruly trees. Amber grabbed her bag and left her car unlocked. It wasn't worth breaking into, so why risk a smashed window for someone to discover that the hard way?

She said, "Bro, you got here fast."

"I know a shortcut." Marcus led her through his gate of interwoven creepers and said, "Sorry, I'm not really into landscaping."

"No, I love it," Amber replied skeptically when she beheld his jungle of a yard.

They left their muddy boots at the side door of the garage and stepped inside. The room was dimly lit by the garage door windows. She took the place in, and said, "Sweet. So, this must be your dojo?"

"Yeah, kind of. I mean, I *do* exercise in here. Mainly a lot of cardio and flexibility stuff, for work you know."

He turned on the hanging lamp and her eyes went straight to the Diūqì Shìbīng. "Oooh. Where'd you get that thing? It looks like something out of *Kung Fu Theater*."

"That is actually, yes, a type of training engine that's not uncommon in kung fu movies."

"Did you build it?" She walked up to it.

"No, Mast—uh, a friend of mine did. It's a long story. I was a kid. It was a gift."

"But I can tell it's been used, a lot. It's got some serious wear on it. So it actually does work."

"Uh, yup, it works." Marcus stood at his vintage desktop computer along the far wall, keeping his distance from the Diūqì Shìbīng for now. He grabbed a remote, aimed it at his classic audio equipment, and pretty soon Marvin Gaye was singing *What's Goin' On?*

O-kay. Amber left the "training engine" alone for now and rejoined Marcus near the center of the room. She hummed and they both sang for a minute.

He was swaying without thinking; dancing to him was like breathing. For a moment they both just grooved, and exchanged juvenile facial expressions. Amber could feel herself blushing so finally she forced herself to stop, un-slung her pack and said, "Okay, okay, so, what were we talking about? You said you were a friend of Sean Dorsey and you believe he was murdered?"

Marcus grabbed the remote and turned it down. He said, "Yeah. You want to sit down?" He led her to the big orange couch along the far wall. Amber whipped out her clipboard and flipped past the concert notes. Then, out of character, Marcus spilled the beans. First, he recited Farah's eyewitness account of the crime on the Sabine Street Bridge almost word for word. Then he told AKK everything he knew about the apparent influx of some violent faction of wannabe vampire a-holes who were haunting north Montrose.

Amber took notes furiously in her flowchart style, and when Marcus stopped talking, she asked him a few follow-ups to clarify. Then the pair was silent for a little while as Amber put the pen to her bottom lip, scanned and tweaked what she'd written. It was more than she could've hoped for, and she had the urge to start researching immediately. She longed for her notebook with wireless internet, but not wanting to take it to the muddy concert, she had left it at work. She could get online with her phone but the screen size would be restrictive. She wanted a keyboard. She looked across the room at Marcus's bulky desktop computer and asked, "Is that thing online?"

"Uh, yeah. It can be." Ting wasn't into upgrading. He wasn't a social networker, and tended to spend his off-time riding, picnicking, training, and meditating. Once in a while, he read a book, particularly if Jaime suggested a title.

Amber frowned at the ancient tube-monitor as she moved the wired mouse erratically. "How can you stand to do anything with this thing? It's super slow."

"Uh, it just takes a little patience. Abusing the mouse definitely won't help. I don't use it to get online very much. I mainly use it as a music reservoir." Marcus indicated the wire running from the computer to his stereo receiver. "I'm not exactly high-tech. But it's good enough for me because I only listen to one song at a time. Though I'm trying to expand on that through meditation." He shot her an ironic smile as he moved to his kitchenette to put water in the microwave for tea, leaving her to decide whether or not she could deal with his trailing-edge technology.

She gave up for now and started to peruse the dojo again, making her way to the garage windows. "So who lives in the house up front? You rent this apartment from somebody?"

Déjà vu. Marcus cleared his throat. "No, the house is mine too. It belonged to my parents. I just don't go in there much."

"It belonged to your parents? Where are they?" Amber had time to regret the question before he answered.

"They both passed away. My Dad when I was only like two years old, and my mom died when I was in the Navy, I guess, like, eight years ago now. I don't have any other relatives around that I know of. My parents were both first-generation Americans who came here alone."

She walked closer to him. "I'm sorry, Ting. Do you want to talk about it?" She reached out, squeezed his forearm, and a tingling sensation traveled up past his elbow. There was a break in the playlist. The wind sighed, and leaves brushed the dojo's exterior walls. "I mean you don't have to. I just—sorry, I ask a lot of questions. I can't seem to separate my job from the rest of my life."

The microwave dinged.

"No no, it's okay. Um, hang on a minute." He reluctantly pulled away from her grasp. The jukebox finished shuffling and played Buju Banton's *Untold Stories*. The song lightened the mood while Marcus steeped tea, sweetened it with honey, and then poured it over the rocks into two tall mugs. Amber had a sip, and the stuff was earthy but cold and invigorating.

Tíng moved to the edge of the futon and sat down. For a minute, he just stared into his mug at his distorted reflection.

She asked, "You okay?"

"Huh? Yeah, I'm fine. I just don't talk much about my family, or lack thereof, you know?"

"Sorry. When I meet somebody interesting, I automatically have to know their whole life story. I'm nosy."

"You're just curious, and that's understandable, especially for somebody in your line of work. I mean, I don't mind telling my sad story," he said with a smirk, "to you. If you're sure you want to hear it. I don't want to be a downer or anything."

"No, I want to hear it. That's why I asked."

"Okay." He reached out for her hand and said, "Come on then, I want to show you something." They went out the side door, stepped back into their boots, and Marcus led her around the south side of the garage-dojo to a narrow path of mossy pavestones barely visible through the undergrowth.

"So, how often do you mow?" she asked wryly.

"Twice a week."

Dry pecan leaves whirled lazily down from the shaggy canopy. The days were getting shorter. A gibbous moon hung low in the west with a thin sheet of pink cirrus for cover. It was too hazy or too early for stars. The two kids carried their mugs to the northwest corner of the house, where a weathered wooden patio creaked as Marcus walked across it to a painted, steel security door that comprised half of what used to be a French door. The other half had been walled over and painted to match. Amber followed at close range. He produced a key, unlocked the door, turned on the lights, and they stepped into a bedroom that was apparently furnished before the demise of disco.

Amber gawked. "Wow, is the whole house done-up like this? I love it."

"Uh, pretty much. This is my mom's old room."

She nodded and waited for him to continue as they stepped out of their boots again.

"The house is like seventy years old, but it's still in pretty good shape.

"I think it's awesome," Amber said, snooping around. She picked up a framed picture of a tall, wiry, happy man with dark skin and short dreadlocks. He held a trumpet in his left hand, and at his right he held a beaming, pale Asian beauty in a baby-doll dress.

"Your parents were gorgeous," Amber said.

Marcus smiled. "My mom's pregnant in that picture."

"Really? She's not showing."

"No, she told me they had just found out like the day before that picture was taken. So they weren't even married yet. But apparently I'm in that picture too."

"Too cute. So your dad was a musician?"

"Yeah. He learned to play when he was a kid. His dad taught him. He grew up in Jamaica. It's actually kind of ironic."

"What's ironic?"

"He ran away from a Kingston ghetto to come here and follow his dream. He wanted to get away from all the bad things that were happening down there. So he gets here, works hard, and then right as his dream starts to come true, he gets shot."

"Oh no. How'd it happen?"

"I only know all this because my mom told me. And sometimes it sounds like a fairy tale."

"I love fairy tales. I could tell a few of those myself."

"Well, Mom told me my dad Jarvis, Jarvis Washington, was some kind of a track star in school, in Jamaica where he grew up. Nobody could outrun him, even though he never showed up for practice. He put all his spare time into his music, his trumpet, which was given to him by his dad. Anyway, Jarvis got on with this reggae band called No Asylum and they were pretty good, but their songs were also pretty political. And the government down there doesn't mess around."

Amber shook her head.

"So when two of his bandmates got shot at a show one night, and Jarvis barely escaped, he skipped town. He skipped the country actually, and washed up here in Houston."

Marcus showed Amber the battered case in the bottom of his mom's closet with a tarnished trumpet inside.

"So he got a job and a visa so he could stay in the states. He worked at a factory that upholstered seats for fancy sport boats and yachts. He did good work, and eventually he got his citizenship. And after work, he'd ride the bus downtown to play his horn."

Amber appeared enthralled so Marcus kept going.

"On the edge of Old Chinatown, right off Dowling Street, there used to be this dive jazz bar called The Wooden Nickel. My parents actually met on the sidewalk right in front of the place while my dad was out smoking a cigarette. My mom walked by on her way home from work, waiting tables at this all-night diner."

"Aww, that's romantic," Amber chimed in.

"Right. My mom's name was Ching Lan. And she wasn't long off the boat herself. She had left a pretty hard life in China, and her mom helped her emigrate here so she could be a dancer. She waited tables at night so she could volunteer at this dance studio in Montrose, trying to get her foot in the door as a teacher."

"Two starving artists in love," Amber said.

Marcus smiled and continued. "So my mom was staying with this immigrant Chinese family and Jarvis was staying at the Y. But she started coming into The Wooden Nickel after work, a lot, to watch him play, and he would walk her home. I guess they fell in love, and pretty soon they got a place together. Then I was born, and they got married. It was just a little private ceremony, but my mom got her citizenship too.

"Ching Lan quit the greasy spoon and stayed home to take care of me. And Jarvis worked his butt off at the factory, and he finally got a promotion to, like, a low-level manager, but it was enough for the two of them to buy this old fixer upper, and move up to the Heights. Mom told me that's when they were the happiest."

Amber's smile faded as Marcus frowned and his tone of voice turned grim. "But unfortunately, The Wooden Nickel was also some kind of meeting place for black political activists. I don't know if Jarvis knew this or not, but it seems like trouble with authority sort of followed him. Because one night, in the alley behind the club, he got shot, along with two other 'black activists' according to the paper. The guy who did the shooting was an off-duty cop, who claimed they were trying to mug him. But my dad wasn't a thief." Marcus was staring at the wall like it bore some invisible message from his past.

Amber touched his leg and said, "I'm sorry. I figured your dad had some deep-seated political views, considering he named you Marcus Garvey Washington."

"Yeah. I'll never know what really happened that night. I guess it's probably better that way. My name's actually Marcus Garvey *Qīngtíng* Washington."

"*Qīng-tíng?*"

He smiled and nodded.

"So that's obviously from your mom's side. Does *Qīngtíng* mean something, you know, in Chinese?"

"Yeah. Dragonfly."

"Dragonfly?"

"Yup. It was actually my uncle's nickname, my mom's little brother. Obviously I never met him. Mom told me he died when he was young. Seems to run in my family. They were rice farmers in south China, right on the Thailand border. It was a tough gig. They farmed by hand and used water buffaloes to pull carts and stuff."

"Wow."

"I know, and apparently, in the wet season, the flies and mosquitoes were unbearable. So they would actually pray for dragonflies. These red ones would show up in swarms sometimes and just annihilate the mosquitoes. Mom told me her mother taught her that the dragonflies got their strength, their honor, and their red color from the villagers' blood, that they reclaimed when they feasted on all the parasites. And since Mom's little brother was always running around outside, half naked and sunburned, my grandma would call him her little red dragonfly."

Amber said, "So *Qīngtíng* was your uncle that you never met because he passed away so young. But literally the name means dragonfly?"

"Yeah, to make a long story short. Mom passed the name on to me. She must have loved him a lot."

"How did her little brother die?"

"I'm not sure. I always assumed it was malaria or something. They lived pretty hard."

"Maybe that was the reason why she left—left home and crossed an ocean to get away from whatever it was."

"Yeah. I remember her telling me, when I was little, that her mom knew it was time for her to go when the dragonflies stopped coming. I'm pretty sure her dad died young too, and her mom pretty much sold everything she owned to get her daughter away from there. I have a few of their old letters, but I think they're all sad because my Mom kept them hidden from me. I can't read 'em anyway. They're in Chinese. Plus, I guess I'm kind of afraid of what they say." Marcus had gone monotone, staring at the floor.

"You okay?"

He nodded. "I haven't shown anybody this for a long time, but—" Ting stood in front of her and turned around, pulling up his shirt.

"Wait. What? Sweetie, you don't have to—" Amber gasped. "Oh my god! Is that new? Is it bleeding?" He held his position and she stood behind him to get a better look.

"No, it's old, and sort of three-dimensional. And the ink is all shades of red. It's what got me kicked out of the Navy."

"Huh?"

"I was stationed on an aircraft carrier, docked in Thailand, when I got a letter from my mom telling me that she was in the hospital. The doctors had told her she had terminal cancer."

"Oh no."

"I know. The letter was three weeks old already, and my ship wouldn't be back in the states for like four months. So when they let us out on shore leave, I thought it was a good idea to get all tore up on this stuff called Mekong. US troops aren't allowed to drink it because it's like whiskey, but they make it out of fermented opium poppies."

"Yikes."

"Yeah. So one thing led to another, and apparently I paid some tattoo artist to do this to me in one night. I don't really remember it much. Unfortunately I ended up in jail in Phuket Town and the boat left without me. So I went AWOL."

"Oh shit."

"Yeah, so a Navy officer had to find me and bail me out. Luckily when I told them my story, the ship's Captain went easy on me. I hadn't even been in for two years yet, and I was just a hull technician on the boat, which is basically a paint chipper. My main enemy when I was in the military was corrosion. So they sent me home with an administrative discharge."

Amber lifted Marcus's shirt higher so she could study the tattoo. The dragonfly's Asian origin was apparent, with bulbous compound-eyes, gem-like exoskeletal plates, and hooked mandibles that clasped Tíng's top thoracic vertebra. Two pairs of veined wings swept back and curled across Marcus's wide latissimus dorsi, giving the perception that the creature was in a steep ascent. Its long, armored tail terminated with a wicked pincer at the base of Tíng's spine.

Amber pouted. It was beautiful yet horrific. The artist was obviously talented, but the scarring could have been done with a soldering iron. She ran her finger along the curved edge of the beast's wing, and goosebumps sprang up over Marcus's back. She placed her palm flat on the spot in a quick attempt to warm it up. "I'm sorry," she said, and helped him pull his shirt back down.

She took a step back, cleared her throat and asked, "So where did you learn martial arts? You were, like, the real Jet Li out there today."

"Jet Li is real."

She shook her head. "Shut up."

"I've had a teacher since I was a kid, the China Man."

"You mean like that convenience store over there close to I-10?"

"Yup, he was friends with my mom, and I used to stay there after school sometimes so she could work."

"Wow. And he's like a kung fu teacher?"

"He's a lot of things that nobody would suspect."

The discussion went from family to politics to existential philosophy and pseudo-science until they had talked their way into a realm of pure speculation, sprawled like a pair of beached starfish on Ching Lan's bed. Amber blew on a green feather boa that had been draped over the headboard for years. Marcus admitted he'd used some of his mother's accessories when he'd first started working at The Fallout Shelter. Amber stifled a laugh.

He grinned and it turned into a yawn. "I think I'm getting delirious."

"Me too." She yawned too, and they lay in silence for a minute, maintaining their incidental contact. Then she said, "Okay, so do you mind if I just stay here, and crash out for a few hours? It's super late, or super early I should say."

"Nah, that's probably a bad idea. You could be a cereal killer. And I'm low on Fruity Pebbles."

"You're such a dork." She smacked his shoulder.

Marcus reached over and turned off a hanging globe lamp, and without another word they rolled up in Ching Lan's comforter and held each other in the last chilly hours before dawn.

Amber awoke once, having dreamt she was alone and surrounded by a blasted world. She felt his arms around her and drifted off to a better place.

He opened his eyes once, in the cool twilight, his face buried in her hair. He closed them and continued to search for her on another plane of consciousness.

12

EAGLE TALON FIST

Amber awoke hugging a pillow, alone like always. For some reason, she hadn't realized the night before that Ching Lan's bed was kind of hard. She rolled off it and stretched. Then she scanned the room wondering where Ting had run off to. She frowned. *He's so alone. Wait, am I falling for this guy? No way. Not that fast. Shit.*

Collecting her stuff so she could bail, she saw a sheet of paper that had been yanked from her legal pad and positioned on the night stand. Upon the page was scrawled *Good morning. I'm back in the garage.*

She smiled.

On the same table was her cup of tea. *Tea? More like loud-mouth soup.* It was still cool and a quarter full, mostly melted ice. She shrugged, swirled it around, then swished and swallowed it. She raked out her bedhead, wiped her raccoon eyes with the insides of her sleeves, and then dug in her pack for a piece of minty gum. She checked her phone. *Whew.* It was earlier than she'd thought.

Amber stepped out onto the patio, and into a cool clear day. The knee-high weeds in Marcus's yard were rife with wildflowers, and the low-hanging trees echoed with the cyclic conversations of birds.

From around back she could hear a faint afro-beat, perforated by the staccato thumping of a couple of nail guns maybe? Walking past the corner of the house, she realized the percussion was actually coming from inside the garage. Maybe somebody had come over to help Ting do some renovating or something. *Great. Dude time.* Oh well, she'd already planned a hasty exit anyway. But as she drew nearer, it sounded more like they were destroying something than building it. She recognized the music now, *Babylon System,* just as it faded out, and another Wailers track followed. This one had rapid-fire congas, and an angry base line. It was *Get Up Stand Up.*

The song set rhythm to her footsteps until the erratic hammering sound returned with a fury, and it was double the tempo of the music now. *What the?* She tiptoed closer.

Tíng's rational brain in the frontal cortex was dissecting this crew of toothy Nazis who'd been victimizing his friends, while his older, primal brain, down in the stem, was directing combat with the whirling man o' lumber that was Diūqì Shìbīng.

Tíng's changing animal-style fists struck and parried the heavy, spinning limbs, while his elbows, knees, and heels bashed the thick pole in the center like wrecking bars. The combatants waltzed violently around the patchwork flooring, and as the battle reached a crescendo, Marcus whimpered, in the background Peter Tosh wailed, and the Diūqì Shìbīng's hardwood limbs flexed and rattled like an oak tree in a gale.

Amber flattened her back against the thin strip of wall between the two big, steel garage doors. The door on the left side was open a couple of feet at the bottom for ventilation, and she needed to know what was going on in there, so Amber ducked down to the side, and peered through the two-foot gap. She had no time to react as a broken hunk of cabriole table-leg came flying right at her. It whistled for a split second as it spun through the air, and then impacted several inches away from her face, leaving a ding in the steel garage door. She squealed, and retreated to her concealed position between the doors.

Marcus glanced in her direction, thinking he'd heard someone. Then he looked back at his sluggishly-rotating opponent. Not one, but two of its limbs had broken off, leaving long, jagged splinters and bent rebar rods in their places. One busted table leg was on the floor way over by the garage doors, and the other, a heavy, angular piece of oak, fell to the deck as Tíng released it from his Eagle Talon Fist.

"Jesus," Amber said, poking her head back under the door again after she was certain the battle had subsided.

"Oh, hey." Marcus walked to the glowing pair of green buttons on the wall and punched one. Amber ducked under and came inside when the dented garage door was about halfway up. Tíng hopped up and slapped the top of the door, and sensing the resistance, it stopped in place.

"Uh, *buenos dias*," he said with a smile. "I'm trying to work on my Spanish."

She used both hands to pick up the jagged piece of lumber that had just tried to kill her. It was heavy, solid, for real. She set it down and said, "Dude you're like, badder than the Centipede, you know, from *5 Deadly Venoms* and shit." Marcus scoffed, shaking his head as Amber walked up to inspect the busted Diūqì Shìbīng. She had only seen it in passing the evening before. She pushed on it, and it only leered at her. She shoved a limb with both hands, the middle section spun, and she heard the hum of steel bearings inside.

Marcus was close behind her. He radiated heat but was hardly sweating. "As you might have guessed by now, the China Man built it for me. Like I said, it's a lot like the ones you've seen in the movies, but this one is definitely the real deal. I think it has some Subaru parts in it."

"Ouch." Amber drew back and extracted a long splinter from her thumb.

"You okay?"

She turned and gave him her hand. "It's nothing."

Tíng pressed the little speck of blood to the cuff of his baggy sweatshirt sleeve for a few seconds. She could feel his pulse. The speck transferred, the bleeding stopped, and he reluctantly released her hand. It tingled as she lowered it to her side. She turned her attention back to the anthropomorphic woodpile and said, "So what did you call this thing?"

"Teacher named it Diūqì Shìbīng. It means, like, *reclaimed warrior* or something like that."

She was touching it again. "I can't believe you can punch or kick this thing at all, much less break it. It would break my hand in a second."

"Yeah well, when I first got it, I thought it was a joke. It hardly moved at all. It felt like a statue. But just like anything else, you work at it and it gets easier. Once you get it spinning though, it gets a little sketchy. It can hit you with two or three limbs at once if you really screw up. Kind of like getting punched by a tree. But it never hits me anymore. I've been doing it for so long now I can just sort of feel it, you know? It's actually a really good stress reliever."

"Yeah, I bet." Amber put her hands on the segmented "torso." "So, I guess these worn-out indentions in the middle are, like, vital points?"

"Yeah, you could say that."

"And you said the China Man built it? How long did that take?"

"Uh, I'm not exactly sure."

"So how long have you had it?"

"I guess like seven or eight years now."

She put her foot on the thing and pushed hard before it started to roll. It was, like, refrigerator-heavy. "Bro. So seriously, for you to break this thing, without a sledgehammer or something, that's like some *Fist of the North Star*-type shit. I would not want to be on your bad side."

"Now you're getting carried away. That dude can fly and shoot lightning and stuff."

"Whatever." She was still transfixed. "So has anyone ever seen you do that before?"

"What, fly and shoot lightning?" he deadpanned.

"No, smart-ass. Has anyone ever seen you do kung fu on this thing before?"

"Um, not much, I mean, no, not really."

"And how long did you say you've been practicing at it?"

"I guess, like, seven or eight years now."

"Every day?"

"Yeah, pretty much. Sometimes I only do it for like fifteen or twenty minutes though."

"*Only* twenty minutes? So how long do you do it when you work out for, like, a good while?"

"I don't know, thirty, forty minutes. But I won't be doing it anytime soon. I broke it." Ting looked at one of the fractured limbs. "You wouldn't think a thick piece of hardwood would just snap like that, especially where it's reinforced with rebar."

"No, you wouldn't think so."

"Anyway, I need to tell Teacher I broke it. He'll probably want to fix it or something."

"Or maybe he's been waiting for this day to come, so he can move you up to your next level of training."

Marcus looked at her to verify she was being serious. "Right. Either way I need to go by and see him. So—"

"So, what?"

"So what are your plans for the rest of the day? You wanna go for a bike ride? Meet some friends of mine, maybe have a picnic?" Marcus walked over and plugged in his griddles.

AKK had plenty to do today, but she wasn't quite ready for this to end yet. "Okay, sure, why not. How can you say no to a picnic with friends?"

"You can't." Marcus was staging his culinary accoutrements. "You hungry?"

She finally left the Diūqì Shìbīng, and wandered over to the sandwich prep area. "Now that you mention it, I'm starving."

He made more tea, poured it on the rocks, and once again explained his relationship with the fringe folks while her heart melted like Velveeta. She helped him expedite the grilled cheeses, and then they sampled a couple from the first batch that were brown, crispy, and gooey.

Amber mumbled, "I could totally write a story about you, you know."

Marcus covered his mouth. "Please don't."

She helped him clean and put things away. Then he packed up and introduced her to the Frankenbike. She assured him she could handle it, so he got on the big trike. They put on their shades and rolled out of the dojo.

Marcus's phone rang inside his backpack while he was unlocking the back creeper-covered gate. "Whatever, I'll check it in a minute," he said, motioning for Amber to go on through first. As she rolled out into the alley, Marcus heard a familiar voice say, "Whoa. I mean, hello."

Amber said, "Hi there," then she glanced over her shoulder to check Marcus's progress.

Bill Cox stashed his phone in his fanny pack. "Oh my goodness, I was just about to leave you a message, Ting."

"Awesome," Marcus replied as he shut the gate and turned to face his new clergyman pal.

"I been out ridin' my bike too." Bill nodded down at his grown-man-Huffy. "I was just out cruisin' and happened to wind up in your neighborhood. It's beautiful 'round here for the most part."

Marcus nodded, bearing a pained expression. He had a vision of a squeaky, superfluous wheel being bolted shoddily onto his front forks. The silence approached awkwardness.

"I'm Amber by the way."

Bill gasped. "Oh, the writer?"

"Yup."

"Well—Will, I mean, Bill. My name is Bill." He straddle-walked his bike over to her, pedals encumbering his steps.

"Pleased to meet you." She shook his hand when it arrived.

"The pleasure's all mine." Bill forgot his manners and blurted, "So y'all gonna go pass out some sandwiches? Can I tag along?"

Tíng forgot his too. "Uh, actually—"

"Of course. Of course you can tag along," Amber chimed in.

Marcus sighed. "Right. Sorry, how rude of me. Amber, this is my friend, Bill. We also just met. He's from down south in Prairie Oyster. He's a Bible pusher."

"I was a minister down in my hometown of *Oyster Prairie*," Bill clarified.

Amber nodded. "Yeah, right, I know where that is. Sweet. So let's go for a ride." She grinned at Marcus who smiled at each of them in turn.

"Alright Bill, we gotta roll by the China Man first. We'll follow you, bro. So you can set the pace."

"Word, Ting," Brother Bill said with pride.

The China Man's parking lot was empty, as was often the case. The China Man himself stood behind the counter, nodding as if he had been expecting them when they walked in. During perfunctory introductions, the China Man studied Marcus and Amber intently. At length Teacher's eyes settled on Tíng, and he said, "So a couple of your pointy-toothed 'monsters' paid me a visit last night." A grin tweaked the corners of his scruffy white goatee.

"Huh?"

"They pulled into my driveway looking for trouble. But when I gave them a free sample, they just ran away." He chuckled. Then the China Man downplayed his violent interlude with the two goons from the night before quite a bit, while he fielded Marcus's and Amber's questions: Are you hurt? What time was it? There were two of them? Pointy teeth? Big guys? Bleached hair? White Van? Decals? License plate? Amber made note of the details.

Bill listened in. It sounded like the same hooligans, but for all the talk, there was really no new info about *who* these guys actually were. *But holy cow that's an ornery little old man,* Brother Cox thought, raising his eyebrows. The interview grew repetitive, and he continued to listen as he browsed the store.

Marcus was thinking about ol' Marty again. Where was he? And what were these goons doing up in the Heights now? Had they come after Tíng himself? He and Nelly had hurt more than their pride that night at the Shelter. What if they were hawking Nelly too, or anybody else they'd seen with Tíng? The dancing duelist stared into nothingness until Teacher and Amber came back into focus. They had been talking while he was zoned out.

"Yoo hoo. You alive in there?" The China Man snapped his fingers so loud Amber flinched. "She said you broke the Diūqì Shìbīng?"

"Huh? Oh. Yeah. Sorry, Teacher."

"With your fist or your foot?"

"Uh, both, I guess, at the same time, mid-front-sweeping-kick with opposing Eagle Talon Fist." He mimicked the maneuver. "I broke it in two places."

"Eagle Talon? Hmm." The China Man pulled at his chin whiskers as he turned and began to pace. "I fear we have been neglecting your training, Qīngtíng. You have become stronger than I imagined. We have much to discuss."

Bill sifted merchandise and eavesdropped.

Amber grinned. *I knew it.*

Marcus felt a lecture coming on. "Teacher, I know I haven't been in much lately, and now's really not a good time either." He nodded toward Amber. "But pretty soon I'm gonna—"

"Yes-yes, you cannot spend your life inside this store like me. But listen to me for one minute." He lowered his tone. "If not for instruction, at least for consideration."

Marcus nodded and tried to appear relaxed. He grabbed an apple from the basket on the counter, inspected it, and took a bite.

Master took a long breath and said, "The body is a circuit, insolent shoplifter. Bolts of lightning may pass through and leave it unharmed. We have discussed this, yes?"

Marcus nodded.

"So we are conductors for certain, but we are also receivers and transmitters: of infrared light, of heat, of electromagnetic waves and electric pulses which inundate us and animate our physical selves, but the line we draw there is an illusion, because separation between matter and energy, like separation between mind and body, is only perceived. Do you understand?"

"Yes, Teacher."

Amber was enrapt.

Bill was trying on a rice-stalk *căomào* (woven straw hat).

Teacher paced away, cropping and condensing lectures in his head. He turned and displayed his interlocked fingers. "So when body and mind are one, and open, a being might find the link to that ambient power, that abstract force only detectable to the detuned receiver. Do you understand?"

Marcus covered his mouthful of apple. "Uh-huh, I mean, in theory."

Teacher continued. "If a being can align itself with this flow of energy, therein lies a limitless pool of undesignated power. It is the fountain of existence. It is the Ch'i. Dormant and active at once, it binds us together as it sets us free. It is the indestructible gel which suspends the universe, the multiverse. Do you understand?"

"Yes. I think so," Marcus said without much conviction.

Teacher searched his student's eyes and sighed. "We are surrounded by a subtle lightning, Tíng. We need only summon it to arc for us. We and all these things, the air you breathe and even less material things, are all in fact one thing. But we are blind to the interconnection."

"So, it's like, we *are* the lightning," Tíng said.

The China Man gave a thoughtful nod.

Amber bore a look of skepticism.

Teacher clapped his hands and rubbed them together. "Your untapped potential is bound by the wall between your mind and the Ch'i. But this wall is not physical. For your skull is not just a vessel. It is an antenna, it is an amplifier, an instrument which can resonate with that force that surrounds us. But we cannot sample this power for even a second, not by some mental trick, or by accident. You must let it inside. You must *be* it. And the focal point is here." Teacher formed his hand into the Serpent's Tail, and leveled it at Marcus's navel.

Tíng tightened up, feeling a slight pressure, though his master hadn't touched him.

"Yes. It was your point of entry to this world—the point from which you draw every breath. It is your core, your generator, your center of gravity, your guts, your will." Teacher grunted as he slowly balled the Serpent's Tail into a fist. His sandals squeaked against the linoleum as his rigid body slid sideways a few inches toward a heavy, metal shelf display on his right, which rattled and groaned as it shuffled toward its Master in kind. Marcus glanced at Amber and saw a look of perplexity—no, mild shock—on her face. The shelf display was crooked now, so Tíng straightened it with his foot.

The China Man relaxed, cracked his neck from side to side, and began to pace again. "You have mastered the Ch'i within your body through use of the Primal Animal Forms, but you have yet to connect with that outside source. Muscle and bone are frail without this connection. A being without it cannot overcome one with it." He stopped several paces away, facing the front door as he mumbled, "And you, my pupil, are so close to that connection." He shook his head, turned, and strode back toward Marcus. "Okay. That is enough for now. I can see that you have ants in your pants, and I have tried to begin ten lessons at once. You must come back soon when you have more time. Now you kids go play, or work, or whatever it is you do."

Marcus nodded as he swallowed the last bits of his apple. He inhaled slowly and said, "Teacher, you know if I see these clowns on the street, I'm gonna have to walk up and have a chat with 'em."

Bill nearly spouted a proverb about violence begetting violence, but thought better of it.

Amber was still trying to rationalize her way through the China Man's human-magnet trick, when a sobering thought pervaded her senses: This could all go very badly, for all of them, but especially for Marcus. *I mean, he's not invincible. Right?*

Marcus asked, "You guys ready to roll?" and almost tossed his apple core into the trash can behind the counter, but then stopped and held on to it.

Bill thanked the China Man as he headed for the door, and Teacher bid him good day.

On Amber's way out, the old man told her, "It is good to meet you, Amber. Come back again soon."

She promised him she would.

Marcus passed the register saying, "Later, Mast—" The China Man caught him by the sleeve quick as a film edit. "You watch yourself dragonfly. I don't want to have to bust you out of the jailhouse."

"Okay, yes Teacher."

Trotting down the front steps, Marcus mumbled something about compost as he tossed his apple core up under the tallow tree. The sun was approaching its peak in the southern sky while thunder rumbled to the north.

Bill took the bridge over White Oak Bayou with more confidence this time, though he still faced front. Amber crossed, only occasionally glancing at the road in front of her, eyes fixed mainly on the bayou down below. About halfway across, she shouted back to Marcus, "Who's that?" as she released her right handlebar to point down at the levee.

Ting stood on his pedals to get a better look. *"Pan-terito?"*

"What?" Amber hollered back, nearly swerving out into traffic. A passing car honked.

Marcus yelled up to Bill, "Bill, pull off to the right when you get past the guardrail!"

Bill threw his head back and yelled, "O-Kay!" then immediately faced front again.

The three of them drove their bikes off the sidewalk, converging in a patch of weeds just past the termination of the bridge. "It is. It's Pan-terito again," Bill said shading his eyes and looking into the distance.

Amber had to ask once more. "Who's Panterito?"

Bill and Marcus just shook their heads as the three of them watched the little man and his dog foraging in a driftwood field a few hundred yards upstream. "What's he doing?" Marcus asked absently as Pan lifted the corner of a rotted wood pallet and harvested something from underneath it. Even at this distance the trio could see that his prize was a giant, misshapen lobe of fungus. The little man held it aloft and admired it for a moment before stuffing it into a burlap-looking bag slung over his shoulder.

"Is he gonna eat that?" Amber asked.

"That seems like a really bad idea," Marcus replied. About that time Pan turned and looked back at them, tipping his hat.

"He sees us," Bill said. His big red dog saw them too, and barked in their direction as it wagged its tail. The three of them waved back, though weakly, feeling slightly disoriented as if some mental fog hung in the air around them. Then Pan turned abruptly and continued to venture farther upstream, farther away from their position with his big red dog in tow.

The two men tried in vain to explain to Amber who Panterito was as they maneuvered their bikes out of the weeds and back onto the sidewalk. Marcus said, "Uh, he's this mystic guy. From Mexico, we think. He's been writing stuff under the bridges."

Bill concurred. "Yeah."

"O-kay," said Amber.

13

KRIST-YON KLEEN

They crossed Buffalo Bayou again, and Bill eased the Huffy and his short caravan to a halt at Allen Parkway to wait for the light.

Amber said, "So *where* are we gonna hand out the rest of these sandwiches? I mean they are the bomb, but I doubt we could eat 'em all."

Marcus pointed up at the rundown building standing stark atop the levee, diagonally across the intersection. "That's the place, right up the hill."

"Really? I drive by here all the time," she said, shielding her eyes as she looked up at the eyesore of a structure.

Marcus nodded. "Everybody does."

The light changed and Bill was on the move. "Y'all comin'?"

When they topped the trail leading up to the village, Amber and Bill were on Marcus's heels, though winded from the effort. Farmer Frank was toiling at the east end of the heap. When he saw the newcomers, he wiped his face with a dirty rag, took a nip from his pint, and walked to greet them. He removed his cap out of respect for Amber, and tried to slick down his thin, sweaty hair. "Hello ma'am, fellers. An' who might this lovely lady be?"

Marcus hesitated. Frank's smile was forced. Something wasn't right.

Bill chimed in, happy to make introductions. "This is Amber. She's the journalist from *The Rag* we're all so fond of. Amber, this is Frank, resident farmer and Southern gentleman."

"Very nice to meet you, Frank." Amber smiled and stuck her hand out.

Frank bowed but not too much because he and Amber were about the same height. "Pleasure's all mine." He took her hand in his rough, soiled one and added, "Who woulda thunk such a sharp writer'd be so pretty too?"

"You're too kind, sir," Amber said with a bit of Southern twang. Like Marcus, she tended to echo the vernacular of those with whom she spoke. "Looks like you've got quite a garden over there."

"Aw well, it's startin' to come together."

Bill couldn't stand it. He had to embellish. He told Amber about the origin of the heap, the fortuitous soil, and the boundless fruit it could potentially bear, hardly pausing to catch his breath.

Frank could hardly get a word in edgewise. He offered a "yep" or an "uh-huh" when Bill glanced his way, but the old farmer's mind was elsewhere.

Marcus couldn't take it anymore, and he interrupted just as Bill was beginning a sermon on cucumbers. "What's wrong, Frank?"

Frank looked at Ting and sighed. "Leo got picked up by the laws last night. They Tasered 'im and knocked 'im 'round a little, but he's alright. They let 'im out this mornin'. He's sittin' over in the shrine. Wants to be left 'lone though. The bastards killed Samson!" Frank was hollering at Tíng, who was already fifteen yards away. Bill and Amber ran to catch up.

There was a gathering of fringe folks seated on the south end of the dock. Jaime and several friends joined hands and helped each other to their feet as Marcus bounded onto the platform from a distance that would give an antelope pause. Amber and Bill shared a look of disbelief as they trotted to the steps at the south end of the dock.

Tíng addressed Jaime. "Dude, they Tasered him *and* killed his dog! What the hell!" He turned north toward the partially open bay door.

Jaime reached out and caught Tíng's arm. "Wait, bro." Marcus stopped lest he drag his frail friend to the ground. "Big Leo's okay. He told me what happened, and I'll tell you about it too. But he also told me he wants to be left alone for a while." Marcus looked at the bay door then back to Jaime, who let go of him and said, "Come on, I'll tell you about it."

Jaime's counsel had always been solid. Plus, the last thing Tíng wanted to do right now was stress out Leo even more. So he settled in with the ragtag congregation, which now included Bill and Amber, whom Jaime and the rest welcomed warmly. Some others were still walking in from the village, but pretty soon, everyone had a grilled cheese in hand.

Amber likened Jaime to a half-starved, careworn Tommy Chong as he sat down Indian style and began to speak. "Leo found a heap of old auto parts in a dumpster. It was a big score for him, lots of good metal. So he piled it onto his trike to haul to the recycling yard. But he was way up on North Shepherd, outside the loop. And a couple of cops who didn't recognize him stopped him to ask him what he was up to.

"Well, apparently Samson attacked one of them. Bit one of the cops, so they say. And one thing led to another. The dog got killed, Leo retaliated, and then both cops hit him with their Tasers. He *is* scary when he's mad. So they arrested him and impounded his tricycle. But one of their lawyers saw the video from the police car camera and decided to let him go. I read his paperwork. They're not gonna charge him with anything. He's a freakin' war hero, after all."

Marcus crept over and peered under the open bay door. He could see Leo across the cavernous room, sitting with his back against the wall. Marcus returned to the group and reported, "He's still just sitting there."

"We just need to give him some time, Ting."

Marcus picked up a piece of broken concrete and fired it way out into the high weeds near the east fence of the village. "I *hate* the damn cops sometimes."

Jaime took a sip of his bottle of cheap wine and said, "And sometimes it seems like they hate us. But hate cannot conquer hate. Only love can do that. Leo's lucky. He could've been shot, or convicted of a felony. Still, it wasn't all his fault. He's still got PTSD. Even though he'd never admit to it." He shook his head and added, "Too much blood on his hands to ever wash off."

Amber came up and hugged Marcus from behind. He tried not to seem tense. When she released him, he turned to her and forced a smile.

Bill was smiling too, though his eyes were moist and puffy.

Farmer Frank puffed smoke from a reclaimed cigarette and said aloud to everyone, "Them busboys are the ones that got off lucky, lucky that ol' bear's so kind-hearted these days. He coulda sent them two greenhorns to the everafter with shit in their drawers."

Amber stifled a giggle, and then asked. "What do you mean?"

Bill saw an in. "Yeah, what do you mean, and how did Leo hurt his leg?"

Frank took a pull off his pint to wet his whistle and said. "He took a round in that leg over in the 'Nam. Me 'n' him chewed some o' the same mud over in that accursed place. Leo was Special Forces, so he's an expert with all manner of weapons. But if you get too close, he can kill ya just as quick with his bare hands."

There was mumbling among the fringe folks, and everyone turned their attention to the partly open bay door. Leo was shuffling out from under it, dragging his stiff leg. He wore his shabby field jacket and had his hood up, despite the mild weather. Silence fell across the rabble as the grizzled giant approached. Many stood and doffed their caps in reverence.

When Leo was close enough he stopped, sighed, looked from Jaime to Frank and said, "Y'all ain't been talkin' 'bout me have ya?"

Frank was on his feet by then, with his pint of booze at order arms. He saluted and said, "No sir!" and several folks giggled.

The congregation slowly dissolved, and fringe folks put their hands on Leo and offered consolation for Samson as they passed. The big man was embarrassed by all the attention, but it went a long way toward healing his giant heart. His feelings intensified when Amber strode up, stuck out her hand, and introduced herself as Ting's friend. Leo smiled and nodded, letting her shake two of his oversized fingers while he silently adored her.

With Leo seemingly returning to normal, Frank turned his attention back to Farah. These past chaotic days had taken a toll on her. She sat huddled up Indian-style, many yards away from Jaime and the rest. Frank was crouched beside her, quietly talking when Marcus and Amber walked up and stood before them.

"How y'all doin'?" Ting asked. "Amber, you've met Frank, and this is Farah." He gave Amber a knowing look, and she received it. Farah was the eyewitness he'd told her about. The one who'd seen Sean Dorsey's murder on the bridge that night.

Farah looked up and forced a smile but said nothing, and then continued to stare down at her own lap. Frank spoke up. "We're doin' fine, sir and ma'am," he said, tipping his cap. Then after a moment he asked, "Ting, we didn't tell ya 'bout the white boots, did we?"

"White boots?" Marcus and Amber said in stereo.

Frank glanced sideways at Farah, but she didn't move so he continued. "Farah wanted to tell ya she remembered somethin' else 'bout the pickup truck on the bridge that night. She can't stop dreamin' 'bout it. Anyway she didn't think much of it, but who knows?"

Marcus was about to shake the details out of him when Frank finally said, "I guess the creeps that night had some white boots tucked behind the cab o' their pickup."

"White boots?" Marcus asked, glancing at Farah, though he didn't really expect her to respond. So he was surprised when she looked up at him and said, "Yessir. I been wantin' to tell you, but with everthang that's been goin' on—"

"It's okay, it's fine. White boots, you said?"

Farah cleared her throat. "Yessir. You know how fellers put their rubbers back there behind the back-glass sometimes?"

Marcus had begun to slowly shake his head when Brother Bill appeared from behind and chimed in. "Shrimpers," he said, somewhat smug. "Lots of people use rubber boots down in Oyster Prairie, and a lot of times they keep 'em tucked upside down right in there behind the cab of their pickup trucks. My buddy Jake, the rice farmer, he's always got a pair stuck back there." Which struck Bill as odd, since Jake was always barefoot. "But the only people I ever see usin' *white* rubber boots, though, are shrimpers. Maybe it's 'cause white is a high-visibility color, you know, in case they fall in the water. I'm pretty sure they float, the boots."

As Amber jotted notes on her ubiquitous legal pad, a smile played across her lips, because she knew the devil was often found in the details.

Bill gasped when he checked his digital Ironman watch, and then announced his immediate departure. He was due at La Estrella de Jahweh Church downtown, where he'd begun volunteering as a counselor. The *hermanas y hermanos* there valued

Bill's passion, and they needed someone with his formal education and command of English.

Marcus was happy the hayseed was embracing the city, but even happier when the holy roller graciously biked away and left him with Amber, who was apparently interviewing Jaime now. The emaciated orator was telling her, "Yeah, so recently the crowd around here has been growing, and the ones who usually tend to wander are sticking around a lot more, especially at night. Everybody's afraid to get caught down on the street by one of these vampire dudes. Some more than others." He was looking at Farah, who was talking to Frank out near the heap. "And we're only slightly less afraid of the cops, you know what I mean? There's a few of 'em who are dedicated to helping people like us, and they're awesome, but they're like, the nerds of the force, you know. They cruise around in this black and white minivan; it's actually kind of funny." He grinned. "But they don't even know we're up here, and we like to keep it that way, you know? Because some of 'em can be real hard-asses, and we don't want to get kicked out."

Amber smiled. "Well, I'm glad you guys called me. We'll figure out who these snaggle-toothed creeps are. It might even turn into a big exposé."

Marcus cut in from the side. "Did you tell him about the China Man?"

Amber shook her head. Then she and Marcus gave Jaime a brief account of the goons' latest regrettable assault. Several folks listened in, and even Leo was grinning by the end of the tale. Jaime said, "Dang. They messed with the wrong little old man."

"Mm-hmm." Leo nodded.

Amber put away her pen and pad and said, "Okay well, I think I've got enough for a good start here. Maybe we should go and mull it over out in the sunshine, while it lasts." She was looking at Ting.

"Word." Marcus had meant to tell Jaime about their chance

meeting with Panterito, but for some reason it slipped his mind. Pan had that effect on folks.

Jaime said he loved the sunshine as well, but he preferred to observe it from the shade. And Leo was already shuffling away toward the steps at the north end of the dock. Jaime hollered after him, "Leo, where you going?"

"Huh? I need to go find my wheels, man."

"Wait bro, we need to look at your paperwork again and figure out where the cops stashed the thing first. If you just go out looking on your own, it'll take forever. And you don't want to be caught out on foot when this wet front blows in." He gestured to the gray sky in the northwest.

Marcus said, "Jaime's right, Leo. Why don't you relax and let things settle down for a little while?" He knew any further discourse between his big friend and the cops could go badly. Leo was intimidating even though he strove to be meek.

Amber said, "I've got a friend with a pickup truck. Don't worry Leo, I'll get your wheels back. Come sit in the sun with us for a while."

He couldn't say no.

They borrowed a blanket from Jaime, which he swore was his cleanest one, though Amber had her doubts. Then the dancing duelist led the journalist, with Leo in tow, back through the hurricane fence on the north side of the village to somewhat of a clearing just east of the path, at the edge of where the hill dropped off. Marcus spread the ratty blanket, and he and Amber sat down with a view of the tree-lined bayou below, and the downtown skyline to the east. She dropped her pack, but didn't move to retrieve her notes.

Leo would take up a king-sized blanket himself, so he crept forward just over the lip of the hill and reclined in the green weeds with his dreadlocks doubling as a pillow and sunshade. He was more at ease concealed by the tall grass anyway. He blinked a few times, and then closed his eyes. But they popped open again when he felt a critter or something infiltrating his hair. He looked up and saw Amber's pale little hands, picking through his dreads.

She said, "Leo, you have grass burs all in your beautiful hair," and she continued to pluck out the spiny debris while the big man tried to relax again. Marcus was smiling, watching her but looking away whenever she glanced at him. This went on for a little while, and Leo was drifting off again when Amber's eyes locked onto something down the levee and she stopped picking.

A small motorcade was pulling in to park a couple hundred yards east, along the bayou, down on the other side of Allen parkway. There was a black, darkly tinted, stretched SUV, followed by an unmarked police cruiser, followed by a silver European roadster. They pulled into a lot alongside a fountain and a small playground amid a copse of tall pine trees.

Marcus followed Amber's gaze and asked, "What's that all about?"

"Not sure." She kept staring.

Leo propped himself up on an elbow to have a look.

A shapely woman in a short business skirt exited the roadster and leaned against it while she traded her heels for walking shoes. She grabbed a touchpad device from behind her seat, shut the door, and hustled toward the SUV.

A lone detective climbed out of the police cruiser with a bit of swagger. His close-cropped hair complemented his polo shirt, utility trousers, and cowboy boots. He took in his surroundings while he adjusted the gun belt around his hips. Then he followed the girl from the roadster.

The driver of the stretched SUV was built like a pro linebacker with olive skin, a black goatee, black suit, and black shades. He scanned the area as he moved to open the door for the VIP in back. The aristocrat stepped out into the sunlight, wearing a beige safari suit complete with Panama hat, and a petite pair of field glasses dangling from his neck.

Marcus scoffed. Only rich people could get away with dressing like that.

Amber's inquisitive stare turned into a frown as she said, "Oh no, I think that might be...."

The khaki-clad man below paid little mind to the fit woman or the cop as they approached him and offered their greetings. Then the VIP turned and strode away toward the small park, dictating and gesturing to the open air. The comely woman fell in at his heels, taking notes on her touchpad device. The cop fell in behind her, taking mental notes of her physique. The eccentric leader stopped when he reached the shade under the pines, and removed his hat to fluff his shock of white-blond hair.

Marcus asked, "Seriously, who in the—"

"I knew it," said Amber. "That's Kristian Klein" She pronounced it Krist-yon Kleen. "I've only met him once in person, but that's definitely him. I was trying to get a quote from him for this piece I was doing about the deregulation of his refineries through the abuse of grandfather clauses. I cornered him at this schmoozy tape-cutting ceremony on one of his yachts at his private harbor down in Galveston. As usual with guys like him, he wouldn't talk to me about it. And when he realized I wasn't invited to the party, one of his goons nearly put his hands on me. Until I aimed a can of pepper spray at his face and found my own way out.

"My friend Ryan Dylan, at the Bayou City Conservancy, Kristian Klein is, like, his nemesis. Ryan's an entomologist and he's one of my go-to PhD's when I write about eco-stuff. You should meet him, Ting, you'd like him. He's got an awesome butterfly garden."

"I bet." Marcus was still looking down the hill.

"Anyway, according to Ryan, Kristian Klein is like this, evil, toxic waste-spewing, chemical overlord who plays himself off as a philanthropist. And from what I've researched about the guy, that's pretty much spot on."

"So is he Klein, like, Klein Chemical, the big, uh?"

"Petrochemical giant. Yup. And he's been in the news a lot lately, dabbling in commercial real estate inside the loop. With his deep pockets, he's got all the corporate brass Downtown and every stuffed suit in City Hall eating out of his hand. I've heard a rumor that he wants to privatize the waterfront along Buffalo Bayou, from Montrose all the way to Downtown. He wants to dredge it deeper, bulldoze these hundred-foot trees, build up the levees with concrete, and put in a ritzy strip mall along both banks. I guess to make it kind of like the Riverwalk in San Antone, but more *upscale* I'm sure. And I can't imagine why he'd be down here in a public park unless that's what he's talking about right now."

Marcus scanned the green, shady strip of waterfront running into the theater district. It was public domain; his domain. "Could he do all that?"

She cleared her throat. "I would hope not. I would hope the municipality would shoot it down, but Klein has so much money, who knows what he's capable of? There's also been some chatter that he's considering a bid for mayor."

"If you can't beat 'em, preside over 'em," Marcus intoned.

"Yeah, and what's really scary is if he could become mayor of H-town, he could become Governor someday, and we know what comes after that. The freakin' White House."

Leo hardly blinked. He was fixated on the sentry down the hill. Klein's driver, in his black suit, blended perfectly with the mammoth SUV that was his charge. He stalked its perimeter as he monitored the actions of the VIP down on the levee. Leo knew that under his broad coat, the driver had far more firepower than any street cop.

The capitalist, the assistant, and the official had walked the perimeter of the playground, Klein talking, the other two following and listening. The trio had circled around and come back up to the parking lot, where they now stopped and stood facing uphill. Kristian dabbed his forehead with a handkerchief. The cop used his sleeves. The fit woman seemed unaffected.

Marcus was looking at a massive cottonwood that was older than any living human, wondering how somebody could just cut down such an ancient lifeform, when Amber poked his leg and said, "Is he looking right at us?"

They sat still as Klein scanned the hill with his field glasses. He laid the binoculars back on his chest and pointed toward the shrine as he spoke and shook his head. The assistant and the policeman on either side of him nodded their heads mechanically.

Kristian Klein turned to the comely woman and issued an imperative along with a condescending hand gesture to send her on her way. She strode back to her roadster, recouping her dignity as the magnate marched back to his SUV, talking over his shoulder to the cop who was trying to keep up. Then Kristian climbed into his armored conveyance without a rearward glance, and his stoic driver shut the door without regard to the police officer.

Marcus stood up and said, "Uh, maybe we should go talk to Jaime about this." He took Amber's hand and helped her up. She shook out the blanket, as if it mattered, and they headed back to the dock with Leo bringing up the rear.

Marcus explained what they'd seen down the hill and Amber filled in the pertinent info about Kristian Klein. Fringe folks once again materialized and gathered to listen. Jaime smiled, despite the grim topic. "Hmm. Yeah, I didn't want to bring it up earlier because there was already enough on the table, but there have been some big guys coming around here, wearing hard hats."

There was some mumbling of consensus, and some of surprise.

"You know, measuring things, kicking stuff around, but

generally ignoring us. It's happened before, but this time it seems like it might be for real. I actually got one of them to talk to me and he said, in a nutshell, that we all might be house-hunting soon." Jaime laughed, and some others in the group joined in.

Amber spoke up. "But haven't you guys been here forever? The doors have been chained for what, ten years? Maybe the owners would lease it, or maybe even donate it, write it off as charity. Maybe you could get squatter's rights while you put a plan together for some sort of nonprofit or neighborhood co-op or something." Judging by the fringe folks' expressions, she thought she must sound ridiculous. She looked at Jaime and added, "We could help."

Jaime smiled. "Thank you for your concern, Amber." He looked at Marcus. "I told you she was something special." Then he took a measured glance at every face gathered around and said, "It's true some of us have haunted this place for more than a decade, but we never presumed it to be ours. In fact, I believe all of us are pretty much forfeit in the game of ownership." He took a sip of wine. "We're fiscal rebels under the boot heels of this capitalist regime." He laughed. "I don't believe any of us could even produce a valid ID card. So I don't think we're going into any bureaucratic office any time soon to stake a claim on a big piece of commercial real estate like this. I'm pretty sure they'd stop us at the door."

She shot back, "Ting can produce a valid ID."

Marcus had been nodding his head, absently agreeing with Jaime. Now he was looking at Amber with his eyebrows raised.

She added, "And so can I."

"And so can Brother Bill," Marcus added. "That dude's itching for a cause to get behind."

Farmer Frank was manicuring his nails with a pocketknife as he spoke up. "Brother Bill already told me he wanted to help us."

"Word," Marcus said.

Amber continued, "You guys are already growing food here.

What if we could form some kind of organization and try to legally occupy this place? It would take some effort for sure, but maybe it could be done."

She knew some people. She was owed some favors. Or was she being totally naïve? When she considered the location and size of this place, it had to be worth a fortune to somebody. And currently, when she thought who that somebody likely was, reality stung her. Now she had everyone's attention, and she kind of regretted it. Was she kindling false hope in people who sorely needed the real thing? She toned down her enthusiasm a bit, but finished with a promise that she would look into it, and do what she could.

It was time to go. All this new info had darkened the mood, and Amber needed to get going on some research. She needed technology and solitude. She needed her cubicle at *The Houston Rag* office space. *The Rag* was only a hop and a skip from their current location, and Marcus's house was way off in the other direction. Tíng was looking at her expectantly when she hatched their new plan. "So, we leave *your* tricycle here for Leo, until we can get his out of impound. You drop me off at *The Rag* real quick, and then you can bring my car up there later. I just need some time to get a little work done. I'll call you."

Leo accepted Marcus's tricycle as a loaner reluctantly but graciously. He couldn't say no to Amber. Then Amber and Marcus said their goodbyes and departed the village. Minutes later, she hopped off the Frankenbike's rear pegs on the sidewalk in front of *The Houston Rag* headquarters. "I'll call you soon," she said. Still seated on his bike, Marcus was about her height, so she swept in quickly and kissed him on the cheek before she turned to go. He was watching her walk away when she looked back over her shoulder and said, "Don't crash my sweet-ass car," with a devious grin. Then she walked into the building and left him there buzzing.

14

OF SHARKS AND SHRIMPERS

While Kristian Klein's underlings carried out their orders, the man himself was reclined in the back of his stretched black SUV, considering his next move in the game of ownership. He grabbed a hardback book from the empty seat next to him and cut two lines of fine white powder across the cover. He snorted one rail up each nostril, mopped up the residue with his finger and rubbed it across his teeth. Kristian's face tingled and he smiled. Within seconds, his body felt lighter, and he was suddenly in the mood for ponies and single malt Scotch. He ordered his driver to head for his private gate at the racetrack.

Irritated they were slowing for another red light, Kristian wondered if he might be able to acquire one of those transmitters that ambulances and fire trucks use to turn traffic signals green. He expressed this interest to his man in the driver's seat. Klein's driver had been a worldly and bloodied soldier before he'd sunk into the private sector for ten times his military salary. He was as good as anyone to consult on the logistics of obtaining such a device.

"I'll look into it, Sir," Argus replied with an indeterminate accent as he glanced at his benefactor in the mirror.

"Good man." Kristian closed the black bulletproof window between himself and his personal mercenary. He looked down at the book in his lap. *God's Economy* by Toby Goodspeed. The business of faith wasn't within Klein's realm of expertise or taste, but the prospect was always explored alongside his other avenues of market research. There's good money in religion for sure, but Klein also liked the dogma of this Toby Goodspeed. And that was rare.

God's Economy essentially homogenized the free market, government, and religion into a unified vision of the American Dream. One might call it a *Capitalist Manifesto*. Plus, this Goodspeed guy had a knack for corralling bums and junkies into his American Missionary churches, and reclaiming urban slums for posterity. After all, Klein wasn't just flipping real estate here, he was engineering a community. And his "Bayouwalk" research team had concurred; one of these American Missionary churches, or shelters or whatever the hell they were, could help shine up the Montrose District. Kristian had other people to do the heavy scrubbing.

Staring at the ruggedly handsome power-evangelist on the book's cover, Klein pushed a button that opened a line to one of his assistants, and said, "Get me Goodspeed." He felt like stirring the pot.

It was an emotional occasion when Toby Goodspeed bid goodbye to his Denver congregation. Of course, it wasn't really goodbye. He'd be back regularly, in fact. It was less than a two-hour flight on the Denver Christian Network's private jet. And the DCN would still be airing his lectures every Sunday morning.

Nonetheless, Toby couldn't help but give himself somewhat of a martyr's send off. It's who he was.

"My sacrifice will be for the greater good. Houston is a strong vertebra in the backbone of our great nation's economy, and God has given me a mission down there that I cannot refuse. A quaint, scenic district in the Bayou City has been overrun by addicts and homosexuals, and it is up to me to take those misguided people by the hand, and turn them into God's servants. Those troubled folks down south just need a little American Missionary amen."

Viewers at home mouthed the words along with Goodspeed. Then they called in credit card numbers, mailed in checks, bought books and videos, and topped off Toby's coffer for the road. His Denver congregation members would drink his Kool-Aid, and soon it would be the same way in Houston. He walked the front edge of his stage, shaking the hands of people who had crowded up there to touch him, before he jogged tearfully into the wings.

An assistant met Toby with a fresh towel as he slowed to a walk and checked his chronometer. He wasn't excited about the climate down in Houston, but it was a bigger market than his Denver and Omaha locations combined. The rustic old building with a view of the Downtown skyline was perfect, and the property value would soar with the projected commercialization of the waterfront below. The ultra-wealthy Klein had plans for the entire district, and he had hand-picked Toby as one of his generals.

Goodspeed dreamed his American Missionary churches would infiltrate and reclaim quaint metropolitan districts (with high vagrant populations) all across the United States, and Houston was a major stepping stone. Heck, with people like Klein on his side, he could take this all the way to Skid Row.

Toby's phone vibrated in his pocket. It was Kristian Klein. He answered it immediately. "Yes sir, Mr. Klein. That's correct, I'll be down there bright and early in the morning."

蛉

The bottomless pool was obstinate, not giving up any answers. Tíng's questions just rippled lazily across its endless surface, lost in its magnitude. In deep meditation, Marcus's physical self was hanging upside down from an exposed beam in the dojo ceiling, maximizing blood flow to his brain. He cradled his dated cell phone over his navel with both hands, maybe to snag a stray radio wave and amplify his astral projection. He was willing her to call.

The phone rang, and Marcus's eyes popped open. He squinted, somewhat surprised it was still daylight. His hamstrings were numb from exertion, and his feet were feeling some serious pins and needles. The phone rang again, and he angled it down toward his face to verify that it was Amber. Tíng swung his head and torso to generate some inertia, straightening his knees just enough to release the beam and not kick the ceiling. He fell gracefully and landed crouched on the floor. Then he answered his banged-up phone as he stood.

"Myellow?"

"I got 'em," said AKK.

"You got 'em?"

"Your friends with the pointy teeth, I know who they are."

"You do?"

"Yeah, so check this out: Third Coast Harvest is a shrimping company that was founded in Louisiana by a Captain Dwight DeSange about thirty years ago. But they've been running a fleet of boats here in Texas now for about seven years. They also have a small fleet of commercial vehicles, some of which are white trucks and vans that haul fresh seafood." She paused but Marcus said nothing. "So this shrimping company, Third Coast Harvest, is also a huge supporter of Ship Channel Rugby, which is like this back-alley sports league. But they have a website with teams, tournament schedules, links, rosters and some player photos. They're all tough looking guys, probably offshore roughnecks, dockworkers and such."

"Awesome."

"Anyway, the Zombies are the team sponsored by the Third Coast Harvest, and looking through some photos of their players, they're all like, these smiling, Aryan-looking muscleheads who apparently filed their teeth to a sharp point. They give me the creeps."

"Yeah, that's kinda their thing."

"Yeah. So you have to see this website. Also, I couldn't match a photo to the team captain, but on the roster, he's listed as *Terror*. That's his name, *Terror*."

"Super scary."

"Yeah. Sooo, I have an address for a Third Coast Harvest in Clear Lake. You think we should go have a look around?"

Marcus grabbed his pack and darted out to the alley where Amber's hybrid awaited. He had learned to drive in his mom's old Town Car, but had sold the smoky, gas-guzzling relic years ago. Still, cars were pretty self-explanatory, and he managed to drive safely back to the *Houston Rag* building.

Amber was already waiting out front. So was Brother Bill, fanning his face like he'd been running. Marcus hopped out and stood beside the car. The minister babbled an explanation as he and Amber approached. "Amber and I were just talkin', and she said y'all were gonna go check out this Third Coast place, and I only live like six blocks that way, so I sort of asked her if I could come along, you know for safety in numbers and whatnot?"

"He called me right after I called you," Amber clarified as she moved to the driver's side.

"Awesome. So you guys talk on the phone now? That was quick," Marcus said as he walked around to the passenger seat.

"Well I'm sorry. I asked for her number. She and I can be friends too," Bill said defensively as he crawled into the back seat.

蛉

The Third Coast Harvest address in Clear Lake turned out to be a wholesale outlet and administrative office. Amber had gone in and posed as a patron to glean this info, and as much data as she could without creating suspicion. Then the three amateur sleuths in the shabby hybrid staked the place out for half an hour. Bill was getting antsy and talking about food when a white, long bed pickup with dark-tinted windows pulled into the TCH lot and followed a driveway around to the back of the building. There were four huge ice chests in the truck bed, and a FISH decal on the tailgate.

Marcus exited the car as the other two began to discuss what they should do. Then they watched Tíng bolt across the busy street without regard for their input. Amber said, "So, I guess we'll just wait here then."

"Uh, yeah," Bill intoned from the back seat.

Obscured by a hedge and the corner of an adjacent building, Marcus watched them unload the truck. He thought he recognized the shorter of the two men even though they wore hats, shades, and coveralls. The burly white dudes chatted while they unloaded their cargo, but Marcus was too far away to overhear. He caught a glimpse of pointy choppers, though, as the roughnecks shared a laugh. The four massive ice chests were taller than the tailgate, and presumably filled with shrimp and ice. When they unloaded the third chest Marcus saw, tucked behind the truck cab, two pairs of white rubber boots.

The two bruisers muscled the heavy chests into the building, and then came back out with ones that were obviously much lighter, empty. They loaded those back into the truck bed. Then they chatted and exchanged paperwork with a muscular, tattooed blond woman who had come out the back door. Their transaction was coming to an end.

Marcus slipped back to the hybrid across the street and reported what he'd seen. Amber nodded and started the car. A moment later the pickup pulled out onto the boulevard.

"Well, there they go. So what do we do now?" Bill asked.

"Follow 'em," Marcus and Amber replied in stereo.

She waited until they were just far enough ahead. Then she whipped out into traffic and applied the tail. Marcus was impressed. Bill was restless.

They followed the pickup several miles south onto back roads dotted with piers, bait shops, and houses on stilts. The shrimpers finally pulled in and parked at a place advertising *Fish Beer Pool* on a partially lit neon sign. Amber pulled into a convenient greasy spoon down the street, and parked within view of the white truck.

Bill spoke first. "Looks like they're gonna get some food."

After a brief deliberation, the trio in the hybrid elected to acquire some sustenance also. Marcus volunteered to watch while they went in first. Amber came back with a basket of onion rings which she'd liberally crisscrossed with ketchup. Bill had a chili dog and fries. Marcus took his turn, and returned with cheese fries smothered in jalapenos. All had iced tea to drink, and they utilized several napkins each.

The trash was thrown, the iced teas were barely ice, and everyone had gone to the restroom at least once when Amber announced for good measure that it had been over an hour. Marcus instructed them to wait here as he hopped out and walked casually down the street. Ten minutes later he hopped back in and said, "Looks like they had their fish but they're still doing beer and pool."

"Seriously?" Bill moaned.

"Seriously. They're in the back shooting nine-ball and drinking beer."

Amber frowned. "Man, they had an easy work day."

"They were prob'ly out trollin' ten miles offshore before the sun came up," Bill said.

"Oh."

The three of them were becoming VIP's at the greasy spoon by the time their quarries shuffled back out of *Fish Beer Pool* and climbed back into their company truck. The shadows were getting long when they got back on the road. And the fresh north breeze cooled quickly with the sinking sun.

They drove southeast, and residential hovels gave way to hulking storage tanks and towering flare stacks. The pickup held a pretty straight line, but accelerated erratically. So it was a little harder to tail than it had been earlier, with a sober driver. Amber was almost too careful, and she had to race to catch up a couple times. Marcus held his tongue. Bill covered his mouth.

They followed a dredged-up highway across an expansive marsh onto an island of industry with a thin barrier of scrub trees. Pretty soon they lost sight of the sun completely. Traffic was sparse and dwindling, with hardly a pedestrian in sight. The kids in the hybrid could hear the horns of commercial watercraft. Seabirds wheeled overhead instead of pigeons. Amber saw a high bridge in the distance, past the stacks off to their right, but she wasn't sure which bridge it was. She said, "We're definitely, like, right on the Ship Channel."

The white pickup came to a T-intersection and hung a left. Amber was zooming up from three blocks behind, and when she got to the intersection, the light was red, but she'd timed it perfectly. They watched as the truck pulled into a driveway a block and a half down on the right. The light turned green but there was nobody behind her, so she waited several seconds before making the turn. Then she proceeded discreetly into an alley half a block away and across the street from where the truck had pulled in. She parked in a deep shadow with a decent view through her rear window.

Marcus said, "Nice work."

She smiled.

The passenger got out of the pickup and opened a wide chain-link gate set upon wheels. The truck passed through, and as the passenger secured the gate, he had to shoo away several large, barking dogs. A few of the canines were vicious, and the brute grabbed a long piece of wood from the truck bed to fend them off before he climbed onto the back and sat atop one of the big ice chests. The driveway ran for dozens of yards to what had to be the Third Coast Harvest boatyard.

The hangar was enormous and white with a powder blue TCH emblazoned on the forty-foot front wall. It was surrounded by several acres of patchy weeds, retired equipment, stacks of pallets, rusty drums, and a few other smaller buildings, all enclosed by a high hurricane fence, topped with three strands of barb wire.

As the white pickup truck disappeared into the property, Marcus popped the passenger door, but this time Amber caught him by the arm.

"Wait. I wanna go with you."

"Uh, you sure?"

Bill foresaw the prospect of being left alone. "I wanna go too."

Marcus sighed, long and deep. "Okay, but stay close to me, and don't make a sound, or those dogs will know we're coming a mile away."

The trio approached from the south, in the shadow of a neighboring structure that appeared to be a massive storage tank. Marcus led them carefully around its edge, scanning for a way to get closer, until he saw what he was looking for. He had to smile. Maybe twenty feet off the ground, a bundle of conduit and thick pipes ran from their cover structure to the roof of the southernmost building on the Third Coast Harvest property—some sort of utility shed maybe. The bundle of pipes crossed a deep, concrete drainage ditch, and passed right over the high barb wire fence of the TCH lot. Maintenance ladders were affixed to the walls at either end of the pipes. It was almost too easy. Marcus was climbing the nearest ladder by the time Bill and Amber caught up. Bill wanted to protest, but was afraid to speak up.

When he got to the top, Marcus signaled the other two to stay put, but Amber was already on her way up, a petite black bag slung on her back. Marcus just shook his head. Then he chose the largest pipe and tiptoed across the sixty-foot span. He turned and waited for her on the other side. The pipe he'd chosen was coated with nonskid paint on the top side, to facilitate maintenance personnel, but there were no handrails. A fall from this height could mean broken bones—and possibly being torn to pieces by a pack of dogs. So Amber crossed more slowly and carefully.

Then Bill sort of inch-wormed across using both his hands and feet while bearing a look of intense concentration. Still, it took some guts. Marcus was impressed. He'd figured both of them would have chickened out and stayed on the other side, Bill for sure. He shrugged and stepped onto the roof of the lesser structure, now officially trespassing on TCH property.

The sky dimmed from rose to violet in the southwest, and the few surrounding streetlights ignited. The mercury dropped along with the sun's sinking halo. Marcus scanned the area for canines. Then he silently stepped off the roof and dropped to the ground. The other two found the opposing maintenance ladder and climbed down.

Ting appeared and led the other two across a dark patch of tall weeds to a door he'd spotted on the near side of the main TCH building. It wasn't locked, so Marcus opened it and they followed him inside. When Bill shut the door, dogs started to bark somewhere out in the yard, and he winced.

They were in a small room where two massive pipes inter-sected at a shutoff valve in the center of the tight space. The only light came from the cracks around another door on the opposite side of the pipes that accessed farther into the building. Marcus tried the door, but this one was locked. He put his ear to it for a minute and heard nothing. So he squatted down widening his stance, then gripped the knob and thrust his shoulder into the door.

Bill was horrified when the door popped open with a bang. But Marcus pulled it back and held it closed. The dogs were really barking outside now, and Brother Cox was *really* starting to wish he'd waited in the car.

Marcus listened at the door again for a response to the sound of him breaking it. Nothing. He stuck his head inside, and then signaled the others to follow as he tiptoed into a deserted hallway. Bill wanted to tell them this was a really bad idea and they should turn back, but he was just barely keeping up, and afraid to make a peep.

The second door across the hall was marked as a stairwell entry. Marcus slipped inside without hesitation, Amber right on his heels, and then Bill grudgingly followed, his head on a swivel. The stairs ascended in two short, opposing flights to a landing that opened into another hallway, this one narrower, carpeted, and enclosed on both ends with three evenly spaced doors along the opposite wall. Marcus tried the closest door. It was locked, but not with a deadbolt, just the knob. Before Tíng destroyed more property and made more noise, Amber produced a spent, plastic gift-card and wiggled it between the knob and the jamb, opening the door with a click.

Marcus smiled at her. Then he ducked down, peered into an unlit, uninhabited office space, and entered the room in a crouched position. Amber bent ninety degrees at the waist and followed. Then Bill crawled in, hands and feet. The far wall was dominated by a row of huge windows looking out into a vast, high chamber with a ceiling crane. Muted voices were coming from down below, so Marcus crept up to the glass to have a look. Amber picked a spot a few feet down, and Bill did the same. Marcus and Amber peered over the windowsill, but Bill waited to see their reactions before he made another move.

The concrete hangar floor was divided roughly in half by an inlet that opened out onto a small harbor skirting the Houston Ship Channel. In the south end, a couple of boats sat dry-docked for maintenance. On the north side of the inlet, yards of heavy line and netting hung from the forty-foot walls. A beat-up yellow fork-lift sat idle, and the whole place was littered with scoops, hoses, tools, and chests. There was an incessant hum in the background, emanating from various coolers, ice makers, and air compressors, and the entire deck was coated in dark nonskid.

Marcus and Amber rose enough to see the termination of the inlet where there stood a group of Zombies, including the pair they had just followed back to the nest. Bill inched up to peer through his section of the window and froze, because at that moment, the obvious ringleader of the goons, a giant among big men, kicked the carcasses of two large dogs into the water. There was no mistaking it. AKK heard and saw the brute bellow the words, "Least we caught the tide goin' out." He laughed and his cohort joined in.

As Marcus studied the scene, movement off to his left caught his attention. There was another human down there who obviously wasn't a Zombie. Standing across the inlet, thin as a rail, clutching a hose and rinsing some ominous dark red fluid into the brine was ol' Marty. He wore a dirty raincoat with the hood up, but by his posture and shaggy white beard, Marcus was ninety percent sure it was him.

Amber was transfixed on the one that had to be Terror. The head Zombie's guttural Cajun brogue was perforated by a toothy hiss. "We need to round up mo' trainin' mutts. These ones ain't been lastin' f' shit." Water sloshed and boiled down in the inlet, and Terror stepped closer. "Aw hell! Lookee here boys! My pets done showed up!" Zombies gathered near the edge, swearing and laughing. The thrashing in the water became so violent that a few of the brutes hopped back to avoid getting wet. Terror said, "Oowee, dat's a bull shark! Look at da head on 'im. He a ten-foota. You put out enough chum, you neva know what you gon' catch."

Ting clenched his fists. Amber fought back tears. Bill decided he liked it better below the window, and slid back down. A huge seabird took flight out in the high rafters, emitting a honking repetitive cry, and Brother Cox panicked momentarily, thinking some alarm was going off. Then Marcus and Amber ducked down too, just as a resounding *pop pop* sounded from within the hangar, followed by the unnerving hum of ricocheting bullets.

"Don't shoot at dat bird in here, dumbass! You break one o' dem windows and I'm gon' feed yo ass to da sharks too!" roared the Terror.

Zombies laughed.

Amber breathed deeply with her back to the wall, angry at herself for not even taking the camera out of her bag. Marcus was still straining to hear what the goons were talking about. Amber prodded him, wide-eyed and pointing at Bill, who was low-crawling for the door.

The dancing duelist assumed the lead again, and half a minute later they were back at the maintenance compartment that led outside. The door was still busted, but Marcus pulled it to, so it would look normal to any passersby. Once inside, Bill said, panting, "Oh my God, there's a bunch of 'em. Those guys are everything we were scared of and more. We've got to get out of here."

Marcus nodded. He would have stayed up there longer if he'd been alone. "Just relax and keep it down. We're not home free yet." He crept to the outer door, eased it open, and made eye contact with half a dozen pit bulls. He shut the door firmly on a cacophony of barking, scratching, and growling. *They're dogs. They could hear us in here.*

Marcus turned back to the other two and spoke calmly, as he lifted one foot at a time onto a huge pipe, tightening and retying his Dr. Martens bootlaces. His co-conspirators were all ears. "Okay, here's the deal. The pipes we climbed in on are over that way." He pointed. "And they're only about thirty or forty yards away. There's a lot of dogs out there, but they only saw *me* just now. So, if I run out and grab their attention, every one of them will chase me. Now, when I take off, you two just wait like five seconds for all the dogs to get moving in the other direction. Then slip out and make for the pipes, okay?"

Bill nodded with a look of incredulity.

Amber shook her head, frowning. "Wait, you're gonna make the dogs chase you?"

He nodded. "Uh huh. And then you guys make for the pipes and climb out. It's okay, they're not gonna catch me. Pit bulls are tough but they got short legs." He smiled and touched her cheek. She clasped his hand, wanting to tell him his plan didn't make any sense, but his fingers slipped out of hers as he turned and kicked the door open. There was a yelp as the nearest dog was cleared out by impact. Then Marcus charged through the rest of the startled pack, flinging the door closed behind him. It bounced off the jamb and Amber grabbed it to pull it closed, but all the dogs were gone anyway. She watched them chasing Marcus out into the yard full of obstacles under the tall, dim security lights.

Feeling Bill at her elbow, Amber grabbed him and dragged him out the door. They sprinted south to the utility shed, climbed up the maintenance ladder, and stood on the metal roof. They spotted Marcus running along the north fence line with what looked like a trivial lead on a pack of killer dogs. There was no way he'd be able to slow down enough to scale a ladder or a fence before they would catch up, clamp on and drag him down.

Tíng loped in a wide loop, trying to align himself with the object that was his ticket out of here—the rusty, white, water plug that he'd seen on his pass by the front fence. It was a foot and a half tall, solid iron, and only about five yards inside the high hurricane fence. He spotted the plug again, lined up on it with a decent straightaway between the obstructions, and bolted straight for it.

Bill and Amber held hands atop the utility shed as they watched Marcus charge toward the front fence. He seemed to catch another gear, and the gap between him and the lead dog was opening up. Amber chewed her bottom lip. *Good God, he can run.*

Marcus took a shortened stride, planted a Dr. Martens boot on top of the water plug, and then he was airborne. The front two dogs leaped after him and bounced off the fence while the rest of the pack clambered and slid to a halt.

Tíng cleared the top strand of barb wire by several inches, came down on his hands, and rolled forward onto his feet in the tall weeds along the ditch on the other side. He turned back to the fence, pointed his finger, and said, "Bad doggies," while the killer pooches snarled at him through the galvanized steel wire and fought amongst themselves. Marcus brushed the grass out of his hair as he hustled to Amber's car.

After the hybrid careened back through the T-intersection and straightened out on the road for home, Marcus began to think out loud before the other two could recover and ask him a bunch of questions. "Well, we found 'em for sure. Evil 'Zombie' shrimpers. But they can't just stay local and be evil down here where nobody cares. They have to drive half an hour up the road and mess with us for some ungodly reason."

Amber said, "They wouldn't be the first haters to come

terrorize Montrose just for the hell of it. And the distance is a perk. It's far enough away so they never get recognized. Don't poop where you eat, right?"

Marcus nodded. "Yeah, but it's not like they're just out randomly hitting the clubs, you know? They're more focused than that. I mean, Sean, the fringe folks, Bill, the China Man. All the attacks have happened in a pretty small area between Montrose and the Heights, right along the bayou. And the only real connection between all the victims is me. They're terrorizing, specifically, *us*."

Bill spoke up. "They could be victimizin' other people we don't know about too." Marcus glanced at him over his shoulder. The clergyman continued tentatively. "But either way, this is out of our hands, right? This is somethin' for the police to handle now. These guys have guns and we know they'll kill people, and dogs."

Amber adjusted her rearview mirror so she could see Bill's face. "There was a cop *down* there, with them, among them." The statement hung in the air.

Marcus looked her way. He hadn't seen a cop there, but he wasn't surprised to hear it.

Bill asked, "How do you know?"

She cleared her throat. "There was this one guy there who didn't have his teeth filed. I could tell when he laughed. He had a black vest and a military regs haircut. He mostly had his back turned to us, but once, when he was stooped over, I know I saw a badge around his neck. It was tucked under his vest, but I caught a good glimpse of it, a gold shield with a black border. It was so obvious, there's no way he was trying to hide it. No way he was undercover."

"Yeah, I saw that dude," Marcus said.

Bill just nodded.

Amber started thinking out loud. "Typically, some kind of

specialized law enforcement would hang his badge on a chain like that. Some kind of task-force member or something." She sighed. "If we get mixed up in this, we could have Zombies *and* dirty cops on our asses. Maybe we should call the FBI or something."

The thought of his name in the mouths of federal spooks made Marcus's skin crawl. "Count me out. Feds are cops too. They give me the heebie-jeebies. Nobody's interrogating me, ever again."

Amber and Bill couldn't argue with that statement.

"So we place an anonymous call and report 'em to the Justice Department, or like Internal Affairs or somethin'," Bill chimed in hopefully.

Amber said, "We'd wanna stay super anonymous."

Marcus added, "Then they'd come down here, start asking questions, make a bunch of noise and get a warrant for what, animal cruelty? The Zombies would probably get tipped off by their local boys in a heartbeat. And the feds would need a pretty good reason to barge through that gate, and possibly have to shoot a dozen underfed pit bulls. By then, they may or may not be able to prove anything illegal's going on."

There was a short span of thoughtful silence. Then Amber said, "Holy crap, so did you guys see the *Terror*? That had to be him, right?"

Bill nodded, his lips tight.

She continued, "He had to be seven feet tall. I would *not* wanna meet that guy in a dark alley."

Marcus would like nothing better. He said, "Did y'all see the dude with his hand in a cast? He must be one of the ones who met the China Man." Bill and Amber smiled and nodded. "What about the skinny old guy, standing over on the other side, with the water hose, did y'all see him?"

Bill shook his head.

"Oh yeah," Amber said. "What was up with him? He looked pretty out of it."

"I'm almost positive that was our friend, Marty, who lives under I-10 in the south part of the Heights," Marcus said.

Bill gasped. "What? Are you sure? Why would they—"

"Looked like they had him doing some of their cleanup work. But there's no way they're paying him. They probably got him strung out on some bad drug or something. Whoever that guy was, I doubt if *he* knew where he was. There's bad mojo all over that place. But what we need is some real evidence."

Marcus and Bill told Amber about the mystery surrounding ol' Marty's disappearance. Then Marcus spent the remainder of the trip home explaining how he'd been able to outrun a pack of pit bulls. He played it down as much as he could.

Amber dropped Bill off at his flat where sitting out front, parked under a streetlight, discreet as a bulldozer, was Jake Bontemps' pickup truck. The lifted dually with oversize mud tires was pine green and unnecessarily muddy. The license plate read SHE REX.

Jake climbed out of his truck as the hybrid approached and Amber whistled. Marcus intoned, "Ooh, it's that handsome cowboy you brought to The Fallout Shelter."

"Yes, it's Jake again. We're childhood friends. He's a rice farmer. Anyway, he loves the city, and he's been talkin' about lookin' around for a place. His fields are only about forty minutes away."

"Mmkay," Amber said as Bill hastily scrambled out of her car. The two childhood friends slapped hands as a greeting, though it appeared Bill had wanted a hug. Marcus and Amber looked at each other, and he said, "You wanna go check out The Fallout Shelter?"

"Okay."

A police cruiser was parked at the front door of The Fallout Shelter, and Marcus said, "Dammit, what the heck are the cops doing here again?"

As Amber did a U-turn in the parking lot, they decided to just head back to her apartment. They passed by the shrine on their way, and it looked peaceful, dark and quiet.

About that time, down on the Ship Channel, two Zombies in a white van pulled out from the Third Coast Harvest boatyard. They took the same route Amber's hybrid had taken earlier, north toward the city. The pair of goons had the day off tomorrow, so it was their night to go cause some trouble.

15

VIOLENT VAGABONDS

Fear of them vampire hooligans had been keeping Farah up at night, but she had finally fallen asleep with a little help from Frank's own personal sleeping tonic. He took himself another pull off the pint of cheap Irish whiskey, and then slipped it back into his pocket. There were flashes way off in the northwest, maybe a storm front coming, but for now the village was still and quiet, save for the snoring. But Frank was edgy. Something was in the air. Electricity from the storm for sure, but something foul as well, like the stench of death wafting up from the bayou. And he felt drawn to it.

Frank passed through the rusted curtain of hurricane fence and shuffled down the hill. He stood for a spell beside the bus stop, scanning the darkness under the tall trees in the park across the boulevard. nothing was moving except for the bats, darting in and out of the streetlights' glow, feasting on the bugs that swarmed there.

Traffic was light and Frank jaywalked across Allen Parkway with no car in sight. Then he ambled farther down the levee, into the brush, close to the water where he could feel it cooling the night air. He sat with his back to a sycamore tree and pulled out his pint. The stench from earlier was gone. The old farmer sipped whiskey and listened to the light breeze in the treetops for a while, until eventually he nodded off.

A wash of grainy memories transported Frank to the fragrant, hilly pastureland of his youth—a flyspeck on a Texas map called Ellund. He smiled, hearing his mother Mary singing an ancient Celtic song on the porch of their plank farmhouse—hardly bigger than the adjacent chicken coop. But too soon the dream sped forward, sweeping the boy away from the green fields of his innocence to the killing fields of the Vietnam War. It was that goddamned war that ruined him, that led to the back-alley living, and the lethal barfight that made Frank what he was today. After all the blood he'd spilled for Uncle Sam, he comes home and snuffs one loudmouthed shit-bird who *deserves it*, and *then* they call him a killer?

His time in the joint had been a long chain of smokes, pills, and humming institutional lights, but the stay had been restorative. It had given the nightmares time to ebb, the demons time to fade. But Frank couldn't meet the requirements of parole. Too damn crazy. So before they could lock him up again, he'd vanished, like a soldier like him could do. He found himself walking the shadows of the concrete jungle, alone, broke, anonymous, and too guilty to ever go home. Then by chance he'd stumbled across big Leo again, and met Jaime and the fringe people, and even Farah. But now 'long come these creeps, and things were unraveling again.

Frank shivered awake and took a big pull off the whiskey bottle in his lap. He stood, but his legs were still asleep, so he hobbled toward the water to work some feeling back into them. He took another pull off the bottle, which was nearly empty, and represented the last bit of money he could spend without dipping into the cash he'd been rat-holing to buy that rusty tiller. That damned war, dysentery, prison, not even the junk could kill him, so why should he be surprised the booze couldn't do it either. God, couldn't he ever die? Frank looked up at the shrine where Farah slept. Where all his friends were. His reasons for living, he supposed.

A big white van pulled into the small parking lot along the parkway at Frank's nine-o'clock, and he froze. He hadn't seen any of these shit-bird Zombies roaming the streets at night, but he'd heard plenty of other accounts, and he recognized the pair of them for what they were. They hopped out of the vehicle and converged alongside it, big, brutish, and pale in the thin artificial light. The two goons stood beside the van and looked right up the levee. They spoke and one of them pointed right at the village and they both laughed.

Frank hollered, "Hey!" before he thought too much about it. *If they came 'round here lookin' for prey, they'll find hell instead.* The drunk old platoon sergeant left the cover of the brush along the water and shambled out into the open, more zombie than they'd ever be.

The creeps shielded their eyes from the streetlights, and searched the darkness for the voice along the bayou as they walked to the back edge of the parking lot. When they got close enough to see Frank, the bigger of the two, who stood slightly in front said, "Who the hell is that down there?"

The big kid had an Irish lilt. Frank grinned. It was true the old man had done too much killin', but for every person who'd call him a murderin' bastard, there were ten soldiers in another life who'd call Sergeant Gaffigan, a goddamned hero. So it was prob'ly best Frank made his peace with the bawdy old Celtic gods of his mother's people. The ones who granted all warriors a trip-ticket to Heaven, in trade for the spilled blood of their brave hearts on the battlefield. *Bless Mary Gaffigan for teachin' me some o' the old ways.* Frank would do himself *and* this kid a favor. *Two fer one, mebbe?*

The Zombies shared a disappointed look. Frank had been

quiet so long they thought he might be in shock. Then his senses returned, and he answered, "It's me, yer ol' dad. I was at yer mum's house, givin' 'er a right good one." He gestured to a dumpster at the western edge of the parking lot, and both goons looked. The smaller one standing in back chuckled, but the bigger man in front wasn't amused. He showed his fangs.

The two Zombies stepped off the pavement, down into the gravelly asphalt that buttressed the parking lot, and Frank walked up to meet them. The hooligans stopped a short distance away from the feisty geezer, and grinned like a couple of hyenas with bloodlust in their eyes. The immense Irish-American kid in front produced a black, aluminum, telescopic baton. He flicked it and it tripled in length. "I'm gonna smash that smartassed mouth o' yours, Grandad."

Unfazed, Frank held up his hand for a timeout while he finished off his pint of booze, save an ounce for his dead brethren. He exhaled a ketone mist, and wiped his mouth on a dirty sleeve. Then the geezer squatted down and tapped his bottle against a shard of concrete at his feet, just hard enough to break the bottom off and make a long, jagged weapon.

Frank raised the busted bottle and inspected it with a daft grin. It fumed, and whiskey dripped from it like *Aredbhar*, the living spear of the Celtic god Lugh. Frank had gone and pulled its head from the opiate draught in which it must slumber, lest it kill incessantly of its own volition. The terrible shank trembled, as if anxious for warmth. Lightning ignited a mountain of black clouds behind the pair of devils, and thunder boomed like a war drum. The storm was coming.

The smaller Zombie reached into his cargo pockets, and installed a pair of chainmail gloves that he used for pulling dangerous creatures out of the nets offshore. His smirk was a snarl as he sidestepped out to the flank. His gloves were impervious to broken glass. With these, he could punch through walls.

The wind whipped and fat raindrops started to fall. Frank winked at the big lad in front of him, and gestured with his busted pint. "Come on then, sissy boy."

The big Irish kid lunged with his truncheon, but in that same instant, Frank's free hand shot forward and let loose a rusty pocketknife. It was the knife he'd learned to stick into a melon from ten paces as a kid, the one that had gone to Asia and back and had waited patiently sealed away while Frank had been in prison.

The slim iron blade made one complete rotation and lodged into the big Zombie's ribcage with a sickening thump. He recoiled as if hit with a hammer, hunched around the spike in his chest, but he didn't drop his baton. He almost panicked and pulled the blade out, but he left it in at the last second, not knowing how deep it was.

Frank had to admire the lad. Most men go straight into shock with a knife in their chest. Then the old vet went for the throat with his broken bottle. Hesitation cost him though, and the baton swept up and shattered his makeshift weapon. Frank still held the bottleneck, but he didn't have a chance to use it before the kid seized him by the wrist and hoisted the little old man off the ground.

The Zombie drew back his baton to crush Frank's bones, but then he convulsed in response to the pain in his chest. The bum had his free hand on the knife, and he gave it a twist. The goon dropped his baton and grabbed Frank's other wrist. Frank could have slammed the blade home with his palm, but he didn't want this dance to end yet. His final dance with death.

The brute wanted to throw Frank off, but that would dislodge the blade and it was in deep. He tried to twist Frank's wrist and break it, but he couldn't do it. The little man's bones were like rebar, and the effort just evoked another twist of the blade accompanied by impish laughter. The big kid cried out as agony, rain, and tears eroded his wicked façade.

A chainmail fist struck the back of Frank's head. His body went limp, and then crumpled to the ground as he released his grip on the knife and his enemy finally let go of him. The big Irish kid had barely enough wherewithal to squat and pick up his dropped baton. His partner, the glove-wearing goon, hoisted Frank's carcass over his shoulder, ran to the nearby dumpster, and tossed it in.

High above, in a vaporous green landscape, Frank embraced the mother goddess Danu, and behind her stood the roguish man-god, Lugh himself, beaming with pride. Frank's father Keagan was there, sober and fit, and his mother Mary urgently wanted to introduce the ancestors.

The wounded Zombie still had Frank's knife in him. He sat back and breathed through his pointed teeth while his buddy drove him to their usual ER near the Channel. Ship Channel roughnecks came in with all kinds of ugly wounds, so the ER surgeon was only mildly suspicious. The brute told the doc he'd been cutting debris from some heavy netting and had accidently stabbed himself. Later a nurse told him the knife blade had stopped just short of a deep pulmonary vein, which would have likely been fatal. They stitched him up, pumped him full of anti-biotics, and sent him home.

The next morning, Toby Goodspeed, Detective Jack Lamonte, and Kristian Klein himself stood before the room-sized window of a vacant apartment, inside a high rise that Klein had recently purchased. They had a bird's eye view of Buffalo Bayou that stretched from the bridge at Waugh all the way down to Sabine Street, and the new American Missionary property was sprawled out before them like a sports arena, just half a block away.

Klein spoke as he looked out the thick, tinted glass through a pair of binoculars. "Look at those queers and junkies gatherin' on the sidewalk along Montrose. Probably none of 'em have jobs. Lots of fodder for your lectures around here, Goodspeed." He put down his field glasses and made a sweeping gesture at the scenery below. "Look at all the frontage you got on Memorial and Allen Parkway. Tons of conservative cash commutes right through here every day, and the traffic lights are long. The bums got easy panhandling down there. Buffalo Bayou's full of parks with public water spigots. They don't need the downtown shelters out here. It's a damned hobo haven. You watch how many of 'em come crawling out of that building.

"HPD's gonna let 'em sleep under the bridges down there until you can get 'em a shelter put up. But they'll come back up here for hot water and free food, no doubt. It's a perfect spot."

Detective Lamonte kept silent.

Goodspeed nodded his assent. "Yes sir. I agree." Toby had planned to go down there and address the vagrants personally, but conditions were less than ideal, particularly with the foul weather. So he had chosen one of his underlings to enter the muddy, rat-infested property in his place. "Looks like they've got a garden down there," he said to himself.

Down below, inside the shrine, Jaime sat up in his blanket and shivered. A wet cold front had blown in overnight and the sky was leaden. But there was something else in the air, even heavier than the hanging mist and ceiling of dark clouds. Diesel smoke and rhythmic rumbling.

Four men shuffled through the big, rusty, partially open bay door and marched into the shrine. Three of the newcomers were big, decked in hardhats and high-visibility vests. The fourth man was more delicate, with wispy blond hair, a glossy gray suit, and muddy white jogging shoes. He strode in front of the three big guys, and stopped just within earshot of some two-dozen vagrants strewn about the concrete floor in varying degrees of awake-ness. The svelte man lobbed a short stack of brightly colored pamphlets toward the cluster of groggy fringe-folks, but none of them moved.

The glossy suit's head oscillated as he read the same printed statement twice, separated by a "once again." His words were fraught with euphemistic legalese, but the message was clear enough. The squatters all had to go, right now. This building was being completely renovated. A temporary shelter would be set up for them very soon, complete with food, electricity, and hot water. But not until some initial sitework, drainage, and grading were completed. Bye-bye. The small man strode away, but the big hard-hatted gents remained.

Amber rolled over in her bed, still half asleep, and reached for Marcus. Instead she found another one of his handwritten notes. *Ugh.* She squinted so she could read his writing: *Took a cab home. Gotta do some stuff at work. Will call you soon. XOX*

Her phone rang on her nightstand and she sat up and grabbed it. *Ting.* But it was Brother Bill Cox calling.

All the homeless people in the shrine, plus a handful of protesters who'd randomly appeared on the sidewalk, were delaying the work crew some. The weather was foul, and nobody down on the site really seemed to care much. But Kristian Klein was watching from above and he did care. He looked sideways at Lamonte and asked, "You gonna do something?"

Keeping his usual bravado carefully in check, the detective made a quick call on his cell, and then snapped the phone back into its tiny holster.

Toby Goodspeed stayed focused on the scene below, overtly minding his business.

Within two minutes a police cruiser skidded to a halt in the village's crumbling driveway along Montrose Boulevard. Two uniformed cops disembarked and strode onto the property.

Marcus was at The Fallout Shelter by request of one of the owners, to come in and pick up his accumulating paychecks. Tíng had just exited the bosses' office and zipped up his pack when his phone rang. *Amber.* He pulled it out and groaned when he saw that it was Bill. The phone always went to voicemail after four rings, but it didn't. It just went silent. So he put it back into his pack. *Dude, I'll call you later.*

It rang again.

Ugh.

He grabbed the thing and answered. "Yes?"

Brother Cox was frantic. "Oh my gosh Ting, there's a big construction crew at the shrine, and Jaime's kinda protestin', and now the cops are here and—we need your help!"

"The cops are at the shrine? Is Leo there?" Marcus could hear the din of machinery in Bill's phone.

"Uh, I haven't seen him yet, but hurry!"

"Okay, I'll be there soon. Don't let anything bad happen before I get there." Marcus almost smiled at the absurdity of his last remark but the situation was too serious. *Dang. Leo's bound to show up sooner or later, and the cops are there.*

Tíng took a deep, cleansing breath as he stashed his phone in his pack. Then he looked down at his plain gray sweatshirt and baggy jeans, utility and nondescript. Good. His Doc Martens boots chirped against the slab floor, and seconds later he alighted in the panic room. There he rummaged through the crates of costume accessories before settling on something that might work.

It was a decent-quality masquerade kit featuring a wide, theatric *cǎomào* with a chin strap and glued-in, shoulder-length, straight black hair. Attached was a Fu Manchu-style adhesive goatee still sealed in the plastic wrapper. He went through the shoeboxes full of costume sunglasses and picked out an oversized pair of *Magnum, P.I.'s* that weren't too scratched up. He wiped down the shades with his sweatshirt and slapped them on. He pulled a work uniform out of his big backpack and stuffed in the costume kit with only a slight bend in the hat. Before he could overly analyze his intentions, he slid down from the panic room and bailed out of The Fallout Shelter.

Minutes later, Tíng skidded to a halt half a block up Montrose from the shrine, and stashed his bike and empty backpack in a weedy, oversized covert. He donned his disguise as he walked toward the village. Checking his reflection in the window of a parked car, he whistled. *Freakish but incognito.* The sky rumbled, and cold drizzle patted on his big straw hat. *At least I don't need an umbrella.*

Jaime knew they would just remove him, like so much debris, if he didn't get up on his own, but it was hard for him to walk very far these days, and besides he had nowhere to go. So he decided he wouldn't resist or obey, just exist. And he was right. After an oddly polite discussion, the newly arrived patrolmen each grabbed an arm and dragged him away.

While bearing Jaime's weight, the cops barked at the remaining interlopers that they had better get moving too. The officers trudged around the north side of the building, and deposited Jaime on the west sidewalk in the public easement. By the time they got there, they were winded and annoyed. Luckily, the other fringe folks had obeyed their orders. They congregated around Jaime, schlepping as much of their stuff as they could carry.

Brother Bill was there too, being supportive and cooperative, especially with his newfound fear of the law. But he'd also called Amber; and she hadn't been there thirty seconds before she'd gotten into it with the senior patrolman, a Sergeant. Promptly

Amber was escorted to the sidewalk as well, while she prattled about "freedom of the press and squatters' rights." She noted the small crowd of local Montrose protesters gathering, and had a suspicious feeling about the lack of any media present.

Marcus shouldn't be here. He didn't *want* to be here. He'd always figured somebody important would come and reclaim this property someday, but now the day had come, and his friends' lives wouldn't be the same. The folks were going to need his help today, so he had to remain objective. The eviction up to this point had actually gone pretty smoothly. He figured it would, except for the possible appearance of one very large brotha with PTSD. *Dang!*

Leo pedaled into the village from the east, on one of the back trails through the tall bloodweeds, and dismounted Marcus's tricycle next to the sprouting compost heap. There he stood in the misty rain, and looked around at the turmoil. The police sergeant saw Leo and marched over to intercept him, hollering and whistling to get the big man's attention. But the giant trespasser continued to stare at the flashing lights, rumbling equipment, and the absence of anyone he recognized.

As the police drew near, Leo's unease was reflected in their faces. This newcomer wore an old military jacket with the hood up and stuffed full of dreadlocks. He was wiry-thin and gray, but also half a head taller than the burly junior patrol officer, the next biggest guy on the scene—who had just trotted up beside his superior sergeant.

The cops stopped and conferred for a moment. Then they walked around Leo's east side, to try and drive him westward along the north wall of the shrine and toward the sidewalk. Both officers drew their batons to show they meant business. They took turns barking commands at Leo to get him moving, and at first it seemed it might work. The big transient recoiled and backed away, dragging the tricycle he'd borrowed from Ting along behind him. But Leo still had burns on his skin from being

Tasered two nights ago, and he refused to turn his back on the two enforcers. So straddling his front tire, backpedaling with his gimp knee, he made such slow progress, it appeared this could take all day.

Jaime and the other fringe folks were still gathered in the public easement near the northwest corner of the lot. Some of them shouted to Leo, but amid the din of machinery and the fog of chaos, the big man appeared not to hear them. The other protestors, farther up the block and sporting a plethora of tattoos and piercings, were Montrose locals. Several had brought umbrellas, and one guy in a slicker held a runny sign that said NO MORE CHURCHES. Ever the interviewer, Amber had just left their ranks to rejoin Bill, Jaime, and his flock of evictees.

The cops were getting annoyed with Leo's lack of progress. They kept getting too close, whereupon he would stop and warn them to stay back. Now the sergeant was spouting something into his radio, probably calling for a paddy wagon. *Crap.* Amber was going to have to march back out there and—

Tíng materialized in the misty wind several yards uphill from the protesters, and promptly he had everyone's attention. He hated being subversive like this, but the cops were already hawking him, even though he hadn't done anything wrong. Deep, cleansing breaths. He was just going to go talk to them, and get them off Leo's back so the big man could get clear. If things went south, then Tíng would fly; zigzag so they'd have trouble aiming at him. He would *not* end up like his father.

As he strode away from the sidewalk, he could hear Ching Lan's voice in the back of his memory: *Qīngtíng, you stay far away from the police. You can fly, Tíng. You have your father's legs. You run from them, you hear me, son?*

He pressed on his fake goatee, pulled down the brim of his *cǎomào*, and tightened the chinstrap. Then the masquerader picked up his pace, and ran in an arc around the south side of the building to meet the pair of cops from behind. He would approach subtly, and not startle them. That was the plan.

Amber and Bill saw the man in the big straw hat loping onto the property from the south side, and both their hearts sank. Only one person they'd ever met could move like that. Jaime also bore a grave expression, shaking his head as he watched the fleet-footed stranger dash around the corner of the shrine. Bill sucked in through his teeth, as if he were about to remove a band-aid, and said, "Yeah, I called him, but I didn't think he would show up all kung-fooey and stuff." The protesters on the sidewalk also openly chattered, and pointed at this bold new presence.

The drizzle was becoming a soaker, and the construction workers sought shelter within their machinery, where they could observe the action in climate-controlled repose.

"Ooh, check it out. Karate boy's about to get shot."

"Thinks he's freakin' Black Belt Jones."

Tíng came to a halt five yards behind the patrolmen near the northeast corner of the shrine. The cops were getting wet, but they couldn't go back to the car and get their slickers yet, so their angst was intensifying along with the rain shower. The sergeant hollered at Leo, who had stopped again. "Hey!" He whistled shrilly. "I'm talking to you, dumb son of a bitch!"

Leo wore a fluctuating mask of anger and confusion, but his expression softened when he saw someone trot up behind the cops, someone who could only be Marcus by the way he moved.

Tíng's eyelids fluttered behind his *Magnum P.I.* shades as he took a long, deep inhale through his nostrils. Stomach distending, he envisioned a tendril of Ch'i spiraling in through his navel, passing chakras and energizing the primal animal spirits in his body. He exhaled. Then he tried to signal Leo to *get the heck out of here,* and that's when the patrolmen noticed him. They had a bit of a kneejerk response to the weirdo in the big hat and sunglasses who had snuck up behind them.

Kristian Klein looked at Lamonte. "Who the hell is that?" The detective shrugged and shook his head.

"What the? Who the hell are you!" fired the sergeant down on the scene.

"Stay back!" the junior officer commanded, pointing his baton with one hand while the other fell to the pistol grip attached to his hip.

On the spot again, Tíng opted to disguise his voice as an added precaution, though this time, for some reason, he invoked the China Man's lilt, that of an aged Bruce Lee. "Uh, hello gentlemen. Might I have a word with you, please?" There was a flash in the east, and rolling thunder warned of an approaching cumulonimbus.

The cops looked at each other with mutual incomprehension. The sergeant replied, "Buddy, I don't know who the hell you are, or where you came from, but you need to clear your ass off this property, right now!"

Tíng opened his mouth, but failed to think of a polite response.

"Did you hear me? I said get the hell outta here!" The sergeant pointed with his baton over to the northwest sidewalk where the fringe people were still gathered, which aggravated the officer further because the band of hobos hadn't taken the hint and moved on already.

Leo hadn't moved either, so the big junior officer encouraged him. "And you, get your ass movin' or we're about to put the cuffs on you!"

"No, y'all ain't!" Leo's backtalk only fanned the flame.

The sergeant turned toward him, smiling and saying, "Bullshit!"

Now Leo had opened his mouth and pricked the cops' egos. Tíng shook his head. He needed them to reprioritize. "Excuse me, please! I just need to talk to you about him for one minute. He is a war veteran." He regretted disguising his voice now, as it apparently created somewhat of a communication barrier. But he had to stick with it, or the weirdness and distrust would only increase. He stepped closer as he spoke so they might understand him better, but that was a mistake.

Dripping wet, the sergeant barked, "Why are you still here? Do you understand English? I told you to clear the hell out! You're trespassing! How 'bout we just cuff both your asses and sit y'all down in the mud! Now turn around, take off that stupid hat and put your hands behind your head!"

Tíng looked past them to Leo and said, "Please leave now and take care of your friends. I will handle this."

"Ok," Leo said, and started to move away.

Both cops seethed, watching Leo get a move on *now*, because this little black-Chinese-lookin' freak told him to disobey their instructions. But they let the big bum go, because something wasn't right about this newcomer. Inspecting Marcus more closely, the big junior patrolman felt an odd wave of nausea.

Tíng's damp, gray sweatshirt hugged his knotted musculature. Water dripped from the brim of his *cǎomào* "See, everything is fine now," he intoned as he backed away. "We are all leaving."

The sergeant was shaking his head. He didn't like the sound or the look of this guy. "I don't think so. You had your chance, buster." He leveled his baton at Marcus and said through his teeth, "Now turn around, take off that hat, and put your hands behind your head!"

Tíng wanted to run, but these two had apparently decided they weren't leaving here empty-handed. If he bolted, they'd probably end up Tasering Leo again. Ching Lan's voice echoed in his head: *You run from the police, Qīngtíng.* Tíng turned his back on the cops and raised his hands, but continued to slowly walk away. He said over his shoulder, "Please gentlemen, there is no need for violence. I am—"

The sergeant spat, "Violence? What violence? Is that some kind of threat? Stop right there!"

That word he understands, Marcus thought.

The patrolman stowed his baton and deployed his cuffs, but he wasn't advancing. So the sergeant ordered, "Dammit Rob, knock that stupid hat off his head and get the cuffs on him!" Marcus was making progress toward the weeds at the back of the lot, but he didn't want to run just yet. Leo was nearing the sidewalk, but these cops were pissed now. So he stopped.

And his heart sank as he heard the heavy policeman shuffling up behind him. The would-be-arrester grabbed Tíng's forearm from behind and swung the open handcuffs at his wrist. But the perp evaded, to say the least. Dropping his hands, lowering his stance, and spinning, he batted the patrolman's cuffs away with an oddly shaped fist, and then swept his legs.

"Ow-sshh—" The big lad's expletive was cut short as he was cut down onto his knees and elbows, his right hand stinging like pins and needles. Racked with guilt, Marcus tried to help the big guy up.

"That's assaulting a cop, you son of a bitch!" The sergeant charged in, baton raised.

The patrolman pushed himself up and dove, aiming to tackle the smaller man to the ground, but Marcus sidestepped him, clipped his feet again, and used his own momentum to send him sprawling into the sodden terrain. *Oops.*

The sergeant's baton arrived in full swing, but it was like a toothpick compared to the limbs of the Diūqì Shìbīng. There was a hiss and a snapping sound as Tíng parried the blow with a spear-shaped fist, *The Serpent's Tail.* The senior officer hollered as his baton fluttered into the tall grass. He fumbled for his sidearm, but his hand felt deadened. So he used his other hand to deploy a long, black flashlight, which he swung at the perp's head. Tíng ducked under the sluggish metal tube of D batteries, and then sidestepped another vertical strike. The fallen patrolman behind him was scrambling to his feet, and Tíng moved just in time for the big lad to catch the sergeant's aluminum flashlight on his head. The blow dropped the junior officer, once again, in his tracks.

The low-hanging rain clouds were obscuring the view from the high-rise apartment, but Kristian Klein could see chaos. He looked sideways at Lamonte. "What the hell's going on down there?" But the detective was already on the phone again. Toby Goodspeed had his hands cupped against the window, peering through the glass.

The sergeant cringed at what he'd done to his partner. He pulled his pistol, but his grip was still weak and Tíng kicked it out of his hand, causing him to swear and stumble backward. The patrolman on the ground had the wherewithal to pull his pistol too, but the same Doc Martens boot blasted it out into the rain as it cleared his holster.

The sarge pulled his Taser with his left hand. It beeped ready, and a few seconds later the patrolman's beeped too. He had rolled onto his side to steady himself, and at this range he couldn't miss. The lasers from both Tasers flitted around on Tíng as he watched Leo step onto the sidewalk with the others, who were all looking on in shock.

Marcus tried to back away again. "I am so sorr—" Tíng hissed as his left hand formed The Serpent's Head, and snared the patrolman's Taser-darts in flight. The pop of the nitrogen propellant activated the sergeant's trigger finger, and his darts also flew.

High voltage infused Tíng's neuromuscular hardware as he watched his right hand, The Serpent's Tail, intercept the second pair of barbs. An arc pulsed from his fingertips that burned the projectiles to ash, as their trailing wires fell to the ground.

The sergeant's Taser sizzled in his clenching grip as his teeth clacked, and he pitched forward onto the ground in a spasm. At the other end of the circuit, the big patrolman shuddered and convulsed in a growing puddle. The perp in the middle was jolted a foot into the air, but he came down on firm gear. Tíng was a fuse that didn't fry. Contorting in the muck, the two cops locked eyes, just lucid enough to see each other's pain and degradation.

Tíng's senses returned with stinging clarity as he stared down at the steaming pair of troopers. Sirens sounded, lightning flashed, and thunder clapped like a starter pistol in the sky. Marcus dropped a pair of Taser darts, which had burned to ash in his hand, and he bolted east into the patch of seven-foot bloodweeds. He found a trail he knew well, flew to the back fence, slipped through a hole, ditched his disguise in the alley, and made his way south toward the Frankenbike, moving like a scalded alley cat.

As they loaded him into the ambulance, the still-shaken sergeant recounted the scenario to Detective Lamonte. The junior patrolman had already been hauled away for observation. A few of the construction workers had shot some sketchy, long-range video of the incident, so Lamonte asked to see their footage. He had a creeping suspicion about the graceful power displayed by the perp as he made monkeys out of two tough street cops. The detective deleted each video before returning the smart phones to their owners. Jack Lamonte surmised that the rain must have caused the Tasers to malfunction. It was the only thing that made sense.

All other witness accounts sounded like scenes from a bad action movie, and everyone swore they had no idea as to the perp's identity. A dozen cops and two helicopters scoured the area. The straw hat with fake hair glued into it was found in an adjacent alley, stuffed under an oil drum and covered in grime, but the man himself was gone. The squatters quietly vanished with the arrival of all the extra law enforcement, and nobody sought to detain them.

CHAPTER

16

CHASING BUTTERFLIES

The displaced villagers crossed the Montrose Bridge as quickly as Jaime could shuffle. On the other side of Buffalo Bayou, they left the street and congregated under the south end of an overpass, concealed among the trees along Memorial Parkway. There wasn't much complaining, because it was all they could do for a while to get dry and warm.

Bill and Amber tried Marcus's phone several times, but apparently it was turned off. So the two of them followed the fringe folks down under the bridge. Then they departed and returned promptly in Amber's hybrid, wearing dry clothes and carrying stacks of towels from their nearby apartments. Working together, they heaped a pile of wet apparel into a blanket and hauled it to a laundromat in Amber's muggy little car. The fringe folks offered up their dollars and coins to pay for the washing and drying, but Bill insisted he had a coffee can full of change for just such a purpose. The north wind was biting, but at least the rain was clearing off, and after everyone was reasonably dry and settled, muted conversation rekindled among the folks.

Jaime hobbled to the edge of the bridge to see if the clouds were breaking up overhead, but his attention was drawn to an unmarked police cruiser moving way too slowly on Memorial Parkway. The driver, a Latino cop wearing a felt cowboy hat, made eye contact with Jaime, tipped his hat, and then sped on by. He turned back to the group and asked aloud, "Has anyone seen Frank?" Fringe folks shrugged or shook their heads. Many appeared worried, particularly Farah.

At the laundromat, Bill and Amber employed a dozen commercial washers and dryers at once and they didn't spare the Clorox. Soon the pair of them were back under the bridge with a warm heap of clean laundry. Both of them had beds to go home to, yet they seemed to be the most worried. They alternated lines in a list of possible solutions meant for all to hear, but directed at Jaime, who at length just smiled, nodded, and raised his hand to quiet them.

He looked to the village up on the far levee, where the construction crew was installing a temporary opaque fence emblazoned with "American Missionary" in fancy letters. A police helicopter flew over again, for about the tenth time, obviously still looking for Ting. Everyone was waiting for their unappointed leader to speak when he finally turned to face them and said, "I think we should keep moving."

"What? To where?" Bill blurted.

"I think up to White Oak Bayou, under the Yale Street Bridge. I've heard it's like a cavern under there on the north side. I-Ten is right there too, big overpasses, plenty of shelter. There's public water in the Heights, lots of big trees. Does anybody else feel like moving out a little farther?" Several fringe folks replied affirmatively, and many more nodded.

Bill was aghast, "But y'all are comin' back right? They said they're gonna build y'all a shelter up there right? It's gonna be a real church now."

Under the rosy, gray, afternoon light, a backstreet exodus of fringe folks headed farther north, up to White Oak Bayou. Amber offered Jaime a ride, but he politely refused. Then he collected his bedding, wine, and a stack of periodicals, and packed them into Leo's cargo basket for transport to the new site. Jaime had scarcely left the village in a decade, but he appeared to know the way, so he took the lead, following the below-street-level bayou trails typically used by varmints rather than pedestrians. Fringe folks fell in behind him, shuffling along in small groups, chatting as they kept Jaime's easy pace. Exasperated, Bill and Amber went to investigate the folks' future digs in her hybrid. *North side bridge at Yale Street and White Oak Bayou.*

The place was nice, as bridges go, with high concrete banks, expansive slabs, and a wide boulevard overhead for tons of cover and concealment. Perhaps most importantly, it was currently uninhabited. The grassy levees to the east were cut with trails and dimly lit by the streetlights above. Upstream to the west, there stood a tall, rickety, old wooden railroad trestle covered in trumpet vine, and the levees were far less traveled, with no artificial lighting or visible footpaths.

The long walk to the new bridge had taken a toll on Jaime. So when he arrived, he went straight to a spot far up on the slab, deep in shadow, and settled directly onto his blankets, which Leo had put there ahead of time. Having brought the cargo tricycle, Leo had traveled at street level and arrived shortly after Bill and Amber in her car. The big man set Jaime up with his jug of cheap sangria and stack of periodicals. Then Leo returned to his favored task, scanning the area for burnable wood and usable or recyclable metal. He bagged any refuse he encountered in plastic grocery bags pulled from his pockets, to be deposited in some nearby dumpster.

Folks easily found cozy, dry places for their bedrolls on the raised expanse of concrete. But there was muffled deliberation about the reason they had come all the way out here. Some said it was to get some distance from whoever'd booted them out of the shrine. Some said it was because Marcus lived nearby. Some said it was to avoid the cops' wrath, since Ting had just done whatever he'd done.

拎

Marcus sat on a bench next to the Frankenbike inside a softball dugout in White Oak Park. He was holed up with a few homeless folks who had also taken cover there, but just from the rain. Ting had barely made it out of the Montrose District before the helicopters had showed up. But he hadn't heard a chopper for a while, so hopefully they were giving up on the search. He'd had a sudden fear of his cell phone after his interlude with the police, so he had turned it off. Now that he powered it back up, he had a ton of missed calls from Bill, Amber, and a couple from an UNKNOWN number. *Probably that crewcut detective, Lamonte.*

Marcus listened to the most recent message from Amber. She sounded more worried than angry: "Ting, damnit where are you?" She sighed. "Jaime's got everybody moving out to the bridge at Yale and White Oak Bayou. Please call me."

They were less than a mile upstream. Marcus issued some handshakes and some greenbacks to the homeless dudes, scanned the sky again for whirlybirds, and then lit out on the Frankenbike. He saw Amber's hybrid parked in the lot of a seedy bar, but he knew she wasn't inside. She had parked there and walked. It was the closest spot to the new bridge Jaime had apparently chosen for the fringe folks. As Marcus coasted over White Oak Bayou on Yale, he practiced what he would say to her.

Ting walked up under the bridge from the west side, the untamed side, his damp clothes hugging his muscular frame. Fringe folks recoiled and backed away until they recognized him. Then many more of them stood, and doffed their caps in reverence. Amber hustled over to meet him. "Nazi vampires, trigger-happy cops, dang, what's next?" Marcus said with a hopeful grin. They embraced, and she squeezed him hard for a long time.

Then she held him at arms' length, looked him in the eyes, and said, "So what the hell happened over there? At first, we were like, 'Holy crap, what the hell's he doing?' And then like thirty seconds later the cops were laid out on the ground, and then *poof* you were gone like a flash. Freakin' helicopters looked for you for like thirty minutes. I tried to call you like twenty times."

"I know. I'm sorry. Like you said, they were looking for me, and I needed to get off the grid for a little while."

She took a deep breath. "Did both of 'em Taser you?"

"They tried to. Must have misfired or something."

"Misfired my ass. What were you thinking, out there smacking the cops around?"

"Smacking the cops around? I barely touched 'em! I was just trying to get 'em off Leo's back. He's had enough rough handling lately, and he doesn't deserve that crap. But they wouldn't listen. And I'm sorry, but nobody's detaining me ever again. I will not—"

"Okay, okay, look, I'm not mad at you. I mean, I kind of am, but I'm not even sure what you are right now. I just know that somehow, you make the unbelievable seem possible, and I don't want to lose you. So next time you drop off the grid, take me with you, okay?"

Marcus parted his lips but no words came out. She pulled on his coat and kissed him, and quieted his roiling psyche. He kissed her back, and startled a squadron of butterflies somewhere behind her navel. Both kids knew in that moment there wouldn't be any others.

Bill covered his mouth, holding back a cheer. In a far corner, big Leo kept busy, smiling.

There was a stir at the center of the camp, and the bulk of the mob tightened into a semi-circle around Jaime, who was coughing his head off for what seemed like a long time. He looked even pastier and more haggard than usual. Fringe folks shared concerned looks until he finally got over his respiratory fit, collected himself, and said, "Oh, I almost forgot to tell you guys, I went to see Panterito last night."

There were whispers in the crowd, followed by shushes as folks continued to gather around their customary orator and get comfortable. Jaime said, "I woke up sometime in the wee hours, right before dawn because something was telling me to go outside, something other than my bladder." There was laughter among the folks. Marcus, Amber, and Bill joined the congregation. Leo hovered in the periphery.

Jaime took a pull off his jug of red wine. "Marcus, bro, you made it! I knew you would." He beamed at his champion, and then continued. "So as I was saying, I walked out into the village, and a storm had just passed over. Everything was wet and the frogs were singing. But there was a break in the clouds, and a big harvest moon was out, and it turned everything pink. I heard a coyote howl down on the bayou, and something else. Something big was down there, bellowing like a gator, or maybe a panther. And I know it sounds weird, but it seemed like the animals were calling to me." Folks exchanged furtive looks. "So pretty soon I found myself on that trail that goes down the hill. It was cool and bright, so there were a lot of critters down there on the water, but they only showed me curiosity. So I kept walking, and I could see somebody standing by a pile of driftwood that was stuck on the roots of that big cypress tree, a little ways downstream. I felt something rub up against me, and I looked down and there was a *big* coyote, like the size of a wolf, sniffing my leg."

Marcus, Bill, and Amber glanced at each other.

"So I told the *lobo* 'hola' and scratched her head, and then we were friends. Then Pan called out to me, because I knew it was him already. He spoke to me in Spanish, and his accent reminded me of my grandmother's, who lived in Michoacán. So I walked over to the driftwood pile, and the *lobo* followed me.

"When I got there, Pan took my hand in both of his and said he had been waiting to speak to me. I asked him why, and he said because, that being a *chamán*, I might understand his story, his reason for being here. I told him I was no shaman. At best I was just a truth seeker. He told me the difference was just words.

"So we sat down on a root, and Pan told me that for as long as he could remember, he had wandered in paradise in the mountain forest that men call Oyamel. He said he remembered other names, in the tongues of the ancients, but that even before the time of spoken word, before the time of men, he had lived in that place, where the butterflies color the trees like flame."

Amber found Marcus's hand and squeezed it.

Bill looked skeptical.

"But he said that recently, a restlessness came over him, and lured him away from the forest, higher up into the mountains, to the shore of a deep and sacred body of water. It was the place he was being drawn to. So he laid down on the bank for a long time, and subsisted on the cold water of the lake that men call Patzucuro.

"As he was telling me this, Pan took something out of a bag he had slung over his shoulder. It was a couple of mushrooms, and they looked purple in the moonlight. He ate one and offered me the other one. And I was starving all of a sudden, so I gulped it down, and it was pretty good."

There were lots of sideways glances in the crowd, including from Marcus and Amber. Jaime cleared his throat. "Okay, so I'm trying to remember all this and translate it the best I can, but his story got a little weird from here."

"*Now* it gets weird?" Bill asked.

"Yeah. So Pan said that he laid there on the edge of Patzucuro for several days wondering why he had come, but his devotion finally paid off. Because one morning as the sun was rising over the lake, and he was staring into the fire-colored water, he saw past the veil that separates existence from nothingness. In that moment, a giant serpent materialized from the depths. The spirit creature asked a favor of him, to help preserve the continuance of life in this paradise, this earth, and its foothold in the universe.

"So Pan accepted before he even knew the task. The great reptile told him that he was to follow the butterflies the next time they left the forest, to see if he could help them along their way. The little flower-farmers were having more trouble reaching their New World breeding grounds with each passing season."

"Monarchs," Amber said. "They migrate through Texas twice a year. A lot of them winter down in the mountains around Michoacán. I've written a lot of butterfly articles for my buddy Ryan Dylan at the Bayou City Conservancy."

Marcus shot her some side-eye.

Jaime was nodding, smiling. "And I've read those articles. So check this out. Last time, when the butterflies left the forest, Pan took off and followed them. He said it wasn't easy to keep up, so he adopted the spirit of the puma, whatever that means. And he stayed with the ones that traveled through the low country, where he could move fast and find water. Then one day, as he was running across a rocky desert, the red *lobo* ran up alongside him. He said he could tell that she had also been sent to help, much like Ting had been sent to help us. So he was happy to have her company."

"Wait, he said that about *me*?" Marcus asked.

"I guess you made quite an impression on him."

Marcus looked puzzled. "I've never even met the guy."

"Anyway, Pan said they journeyed far through some rough country—him, the *lobo*, and the Monarchs. And along the way, he was surprised by the number of butterflies that just got tired and died. But he said new ones were being born along the way too, from cocoons that must have come from the eggs of butterflies past. And the newborn *mariposas* knew which way to go as soon as their wings were hard enough to fly.

"He said they could predict the weather, so they knew when to rest and when to move, but mostly they moved. Until one day, the cloud of butterflies that they had been following came to a rest in a big stand of pine trees not far south from here. The day was young and the weather was fine, so Pan couldn't understand why they had stopped.

"They stayed long after he thought they should have moved on. No newborns had joined them for a long time because of miles and miles of poisonous farmlands. Too many of them were starving and dying-off on this island of sterile pine trees. He thought, for the first time in their journey as a whole, that they were confused.

"Finally, what was left of the group split up, flying east and west, instead of north, so Pan let them go. For creatures that found passes through mountain ranges, this city, this collection of barren fields and monuments, shouldn't be such an obstacle. So he thought this was definitely a place where they could use some help."

Jaime pulled a brown, woven pouch from within his blankets. "These are seeds Pan harvested from a marsh far to the south. He said they were from a plant that would attract butterflies and breed new generations, right here in H-town. My translation may not be perfect, but he called it like, a purple hemp flower.

"Anyway, he gave me this pouch full of seeds and told me to plant them around here, but not right on the bayou's edge. Not yet. He said the water here was a little tainted. He also told me that we should plant some right up there in the village. He said the soil up there was rich and it ran deep. But we would have to wait until the trespassers are gone."

"After *who's* gone?" Bill asked. But everybody was thinking it.

Jaime shook his head. "I don't know. I guess those, uh, American Missionaries up there. I guess he meant in the future. I don't know how he knew that, but Pan seems to have kind of a different sense of time than we do."

"A different sense of reality is more like it. Runnin' across the desert, chasin' butterflies for hundreds of miles? I think he's been eatin' too many of his hand-picked mushrooms."

"Could be. I know that little *hongo* gave *my* reality a good shake. Oh, and that's another thing. Pan said the mushrooms around here are doing a good job of cleaning the water's edge, but he told me that only a shaman should eat them for now." Jaime chuckled and coughed. "Not that any sane person would eat the *hongos* around here."

Marcus said, "But you did. He picked you a weird mushroom down by the bayou? And you ate it? You're lucky it didn't kill you."

Bill interjected, "Only a shaman, he said? So he thinks you're a medicine man or somethin'?"

Jaime nodded at Marcus. Then he turned to Bill and said, "I think he meant the *hongos* were only safe for somebody with, like, an open heart, an open spirit."

"An open spirit? Jaime, hallucinogens don't make you more spiritual, they trick you into seein' things that aren't there. They're poison."

Jaime cleared his throat. "I can see how one of those mushrooms might whip up a nightmare for somebody, maybe drive them insane or give them a heart attack or something. But as I was saying, for somebody who doesn't worship the material things in life, for somebody who hasn't been fooled into believing there's no magic in this world, for somebody who understands that the most important lessons can't be learned with the physical senses, they might just offer a more heightened perspective. Maybe for somebody like you, Bill."

Bill was caught off guard, and also glad Jake Bontemps wasn't here.

Marcus said, "Bro, I think that was a compliment."

Jaime continued, "I can't describe what I saw in the clouds over the lights of Downtown last night, only that it was all I could imagine. And the images I saw reflected in the Bayou were from the other side of the veil. Yet somehow, I cheated and remained. I lived."

Barely, thought many in the crowd.

"And now we too have a mission from our mother, the earth. To plant these seeds. Pan told me that the wind still speaks to people, only they have forgotten how to listen to it. He said he would help us remember, that we'd know what to do when the time came, and I promised him we wouldn't fail. So I'm giving half of these seeds to you all, and I will reserve half in case any of us lives to see the day when the village is no longer buried under a parking lot."

The grapefruit-sized pouch was full of rare purple hemp seeds, and Jaime distributed a healthy pinch into each person's hand, holey pocket, or purse for scattering. They would grow on these levees eventually. Jaime had seen it in his vision. Marcus and Amber took some. Bill came and got his last.

Jaime smiled and said, "I hear you got on with La Estrella de Jahweh church, Brother Bill. They're good people. Christians who truly emulate Christ. Thank goodness for that." Jaime raised his voice, and once again Amber saw him as a bizarro Tommy Chong. "And what are we if not apostles? Certainly imperfect in every way, but living for each other just the same. Out here, there's no insurance, no sales tactics. Nothing's business and everything's personal. Some people see us as a burden on society, but the truth is we have almost no impact, no carbon footprint. We live like the ancestors, in deference to Mother Earth. The men sitting over in those glass towers, the ones who own the refineries on the other side, it is they who hold the future of all us earthlings in their hands, humans, animals and plants alike. Out here, we're reduced to the raw state, and yet we don't regress. We find, under these rags, the spirit of humanity, not the fangs of predation, of profiteering."

Jaime's speech inspired fringe folks to look around and consider each other warmly. Some shook hands, and even hugged as they milled and mingled, discussing the strangeness and where they would plant their seeds. All but Farah. She stood apart from the crowd, looking restless and worried. Brother Bill approached her "Farah, you okay?"

"Not rilly." She sniffled. "We ain't seen Frank all day. Wonder if he even knows we're here."

Jaime overheard. Looking to Marcus and Amber, he said, "I've been worried about Frank too. He wasn't at the shrine this morning. Sometimes he wanders off on his own, but he usually doesn't stay gone too long. And, I know this is weird but, I saw him in my vision last night. Like, saw his reflection in the bayou." Jaime had most everyone's attention again. "He was younger, and he was standing on a grassy hill, but I'm pretty sure it was Frank."

Amber said, "Okay. So, let's go out and look for him. He can't be too far."

Marcus said, "I can check underneath I-10 and along White Oak Bayou, but I'm staying away from the village for a while."

"Then we can split up," she said. "We'll find him faster anyway. I'll go look close to the village and work back this way."

Marcus took the Frankenbike east, backtracking toward White Oak Park as he explored the vast area underneath Interstate Ten in that direction."

Bill piled into the hybrid with Amber, and they headed south on Yale back toward the village, scanning the sidewalks and under-passes as they went. It was a short drive back to Buffalo Bayou and they hadn't seen anything on the way. Amber hung a left on

Allen Parkway so they would pass right by the village. As they crossed Montrose, Brother Bill looked up at the shrine through his window, but he couldn't see much except for the temporary construction fence surrounding the property, with "American Missionary" on it in letters three feet tall.

On her side, Amber saw two police cruisers, lit up, plus an unmarked sedan in the small parking lot coming up on the left. "Oh my god."

Bill followed her gaze and gasped. As they drove by the lot, they saw two uniformed cops muscling a body out of a dumpster. It was Frank. Cars honked and Amber had to speed up.

"Was he dead?" Bill asked.

"I think so," she said as she performed a sketchy U-turn, causing Bill to grit his teeth and grip his door handle.

They pulled into the little parking lot, and immediately attracted the attention of the two uniforms. One of them approached while the other stayed put, guarding a stuffed body bag that was on the ground. Detective Lamonte was on the phone, pacing beside his unmarked sedan. Amber recognized him immediately. He's the one she had interviewed for her article about Sean Dorsey's *murder*. The one who seemed to pop up lately whenever Kristian Klein was involved.

She dug a press ID out of her purse, looked at Bill as she popped her door open, and said, "Sit tight."

"Okay."

The scene was blocked off by the police cars, and an approaching uniform met her several yards on her side of the barricade. Amber rattled off her name, flashed her press ID, and turned on the charm. "What happened here, officer?"

The patrolman actively chewed his gum for a few beats, and then answered guardedly. "Old homeless guy fell in the dumpster. Cracked his head and died."

"Do you know who he is?"

"No ID. But we'd notify his family first anyway. If he's got any."

"So, how exactly do you fall into a dumpster? That thing's what, six feet tall?"

The cop smacked his gum, studying her. "He *climbed* into the dumpster last night, prob'ly when this wet front blew in. He was trying to get out of the weather, but he was drunk and he fell over the edge. Unfortunately, the dumpster was pretty much empty. So he cracked his head when he hit the bottom. He's got trauma to the back of his skull. Lucky for him though, he probably just died in his sleep. He was drunk as a skunk. You could smell the whiskey on him a mile away."

Amber noted the dumpster had one of those sliding, easy-access doors on the side. She pointed at it. "Why wouldn't he have just crawled through that side door? And if he was old and drunk, could he even climb over the front lip of that dumpster. It's, like, a foot taller than him." The cop didn't look back to weigh her assertions, just shrugged his shoulders. He was getting bored, his eyes wandering from Amber's head to her toes.

Detective Lamonte said, "Yessir, Mr. Klein," and hung up his phone as he strode up behind the patrolman. *Her again.* Before Amber could formulate a probing question for the high-ranking officer, he pointed at her hybrid and commanded, "Move your car! You're blockin' the coroner!"

An ambulance was trying to back into the tiny parking lot, and she was in the way. "Oh, sorry!" she said as she hustled back over to her car.

"And keep clear of here! If you want a printable statement, you can come get it from me at the station," he hollered. She nodded her head without looking back.

Bill's apartment was only a few minutes away, so they headed that way. As Amber pulled back out onto Allen Parkway she said, "According to that policeman, Frank crawled into the dumpster to get out of the rain last night. But he was drunk, so he fell in. And the dumpster was empty, so he hit his head on the bottom and died in his sleep."

Bill frowned. "Frank's wiry, but he's pretty short. You think he could climb into that thing, drunk?"

"I don't know." She glanced at him, and then faced the road again. "There was one of those sliding doors on the other side. He could've just crawled in right there."

Bill looked at her. Then he also faced the road again, brooding.

She said, "I gotta call Ting. But I'm gonna wait until the cops are gone from there. Looked like they were about done. That ambulance was a coroner."

Bill pouted at the finality of those words. Then he said, "Uh, yeah. Let's keep Ting and the cops separated please."

The She Rex, Jake Bontemps' monster truck, was parked in front of Bill's apartment again, so Amber threw him a sideways smirk. Bill was defensive. "It won't stop rainin' so there's not much work to do in the rice fields right now. And he likes the city. We're just friends."

"I didn't say anything," Amber replied, her voice pitched higher than normal.

She kicked Bill out, and then cruised back by the scene. Everyone was gone except for Lamonte, talking on the phone again, sitting in his unmarked cruiser. So she gave it ten more minutes. When she came back again, the Detective had finally left, so she pulled into the lot and called Marcus.

17

DEVILS IN DETAIL

Ting entered the parking lot from the tree-covered levee instead of the sidewalk, and spooked Amber when he appeared. Then she wondered why she had expected otherwise.

He lingered at the dumpster, inspecting it, resisting the urge to run over and embrace her. She had given him the details of the cops' assessment when she'd called him on the phone. "See what I mean? That thing's pretty tall," she said as she approached. "And the detective on the scene when I got here was the same one who investigated, or *didn't* investigate, Sean Dorsey's murder."

Marcus looked at her. "Lamonte."

"Yeah. And I know that's not a coincidence unto itself, but I can't tell if he's actually corrupt or just lazy."

Ting shrugged and shook his head. "I'm not going anywhere near him."

She walked to the edge of the dumpster. "And check out this side door. Why wouldn't Frank have just crawled in through here?"

"Maybe he didn't notice it. It was dark and rainy," Marcus said. But he was thinking something totally different. Frank wouldn't climb into any dumpster, not with the shrine right up the hill, no matter how hard it was raining.

"You think somebody put him in there?" she asked, watching his expression.

Marcus shrugged. "It's hard to say without any proof or any witnesses." He was still trying to protect her, he guessed. The pavement had been washed by the storm and trampled by flat-footed policemen, leaving the prints barely detectable, but Marcus could see them clearly enough. A few ghostly tracks from a huge pair of combat boots ran to the dumpster and back, starting from the muddy gravel at the back edge of the parking lot where Tíng had stashed the Frankenbike, and where he'd also seen the broken bottleneck from a pint of Irish whiskey. He knew the crew responsible for this. He knew where they were. He scanned the area, hoping the guilty party might return.

Amber took his hand. "What are you thinking, baby?"

The question was stirring, but before he could answer, something behind her caught his attention—a long, black SUV, moving too slowly on Allen Parkway. "Is that what's-his-name again?"

She looked over her shoulder, and then turned back to Marcus. "I think so. I think that's Kristian Klein." A chill ran up her spine.

The skulking, monstrous vehicle was giving him the creeps as well. Tíng looked her in the eyes and said, "I think it's time to go."

She nodded.

He moved slowly to keep Amber between him and the SUV. "This is dumb. I'm way too close. I had on a big hat and sunglasses a while ago, but I'm still wearing the same clothes. I need to get home and change, maybe go by and check on the China Man. And I need to go break the news about Frank to Jaime, and the rest of the folks." He sighed. "Leo's gonna be real upset. Can I call you later? Maybe we can meet up at the Shelter or something?"

"Okay, yeah, go, take care of your stuff. I think I'm gonna go hassle the cops some more. See if they change their story." She made a pouty face. While Marcus was worried about everyone else, Frank's death was affecting him too. She pulled him in for a quick kiss, and then let him go.

Kristian Klein was in the back of his big black, armored conveyance, talking out loud. "I don't know where your hobos ran off to, Goodspeed. Look, just get your shelter built, and they'll probably come right back up there. If they're not down there panhandling, what are they gonna do for food? They gotta eat, right?" Klein pressed the button to hang up the speaker phone. "Damned Jesus Freak," he said as he lowered the black glass separating him and his driver.

Glancing in the mirror, Argus informed his benefactor that there was a Chevy Impala tailing them, but it had no detectible surveillance equipment.

Kristian swore under his breath. "Lose 'em. And then find me a damned pay phone."

"Yes sir."

Minutes later the soldier behind the wheel said, "All clear, sir." They were northeast of Downtown, off Lockwood, in an area where Kristian was certain nobody would recognize him. Argus had done well, as always. A couple of addicts eyed the long black SUV with a mix of fear and anticipation as the driver opened the door for the mogul in back.

It was rare that Klein used payphones anymore. There were hardly any of them left, but he knew of a few, and Argus had assured him that they were still the hardest lines to trace. Kristian bathed the receiver in hand sanitizer and dried it with a silk handkerchief, which he also used to punch in the numbers before he dropped the soiled cloth onto the ground. He let it ring, hung up, and checked his chronometer twice before the payphone rang back. He lifted the receiver, but only listened.

"Almighty Zeus?" said a deep, grating voice with a Cajun drawl.

"Who's speaking?"

"Hercules."

"I just got a call from my boys on the force. What's with the dead bum in the dumpster?"

"Jus' keepin' 'em off da streets, like you say. Mean ol' sumbitch put up a fight. Had a blade on him."

"Alright, fine, but I need your boys to back off from that new property now. We want the dregs to feel safe up there again. That candy-ass Goodspeed needs a yard full of hobos for his friggin' missionary project. And I need the bums to stay out of my streets and storefronts. Unfortunately, we can't kill all of 'em. So it's time to put 'em back in the corral.

"That dead queer floatin' in the bayou was a nice touch. But a little bit of fear goes a long way. So I need you to get your dogs on a tighter leash." Klein loosened his tie. "Now, listen up. There'll always be more guns and drugs to peddle, but they're not making any new real estate. So he who owns the land is king. I've got a little reinvestment for you, but there could be a lot more down the road when I turn that muddy ditch into another Riverwalk. Show me you're ready for bigger projects, you hear?"

"Yessa."

"Now, speaking of unleashed dogs, y'all got fights down there tonight, correct?"

"Yessa."

"Then I'll be there. You can place my bets. And you better pick me some winners." Klein smiled.

"Yessa." A leviathan in a camo utility vest hung up a pay phone near the Third Coast Harvest boatyard and grinned with his jagged teeth.

Several more devious-looking neighborhood characters had appeared in the vicinity, inching subtly closer to the big black SUV. Kristian Klein paid them no mind as he strode back to his vehicle and climbed in. Argus held the door open with his left hand, while his right rested on the submachinegun strapped under his black sport coat.

蛉

Upstairs in his garage apartment, in the glow of the bathroom nightlight, Tíng stood before a mirror wearing a black poly-cotton pullover, dark blue dungarees, and his oxblood red Doc Martens boots. He covered up with his dark gray trench coat and Kangol. He snapped the lid onto his big Tupperware, packed with umpteen warm grilled cheeses, and slid the container into his big black backpack. Then he slung it over his shoulder and climbed out the window.

The dancing duelist scanned the area from the top of his big oak tree. Then he dropped silently into the alley and found the Frankenbike where he'd stashed it. He had a little time to kill, and once again he was disgracefully overdue, so Marcus went to see his master.

As usual the store was devoid of customers. The China Man was dusting in a corner behind the counter with his back to the door as he spoke. "Ah, the prodigal grandson returns. Do you seek knowledge or sustenance?"

Marcus set his pack of grilled cheeses on the counter. "Uh."

Teacher turned to face his pupil. He frowned and said, "They are one in the same."

A moment of silence passed. Then Marcus began to gush, recounting a ten-minute tale of spying on the dog-fighting Zombies, being Tasered by the cops, and ending with the circumstances surrounding Frank's death. He left out the clue of the muddy boot prints in the parking lot, and the fact that he was going back down to the Ship Channel tonight. Of course, he was dressed like a ninja, and his teacher was no fool.

The China Man put down his feather duster and listened until Marcus was done. Then the little old man asked, "Two Tasers? And yet you stood?"

"Uh, yeah. I mean, I didn't go down, but it was weird, like I sort of watched it happen from outside my body for a second, you know?"

The China Man nodded and pulled on his chin whiskers. "Yes, I know." He came from behind the counter and started to pace while Marcus remained still. "My pupil, as I have told you before, most people believe they are trapped inside this—" he looked down at his own body "—physical shell, unaware of their *access* to that greater thing, which cannot be contained."

Marcus checked the clock on the wall.

"Very few beings break free to discover their connection to the universe, to the multiverse. Of these few, some become conquerors, tyrants, devils. While others live as ascetics, silent devotees in a state of constant meditation. And then, there are those who use their power to do good, to protect those who suffer, to balance those forces from the bad, those forces of evil. And these beings live with eyes and mind open as the Ch'i flows through them like warm summer rain. These are the heroes, the angels. They have been called many names. Do you understand, Marcus?"

Heroes, devils, angels? Marcus nodded with a quizzical expression. He'd never heard his master stray so far from his typical, quasi-scientific path of logic.

"Open yourself to the multiverse, string bean. Everything is real, or nothing is." Master searched his student's face for understanding but Marcus's focus had drifted to *Iron Monkey* playing quietly on the little TV at the far end of the counter. Teacher had been expecting him, as always.

"So like, even *Kung Fu Theater* is real, in a way," Marcus said. Then he frowned. That was stupid, wasn't it? He looked at his master. "Teacher, what really happened that night, with those two thugs out in the parking lot? Who are you, Master?"

The China Man had a brief flash of himself as a young cleric at a temple in the Mufu Mountains, in the time of Hu Yaobang, before he'd had to flee his homeland. He sighed. "In this dimension, I am just a poor shopkeeper. Yet from certain planes of existence, I begin to see this shopkeeper's destiny." He looked Marcus up and down. "But more importantly, for now, I can see what you are up to." He prodded Marcus's shoulder. "So go, do this thing, whatever it is you must do, if it is the right thing." Teacher frowned, his tone becoming stern. "But mind your power. You have been long untested, Dragonfly."

The leaves on the tallow tree out front were turning red, its gnarled limbs peppered with dark, toxic berries. Tíng's ride to the Ship Channel would be meeting him at The Fallout Shelter soon, but he still had to pop up under the bridge and see Jaime and the folks along the way. He needed to hustle.

蛉

Leo had a barrel fire going, and it flared blue-green as he added an armload of tainted driftwood to the flames. The big man looked up and said, "Brotha Marcus," as his young friend walked up under the bridge. Tíng stopped and smiled sadly at Leo and the rest of the folks, his eyes finally settling on Jaime. His face said it all, but he had to put it into words. "Everybody, Frank is no longer with us."

Farah started to sob, and a few folks moved to console her.

"The cops found him down in the park along Buffalo Bayou. They say he fell down and hit his head, that he passed away peacefully while he was unconscious," Marcus said in Farah's direction. For her sake, fringe folks kept their questions to themselves, though their skepticism was palpable.

Marcus mechanically distributed grilled cheeses to everyone, but nobody started to eat. When he got to Jaime, he took a breath and said, "So yesterday, me, Amber, and Bill followed a couple of those vampire-looking goons back to the place where they work." Everyone was listening. "We were right. They're shrimpers, and there's a bunch of 'em. They've got a big boatyard down on the Ship Channel. Anyway, we sneaked in there to see what they were up to, and they're definitely into guns, drugs, and dog fighting. And you remember old Marty?"

Jaime nodded. "He went missing, just like Frank."

"Yeah, well I swear I saw him down there. He looked really out of it, like they had him strung out on drugs or something. Looked like they had him doing some of their cleanup work." There was conversation among the folks, but they quieted when Marcus added, "So, I'm going back down there, tonight." He produced a small digital camera with a protective case and showed it to Jaime. "I'm gonna sneak back in there and see if I can gather some evidence against 'em. Maybe turn it over to the Feds so they can go down there with a warrant or something."

The uncertainty in Tíng's voice was reflected in Jaime's face. "Dude, what if they're having a big drug deal, or hate rally or something? There might be a whole lot of 'em, all armed to the teeth and whatnot."

"Well, that's what I'm hoping for. That's the point. To film these a-holes doing something bad, and then give the video to the cops."

Jaime had no faith in those words, and it showed. He was just worried about his friend. "Why can't you just tell the cops where they are and they can get their own evidence?"

Marcus sighed. "At least one of them *is* a cop, maybe more."

Mumbling returned among the folks.

Jaime took a deep breath. "Well, I guess you've made up your mind. But if something goes wrong you can just, escape, right?"

"Of course. You know those big white boys can't catch me." Marcus grinned but Jaime did not. "Look, I need to get down there and get this done before something else bad happens. And because I don't know who else can do it." Marcus sighed and added, "Plus, I need to get some kind of closure for my friend, Sean."

"And for Frank too," Jaime added gravely. Fringe folks showed signs of concurrence. They all doubted Frank's death was an accident. But they couldn't do anything but trust that Ting would handle it.

"But for real, I'm just going down there for reconnaissance. Gather up some evidence. The cops are gonna handle all the dirty work."

"Yeah, well, you know what they say about the best-laid plans." Jaime said hoarsely. He cleared his throat. "I was thinking maybe you could take Leo along too, you know maybe as a scout or something."

"I'm not going alone. Big Nelly's my ride."

"Yes, but Leo has reconnaissance experience."

Marcus shook his head. "This recon tonight will be a lot different than the kind Leo used to do."

"Are you sure?"

Marcus heard the shuffle of giant feet, and then he felt Leo's heavy paw on his shoulder. He looked up at his big friend, and could see the anguish over losing Frank. Marcus smiled weakly, defeated. He turned back to Jaime, sitting in his Drunken Lotus position. The unlikely sage grinned at his two friends and had a sip of wine. Ting would be safer with Leo as backup.

It was dark but still early, so the parking lot was empty as they rolled up to the west side of The Fallout Shelter. Nelly was running late too. Marcus hopped off the Frankenbike and undid the lock and chain he kept hanging on the rusty bike rack. Leo stepped off his trike, took an immeasurable breath, and stretched his arms up over his head, twisting his torso. Big bones and joints cracked and popped as he loosened his muscles. Marcus had a vision of the China Man's tallow tree, flexing in the wind, and it dawned on him that Leo might have his own reasons for going down there. Of course, the dancing duelist didn't dare examine his own motivation too closely either.

He chained up the Frankenbike along with the big tricycle, and gave the lock a tug just as Nelson Riley wheeled up in a sleek SUV. Although he'd seen Leo around and knew Marcus held him in high regard, Nelly was not excited to discover the gent would be occupying the back seat of his new Audi on this little venture. Then he chastised himself internally. *It's just a freakin' car, Nelson.* Plus, to Nelly's surprise, Leo didn't smell bad—kind of like earth and damp leather. The interior was roomy but big Leo still had to ride sidesaddle.

As they entered the freeway to head south, Marcus asked, "So what were the cops doing at The Shelter last night? Me and Amber rolled by there, but we didn't come inside because we saw a cruiser parked by the front door."

Nelly gave Tíng a sideways glance. "They didn't give a name, but they were looking for somebody. They cased the place pretty hard, until we started flirting with 'em. Then they finally left. Were they looking for you?"

"Probably so."

They drove a couple miles in silence. Then Marcus went over his loose plan. "I'm gonna sneak into the building and do some filming, alone. You two are just here for backup. Stay out of sight, and if something goes wrong, get out of there quick and we'll rendezvous later." Nelson agreed and Leo nodded. Tíng was thinking again that he should have just come alone on the bus.

Nelly was a speedy driver, and soon Marcus directed him into the same alley where Amber had parked the day before, just up the block and across the street from the Third Coast Harvest boatyard. Nelson pulled down his visor to use the mirror. Marcus turned in his seat and opened his mouth to speak. But he was rendered mute as he watched his big friend in the driver's seat quickly apply an unreasonable amount of makeup to his face—to the point of appearing mime-ish.

Ting had to ask. "Dude, what are you doing?"

Nelly stared into the tiny mirror, blackening his eye sockets with an eyeliner pencil as he spoke. "Ting, I hate to overstate the obvious here, but what we're doing right now isn't exactly *legal*. Plus, these are bad dudes. If they get a look at you, it would be better if they were never able to recognize you again." He turned toward Marcus and sighed. "And I know you're not gonna wear that Kangol in there. It makes your head too big."

Marcus frowned and took off his hat. Then almost without thinking he reached into the pocket of his trench coat and pulled out one of his favorite accessories for work, a deep-vermillion eye mask that fit snug, and covered the top half of his face, but didn't obscure his vision too much.

Nelly nodded, saying, "Yeah, there you go." Then he popped open his door, wet his fingers with a bottle of water, and raked his ample bangs straight down over his face, leaving vertical slits so he could see. Residual hair products held the creation in place. He turned to Marcus for approval.

Yikes. "Wow, that looks like it should work. But remember, you're just here for support. You two can be my lookouts, but don't come too close to the property. If something goes wrong inside the building, you'll know. I'll cause some kind of diversion, and then I'll fly. But if you see them coming first, get out of here. Don't wait for me. I'll give these clowns the slip and we can meet up later."

Marcus slipped out of his trench coat and stuffed some cash, his mask, and his bus pass into his dungarees pockets. "I'll be back in less than an hour. Hang tight." Ting exited the vehicle with his little pawnshop camera in its case, the lanyard strapped to his wrist. Then he dashed from the alley and into the shadows across the street. The two huge men looked at each other. Nelly sighed, Leo shrugged, and then they both got out of the car.

The Zombies had taken some lumps at the hands of lowlifes lately, and some bore injuries as constant reminders. The scuffle at The Fallout Shelter, the scenario at the China Man and the fiasco near the American Missionary thingy, had sent ripples of unrest through the Third Coast Harvest. The Zombies were not accustomed to defiance. They were the defiant ones. Plus, they had discovered the door that Marcus had broken on his previous visit to the TCH boathouse. They'd been infiltrated. So tonight they kept their weapons close and stayed on alert.

Tíng's pockets were too small and too snug to store the camera without risk of dropping it. So he cinched its leash tightly around his wrist, and let it hang so he could climb. With nobody to slow him down, he crossed the big bundle of pipes over the high fence in no time flat. He scanned the area from the top of the utility shed, but didn't see a single guard dog this time. *Hmm.* There were also a lot more vehicles parked here than last time, mostly muscle cars and four-by-fours. But there was also a big white van, three white pickup trucks, and a long black SUV. *Freakin' Klein?* Anger boiled inside Tíng, but he tempered it with resolve. *Stick to the mission.*

Studying the hangar, Marcus spied a ground-accessible ladder that went all the way to the roof, and decided this time he would try a different approach. He dropped off the shed and crossed the yard in seconds. Then he mounted the ladder and scaled the boathouse to the top, where he stopped and looked around to get his bearings. To the southeast, the Ship Channel stretched out a half-mile wide. Due south, in the distance, he could see a high arching bridge, still lined with cars, though they were moving along at a decent rate. The horizon was dotted with burn-off stacks, flaming like giant torches, constantly warming the atmosphere. Above, the dark sky was opaque, no stars visible behind the cloud layer that had moved in. Tíng could smell rain on the breeze, and he saw occasional flashes in the north. The droning of tugboats was perforated by honking foghorns and the piercing cries of nocturnal birds.

Returning to his task, Marcus followed a catwalk to a square manhole, one of several spaced across the vast metal roof. The entry was padlocked, but the attaching hardware was corroded from exposure to the salty air. Marcus gave it a good twist, and the whole shebang wrenched right off. *Oops.*

He cracked open the hatch and immediately heard a cacophony of barking, growling, arguing, whooping, and hollering, over a soundtrack of angry-white-boy music echoing from the far end of the hangar. He gave a quick look and then slipped inside. Just as Marcus had hoped, the manhole he'd chosen entered just above the office spaces they'd infiltrated on his prior visit. The top of the internal office structure was only about ten feet beneath the catwalk upon which he stood; a makeshift walkway of plywood spanned the ceiling-joists below from one end to the other. It was almost too easy.

Tíng hung by his hands and silently dropped down onto the plywood walkway, and then moved carefully toward the racket. He didn't see anyone working in the hangar, but there was a lookout posted at the south bay door where he'd just come from. Luckily the guy hadn't been looking up. Judging by the noise, everybody was pretty much in one location, just beyond the termination of the office structure where Marcus was headed. He got down low, and worked his way up to where he could peek over the edge. *Freakin' dog fights.*

About two dozen big, tough-looking white dudes were gathered near a crude grid of hurricane-fence kennels. Many pit bulls were present; most were in the cages, others on short leashes of heavy rope or chain. The human crowd was comprised of the Terror himself plus a great many Zombies and their ilk, including the man Amber had identified last time as a cop. Random military garb was sported throughout the mob, along with mix-matched roughneck attire. All wore boots, a handful of which were white rubber.

Marcus crawled back from the edge and breathed deeply as he got his little video camera ready to go. He eased back to the precipice ready to film but stopped cold as he heard the voice of the Terror, coming nearer to his position. There was no mistaking that gravelly Cajun drawl, with a lisp born of pointed incisors.

The head Zombie and his friend the cop were walking away from the revelry to have a semi-private chat, and in doing so they were working their way closer to Marcus's hiding spot. He kept his head back from the ledge, but stretched the little camera out far enough to fix the pair of villains in the little display at full zoom. Luckily he was above the floodlights which illuminated the thugs' makeshift arena, so Marcus was fairly undetectable as long as he kept low.

Then Kristian Klein walked out to join them. The mogul must have been inside the office space right below, with the big windows, the one Marcus had infiltrated last night. A few steps behind Klein was his "driver" in his black suit and perpetual sunglasses. He was several inches shorter than the Terror, but Marcus knew if there was anyone down there who could take down the giant Cajun monster, it was Kristian Klein's bodyguard.

Terror was so close that Marcus got the gist of what he was talking about in snippets above the turmoil. The cop's voice was lower and harder to decipher, but he generally agreed and nodded approval at whatever Terror was saying. It was a progress report concerning the Zombies' various enterprises. From cooking and distributing crystal, to smuggling weapons and Mexican angel-dust in shrimp boats, to dog fighting, loan sharking, and racketeering, business was good. Apparently the heat was taking a cut to let things slide.

Tíng bit his lip when he heard the Terror distinctly comment on "roustin' them bums and queers downtown." For the first time, Klein shook his head side to side and spoke while the others listened. His back was to Marcus so his words were inaudible, but the petro-baron was in this up to his starched white collar. The conversation ended shortly, and the alpha Zombie and the cop returned to the fun. As Klein and his driver turned and walked back into the office space below, the camera finally caught a brief shot of the mogul's face.

Jackpot. This was more than Marcus could've hoped for. The audio was weak, but surely the feds with their technology could clean it up and hear every incriminating word. He had enough proof to get some real cops down here with a warrant and start hauling these jackasses in, but he was still filming. The crowd was getting riled up, and so were a couple of the dogs, forcibly. Two Zombies with axe handles were prodding the caged animals, as they snarled and gnawed splinters off their objects of torment.

Marcus clenched his jaw. These two serially abused animals would soon fight to the death for the pleasure and profit of these miscreants. He was torn. The objective thing would be to keep filming. The dogs were being led into a stained cinderblock "pit" alongside the saltwater inlet, where the loser would be fed to the sharks. In a minute he would have graphic evidence of wrong-doing. The footage could be played in court, and maybe bring about more severe sentencing.

Tíng sorely wanted to go down there and prevent the blood-shed, though, and a lot of Zombies would have to fall in the process, hopefully the ones who'd murdered Frank and Sean. But he couldn't take them all down. And even if they didn't catch him (or shoot him), his cover would be blown, and they'd be on guard when the cops came. It would ultimately do more harm than good.

Still, these dogs were being tortured and forced to kill each other. How could he watch, or even just walk away?

Marcus pulled the camera back and stopped filming when he heard Nelly shout, "Hey, be careful with that thing!" Tíng peered back over the ledge to his right, in the direction from which he'd entered. There were his two lookouts, Nelson the hulking, gothic man-child, and big Leo, being marched in side-by-side from the south bay door at gunpoint.

Dang! Nelly probably came snooping around and found a sentry. Marcus sighed. It didn't matter now. He put the camera back in its case and cinched it tight around his wrist.

18

BRAWL AT THE BOATHOUSE

Amber walked out of the police compound in a huff. She had waited an hour to see Lamonte, and then he'd ghosted her completely. Apparently he'd had another pressing engagement, and left the building without telling anyone. She'd had to settle for an interview with a grandfatherly sergeant, who'd read straight from the report and couldn't answer any of her additional questions. But the story hadn't changed: The nameless old man was trying to climb into an empty dumpster to escape the weather. Being intoxicated, he fell in and suffered a head trauma that, without medical treatment, killed him as he lay there blacked out. There had been no witnesses or any evidence to suggest otherwise.

Walking through the parking lot to her car, she called Ting, but it rang four times and went to voicemail. *Ugh.* She hung up, climbed into the car, shut the door, and put the key in the ignition. She took a deep breath, and fought the urge to call him again. He was dealing with Frank's death right now, and needed a little time and space. She didn't want to go home, and she didn't want to go stalk Marcus at his house, so she decided to cruise by the bridge at Yale and White Oak Bayou. Maybe he was there, still breaking the bad news about Frank to Jaime and the others.

She parked her car at the seedy bar and took the sidewalk down to the bridge, gripping the small can of pepper spray attached to her key chain.

Under the bridge at White Oak Bayou and Yale Street, Jaime caved quickly under Amber's interrogation tactics. He spilled the beans on Ting's whereabouts and questionable motives, plus the fact that pretty much everybody figured the Zombies were responsible for Frank's death.

I knew it!

Promptly, she was giving the hybrid hell, merging unsafely onto I-45 South, worried sick but angry too, so she wasn't crying. The one and only person Amber wanted in this car with her right now was already down there on the Ship Channel, sneaking around risking his neck without her. They should have planned this together. She knew he trusted her, so he must have gone down there without her to try to keep her out of trouble, to protect her. It did make sense. But she was still pissed. Amber grabbed her cell. At least one person she trusted needed to know she was going down there.

Brother Bill Cox checked his caller ID and then answered his phone. "Hello there—"

"Ting went back down to the Third Coast Harvest boatyard with Nelly and Leo."

"Huh?"

She hastily synopsized everything she'd squeezed from Jaime down under the bridge. Bill could tell she was driving. "Amber, do not go down there. Stop somewhere and call the police."

"We *can't* call the police. They're *in* on this crap, at least to some degree. And the bad ones will be the first ones on the scene, guns drawn, ready to cull witnesses. Promise me you won't call the cops either."

Bill sighed. "Alright, fine. So come and get me, and I'll go down there with you," he said grudgingly.

"I can't do that either, sweetheart. I'm already halfway there. You stay put and I'll call you when I have more info. Supposedly, he just went down there to shoot some video. And you know Ting, he'll probably sneak in and out of there right under their noses. I gotta go." She said goodbye and blew him a kiss over the airwaves.

Yeah, I do know Ting. Dang! Bill hung up the phone and stewed for a couple of minutes, pacing and chewing his bottom lip. He needed a dang ride. Jake had been gone about an hour. So he'd be back in Oyster Prairie by now. Plus, if he got Bontemps involved in this, a full-blown war might ensue. Brother Cox stood in place and tapped his foot for another moment, then he looked at his phone and dialed his childhood partner in crime.

Bontemps was in BFE, on a muddy road, cruising slow and shining a spotlight out into his rice fields when his phone rang. It was Bill so Jake answered, "What up, chicken butt?"

Bill skipped the greeting and feverishly rattled off a third-hand account of the situation down on the Ship Channel.

"I'll be there in thirty," Jake said, and then burped.

It had been raining, so of course Jake had been drinking. "Wait!" Bill said to the empty line. Too late. Jake was coming, and trying to dissuade him while he was driving would only make it worse.

蜻蛉

Bill popped open the door and swung up into the She-rex as he'd done countless times, and almost swore as he sat on an AR-15 with a banana clip installed. The thing was still warm, and the cab smelled of beer and gunpowder.

"Oops, sorry. Saw some hogs out in the rice," Jake said, grinning. He grabbed the banged-up assault rifle and shoved it up under his bench seat.

Bill sat back down and kicked three crushed beer cans discarded on the floorboard. There were two tall cans remaining in the six-pack beside Jake on the seat, and he had one open sitting in his cup holder. Bontemps was legally intoxicated, and Bill demanded the driver's seat. Jake laughed, but he also complied since they were in the city and he didn't know where they were going. So the two skinny country kids swapped positions in the cavernous cab without opening the doors.

Bill put the big truck in gear and stepped on it like he was driving his Grandpa's old Ford Fairmont. His skull thumped back into the headrest, and Jake hollered, "Woohoo!" as the She-rex kicked up a rooster tail of water vapor and burnt rubber on the saturated pavement. Brother Cox gripped the wheel at 10 and 2 and blessed the She-rex's whistling turbo diesel.

蚣

Marcus wasn't sure what to do. Cause a diversion? That's what the heroes on TV did when they were outnumbered and outgunned. He'd left his phone in his trench coat in Nelly's car. But what would he do with it now anyway, call the cops? He felt like the worst kind of fool bringing Nelly and Leo down here. He should have just gotten on the bus and come alone. He wasn't a crime fighter. He was an idiot, and now his friends might be killed because of it. Ting breathed deeply and tried to center himself. He closed his eyes and focused into the bottomless pool until his thoughts became clearer:

This uncertainty, this fear, wasn't for himself, but for Leo and Nelly. Marcus would risk his life right now to save his friends, and with that realization came power, because Ting knew he wouldn't go down easily. The heroes on *Kung Fu Theatre* didn't cause diversions. They waded into an onslaught and left piles of evildoers in their wake.

He opened his eyes and studied the situation with grim determination. The intrusion had brought weapons out into the light, a couple of handguns and one assault rifle Tíng could see for sure. He'd have to get close to those guns if he was going to dispose of them. The rifle was a menacing thing that looked like an AK-47 with a banana clip. It had to go first.

Tíng retreated from the edge of the building so he couldn't be seen as he stood up. He pulled the dark red mask from his pocket and put it on. Then he leaped up, grabbed the catwalk overhead, and pulled himself onto it. He followed it to a point where he was above the big boats in dry dock. Then he slipped over the rail and dropped twenty feet onto the wheelhouse of an eighty-foot trawler.

Nobody heard the thump of his landing over the raucous crowd and barking dogs on the hangar floor. The camera took a bump when Tíng put his hands down to absorb some of the impact, but the little gadget appeared to be okay. He climbed down to the foredeck and took the camera off his arm, stashing it within a coil of heavy rope. He would try to come back for it if he survived the next several minutes. For now, he needed his hands free.

Something big caught his attention, scuttling through the dark rafters high above, but it obviously wasn't human. Probably a raccoon or a possum. Marcus disembarked on a maintenance ladder. Then he crept toward the machine gun and imminent chaos.

The dog fights were put on hold, and Terror bore a puzzled but pleased expression as he strode toward his two new guests. The alpha Zombie was bigger and more muscular than any man present, and that was saying a lot. He raised his hand and promptly quieted all other conversation in the hangar, along with the music playing in the background. "What da hell you freaks doin' sneakin' 'round my property? *And* wit no ID's on y'all? Y'all don't look like y'all lost. Not yet."

Leo stared at the ground, mute. Nelson had never been so afraid, but he knew Ting was in here somewhere, hopefully about to do something, and he didn't want to give it away. So he played it tough. "Uh, yeah, sorry, we were just out looking for our dog. Maybe you guys have seen him. He's a rescued pit bull about this big."

Terror's laugh echoed through the boathouse, so gravelly and baritone that it sounded inhuman. Then the giant man said, "Well lookee here ever-body. We got us a couple o' tough guys." He snapped his fingers at one of his henchmen. "Bring dat mutt ova here." The lesser Zombie walked up with a heavily scarred pit bull on a chain. Terror took possession of the animal and said, "Y'all got some kinda bidness y'all wanna keep secret, I see. But dat don't matta. You'll tell me what I wanna know when dis dog gets a hold o' yo kneecap. Y'all done stumbled into my world now, boys. Nobody'll hear ya screamin' down here."

Kristian Klein observed from the elevated office window with his arms crossed, one hand stroking his chin. He was concerned about this intrusion, but also a bit excited, in a Roman Colosseum sort of way. Argus, his driver, stood beside him at ease.

Nelson wanted to back away, but there was a gun behind him, which meant certain death. His mind was swimming, but then he saw something even scarier than the pistol or the approaching pit bull. Something in his peripheral caused his head to turn and his jaw to drop, as did the jaws of all the Zombies, and Marcus too.

Leo had feigned scratching his stomach for a second, and then completed the gesture by pulling a hand grenade out of his oversized trousers. He made sure everyone got a good look at it as he expertly pulled the pin and flicked it away.

Terror instinctively stopped his advance and slowly reversed course.

Kristian Klein said, "Get me out of here."

Argus replied, "Yes sir." The two of them hastily departed the building.

Leo wished he had an HE grenade, but the best his old buddy at Guns N Surplus had been able to do was a flash grenade. It was a bulky, antiquated, Russian-made device, but it looked ominous. So nobody called him on it. Leo's friend at the surplus store, a fellow Vietnam Vet, had ensured the grenade's integrity. He'd kept it packed in ether, and guaranteed it would still "pop and fizz."

Terror slowly backpedaled, saying, "Awright, easy now, boy." He smiled, but his eyes were calculating. The dog at his heel backed away too, sensing the change in atmosphere the grenade had brought on. Leo looked into Terror's eyes, and the big Zombie's smile vanished. "Now you wait a minute, boy. Let's just—"

Leo released the spring-loaded lever with a ping that everybody heard. Then he lobbed the little bomb over Terror's head into a nearby collection of steel drums that were fenced off and marked WASTE OIL.

Zombies dropped leashes and scattered; sensing their fear, pit bulls chased after them. Terror shielded his head and ran away from the impending blast, as did Nelly and Leo, but in a different direction.

The flash grenade exploded and it was pretty impressive, but not worth the preemptive panic it had caused. Still, the charge kicked around some barrels, and the flash of white phosphorous ignited a plume of spurting oil. A pool of flame spread beneath the toppled drums. Many who'd fled the initial blast stopped and looked back, but then turned and kept on running out to their vehicles.

But the assault-rifleman was worth his sand. He recovered quickly and raised his weapon, spotting Nelly and Leo scrambling across the hangar.

Tíng felt impossibly light as his core pulled him like a magnet toward the AK-47. The rifleman heard the flapping of bell-bottom pant legs, turned, and saw the masked freak coming fast out of nowhere. He tried to engage, but only had time to grimace as a blood-red Doc Martens boot arced up and cracked the hardwood stock of his AK. The weapon fired as the rifleman lost his grip on it, and the recoil sent what was left of it hurtling through the air. The Zombie's empty hands stung for only an instant before a matching boot cannonballed into his chest, knocking the wind out of him and launching him backward into a stack of wood pallets.

Terror pulled the pistol from his leg holster and was about to take a shot at Leo when a short volley of rifle shots whizzed over his head. He ducked and turned his weapon toward the shooter, but then hesitated when he saw his rifleman go down hard. There was a new player. A queer-looking masked weirdo had entered the fray and done some damage. Now the little bastard was releasing all the dogs from their makeshift kennels.

But the freak's good deed cost him, because soon he was surrounded by several of Terror's underlings, armed with wrenches, pry bars, and cheater pipes. The pack of Zombies descended on Tíng like bad kids with a stolen piñata. Men grunted, tools pealed and spun through the air, and Terror watched in amazement as his soldiers were pummeled to the ground by a barrage of flamboyant, bare-knuckle strikes and kicks. *They didn't even touch him.*

Then the violent fairy in the red mask and boots bounded away, chasing after his apparent friends, leaving his assailants in a writhing, semi-conscious heap. The fairy was unnaturally fast, and the freaks were nearing the double exit on the opposite end of the boathouse, but Terror still had time for a couple of pot shots. He raised his pistol just as a flaming barrel burst and sprayed burning oil in his direction. The giant hater hit the ground and rolled to put out the flames on his clothing, and when he rose again the intruders were gone.

The fire had spread to the top of the office structure. Smoke was clouding the ceiling and blacking out the lights. Expanding metal groaned overhead. Terror kept the fire alarm disabled for this very reason. There was way too much contraband around here for a mediocre fire to attract attention. But this fire was no longer mediocre. His men had spent their portable extinguishers on the blaze, but it was too widespread from the explosion, and the splattered black oil burned like napalm.

Tíng caught up with his friends outside, but they were on the wrong end of the building, cut off from Nelson's ride by fences, flames, Zombies, and wandering pit bulls. So the trio paralleled the Ship Channel for a couple of blocks as fast as Leo could hobble on his bad knee. Then they turned inland, up a washed-out lane that reeked of decayed sea life.

The Zombies who had tangled with Tíng hosted an array of debilitating injuries, from wrenched joints, to deep bone bruises and deadened nerves. It was all they could do to drag themselves out of the boathouse to escape the fire. Now only four of Terror's best lieutenants remained, still fighting the blaze with everything they had, but it was a losing battle. There were drugs and weapons galore around here, the friendly cop was long gone, and because of the fireworks, officials were probably already in route. Terror kept a speedboat docked less than half a mile down the Channel, always fueled up and ready to go, but he was loath to use it. His losses here would be massive.

The alpha Zombie looked up to the office windows, but he knew Kristian Klein was long gone. Terror's bosses were tycoons and diplomats in the public eye, but they called themselves

Dragons and *Wizards* in private. To lose this stronghold in a fire would be a tragedy, but if the law connected the Organization to this little crime ring, it would be unforgivable. Most importantly, the ones responsible could not be allowed to escape.

The giant killer hollered, "Let it burn goddammit! Just let it burn to da ground! Come on! Let's go catch dem freaks befo' dey get away!" Terror's four best men followed him out of the building at a run.

Shuffling and panting on the wet asphalt, Leo said grimly, "That big one, he was the Devil. F' sho."

"You mean like freakin' Satan?" Nelson gasped, even more winded than Leo.

"Uh-huh. I met him befo'. He take any shape he want to. But you know it's him when he come fo' ya."

Marcus was in the lead, trying to maximize their pace, which seemed painfully slow. The lane ahead of them was clear all the way to a fenced-off industrial park that appeared to be under-going some structural renovation. What they needed was a left turn, so they could loop around a few blocks, avoid the scene alto-gether, and come back to Nelly's ride from the north side of the TCH property. But every turn in that direction seemed to be an alleyway, one after another, blocked by fences, dumpsters, equip-ment, and maritime junk. Ting could get through easily, but his companions weren't climbers. To their right was the Ship Channel, and behind them—

"I got 'em!"

A Zombie materialized in the gathering darkness, running at an easy pace and catching up to them fast. Then two more joined him, only slightly farther back. Leo stopped shuffling and turned around to face them, as did Nelly and Marcus without a word. Crime wasn't a problem around here. Cranes and tugboats were hard to steal. There were only a few security lights in the area and a descending mist dampened their glow. The place was deserted.

There were five Zombies now, and only Terror himself was empty-handed. The others had acquired bludgeoning devices of one sort or another on their way out of the hangar. The four lieutenants formed a skirmish line as they approached, and their commander moved to the center. Terror addressed Marcus directly. "Well now. Dat's a cute little mask you got on, boy." His men cackled. The brutes were barely winded. "Let's try dis one mo time. Who da *hell* are y'all and what da hell y'all doin' 'round here!"

Tíng couldn't help but respond. "Who the hell are *you*? You're the one who brought *us* down here, you freakin' Nazi! You and your little *thugs* coming up to the city, hurting and killing people, and for what? Is it just hate? Is it money? Some kind of twisted social cleansing?"

Terror had to laugh. "So dat's it? You just some kinda goddamned queer vigilante? You black-lookin' little mutt! You think you can come down here and burn *my* house down? Do you know what you just cost me? Do you know what da hell I am? Afta I break yo arms and legs, I'm gonna pull yo heart out and show it to ya befo you die! And nobody's gonna cry for ya 'cause they'll be dead too."

Terror stepped forward, but Marcus stood his ground and pressed on. "There was an old homeless guy here not long ago. Your goons must have kidnapped him. Where is he? And what did you want with him?"

"Huh? What you say? Jus' how long you been spyin' on us, boy?" Terror snorted. "My men got mo' important stuff to do dan scrape barnacles and shovel dog shit. You'd be surprised what a junky can do wit a little crank in his veins. When dey can't get up no mo' we just dump 'em in da Gulf wit a pocketful o' scrap iron. Nobody misses 'em. Dey da scum o' da earth, just like you are, boy." He glanced at Leo then back to Marcus. "Look like da sharks gonna get some dark meat tonight, boys."

A compact car, covered in debris and dragging a section of chain-link fence, came crashing out of a recently blocked alleyway, and careened toward the Zombies—playing chicken with the goons to make them scatter. None of them flinched. As the vehicle quailed, braked, and skidded sideways into their skirmish line, the nearest thug sidestepped the little car, busted the left front window with a pipe and grabbed the driver by the throat.

Amber barely had time to slip the hybrid out of gear and undo her seatbelt as her neck began to stretch. She grabbed onto the thick forearm of her captor as he dragged her out through her broken window with one hand. Somehow, she'd managed to hook her key ring with the pepper spray attached, and she discharged it wildly where she thought the goon's face was.

But he'd been pepper sprayed before, and stabbed and beaten and burned, among other things. With one hand still on Amber's neck, the brute dropped his steel pipe, tore the car keys from her grip, and tossed them on the ground. With both hands around her throat now, he laughed wickedly and hauled her face up near his. She clung to his wrists to take the weight off her neck, her feet dangling a foot off the ground. "I'll pop your head off, you little bitch!"

Marcus was too far away, and by the time he recognized her, it was way too late. "No wait—please don't!" He almost shouted her name.

Amber was fighting just to breathe. Pinpoints of light crowded her vision. The Zombie looked to his commander.

"Hold on a minute!" Terror hollered over his shoulder. "Dis yo little girlfriend, boy?" he said, studying Marcus. "Jus' hang on to her a minute! I want her to see what I'm gonna do to him first. Den we'll take her wit us and find out everythang she know."

Amber's toes were thankfully back on the ground, and the goon transferred her into a choke hold. Tears flooded her eyes.

The pepper spray was affecting her more than him, but she wasn't going to struggle. Not yet.

If Tíng rushed the Zombie who held Amber, the others would step into his way. The thug could break her neck before he could get to her. As if he knew what Marcus was thinking, the lumbering punk backed away even farther, dragging Amber with him. Marcus shouted, "Don't worry! Everything's gonna be alright!" She wanted to believe him.

19

DRAGONFLY

A flash brightened the sky, there was a resounding boom, and everybody knew it came from the TCH boathouse. Rage coursed through Terror like a hot wire. He pulled a vial from his pocket and poured a thick line of bright white crystal onto the back of his hand. Then he snorted it up both nostrils, looked skyward, and roared like a wild animal.

Leo confirmed to himself that this wasn't just a man, but the Fallen Star crammed into a human shell.

Terror charged with a jagged maw and black eyes, like those of his pets swimming down in the Channel. Marcus had to wonder, *could this guy be the devil?*

"Ting!" shouted Nelson and Leo as they tried to step to his aid, but both were intercepted by other Zombies. Amber couldn't draw a decent enough breath to scream. She tried to stay calm, had to think her way out of this.

Marcus snapped back to reality just in time to repel a combination of piston-like punches. He slapped away a jab that would have smashed his face in, ducked under a whooshing left hook, and then arched backward, tucking his chin to narrowly avoid a crushing uppercut. Tíng spun away to the side as a massive, clawed fist raked his back, ripping his shirt and leaving four ugly scratches across his dragonfly tattoo. But Terror had overextended for that last strike, and left his big mug exposed. Tíng still had rotation when he released a simian cry and clubbed Terror's jaw with a Monkey Style Fist that sounded with a crack. The giant's head snapped to the side, but he didn't stagger.

Marcus moved away several paces and tore off what was left of his shirt. He could feel the claw marks burning on his back. His hand throbbed as he frowned at Terror. That Monkey Style hook would put a normal person in the hospital—or the morgue.

Terror shook his head and sneered, a small trace of blood in the corner of his mouth. "You a quick little mudda, ain't cha? What's dat tattoo on yo back, a butta-fly?" He sniffed the part of Marcus's ruined shirt that was still in his hand and said, "Smells like mutt blood." He dropped the rag on the wet asphalt, and ground it in with his boot.

Nelson Riley wiped his eyes beneath his drooping bangs. His excessive makeup was ghastly now, diluted with sweat and misty precipitation.

"Biggest woman I ever saw," his adversary said, grinning through his honed choppers. Of course, he was big too, and built like a brick shithouse. The Zombie edged closer at a calculated angle. If he could do some damage with the sledgehammer he'd brought from the boathouse, he might not have to touch this big, sweaty homo. *Sucker might have AIDS.*

Nelly pulled off his wide, studded belt and wrapped it around his big right hand three times. The leather creaked as he gripped it tight.

The Zombie picked his moment but didn't cock back too far, just a quick, overhand shot to the right side. It'd be hard to dodge, and his hammer would snap that collarbone like a pretzel. But Nelly didn't try to dodge. Instead he lunged forward and attacked as well. The hammer's fifteen-pound head overshot and bounced off that meaty region where shoulder meets neck. It was a glancing blow that didn't affect Nelly's momentum, and he led with a stiff left jab.

Tucking his chin saved the Zombie somewhat as his chest absorbed a bit of the impact. Still, the hater was knocked backward, his equilibrium shaken. When his vision cleared, he wasn't sure what he'd been hit with or when he had dropped his hammer. Uncertain of his ability to speak, he growled as he pulled a set of brass knuckles from his black utility trousers and slid the weapon onto his left, power-punching hand.

Big Nelly ached from his earlobe to his shoulder blade from the hammer strike, but he refused to show weakness. He assumed an opposite stance with his heavy, studded right fist cocked back. Cold heavy raindrops started to fall.

Leo was one in a million, a walking genetic bottleneck. All the physical traits that had been selectively bred into his enslaved ancestors had come up dominant in Leo's DNA, granting him the capacity for heroic strength and endurance. And decades of farming, fighting, killing, pedaling, scrapping, and crushing a sea of cans had made Leo harder than Chinese Algebra.

As a pair of Zombies circled him, each wielding an axe handle (their preferred dog-training implement), Leo weighed the odds that it was one of these two who had killed Frank. The old vet peeled back the hood of his coat, and his dreads uncoiled like black and silver tentacles. He unzipped his old field jacket and tossed it to the side. Few had ever seen him without it. He was thin as a wraith, but his gangly frame was fixed with knots of muscle that protruded through his threadbare T-shirt. Leo raised his fists, knuckles like two short rows of ball-peen hammers, and he grumbled, "Which one a y'all killed my buddy Frank?"

The nearer Zombie said, "I don't learn spooks' names, boy. I just kill 'em." He stepped up and swung his axe handle with a high whistling stroke to the head, but Leo caught the blow on his forearm, and the hickory rod snapped like a switch. The goon was surprised, but he was a seasoned brawler, and he followed with a powerful kick to the groin. Leo shifted his hips and took the boot on his thigh instead, while his left hand clamped onto his attacker's ankle and wrenched it upward like a machine, hyperextending the kicker's knee.

The Zombie's wail was cut short as Leo dragged him close and tapped him with a wicked, downward right. But his gnarled fist was forgivingly unclenched, and what could have been a bone-crushing punch became a stunning, open-hand chop. Leo dropped the dazed thug on the wet ground, and a half-breath later, the other hooligan hit him in the back.

The Zombie smiled when he felt something give and heard that resounding pop, but then he realized it wasn't Leo's spine that had fractured, but his axe handle, so he dropped it. Leo had the wind knocked out of him, but he kept his feet, and turned to face his opponent. The Zombie said, "Perfect." He wore steel mesh gloves, and he stuck Leo with a wicked short-right that would crush his face.

Leo couldn't get his left up in time, and the punch was coming, so he thrust his forehead down to meet it. Hammered between knuckles and skull, the steel mesh glove pealed like a bell. The hater felt as if he'd punched a statue. Leo's vision blurred, but the sharp pain above his eyes kept him lucid. A big speed-knot popped up behind his matted dreadlocks, but his cavernous lungs were refilling with cool dense air. The old killer's vision cleared, and he put up his dukes to see how much more he could dish out for Frank. But this Zombie had also fallen at the old vet's feet, curled up around his ruined right hand—still in the mesh glove but beyond useless, since he had just shattered it against Leo's cranium.

Leo picked up a fractured axe handle and pulled it in half,

making two long, hickory spikes, perfect for dispatching a couple of wannabe blood-suckas. He glared at the whimpering kid with the broken hand, and then at his partner who was dragging himself away, still half-dazed and with a blasted knee. Leo realized that he wasn't a killer anymore, like he had been in another life. He tossed the sharp sticks away and hollered at the two wounded punks, "It ain't too late for y'all boys to start ackin' right!" Blood thinned with rain trickled down to mix with his salty tears. Leo scanned the area, looking for Marcus, so he could go help him fight the Devil. Then lightning struck, way too close.

The Zombie lieutenant was tired of taking lumps from the heavy left jab, and his brass knuckles didn't seem to penetrate Nelly's factory insulation. *Play time's over.* The goon pulled a T-handled knife from his belt buckle, and gripped it so that the blade protruded between the fingers of his right fist. He shuffled forward with the shank out front, brass knuckles cocked back. Through bloodied pink fangs, he managed to hiss, "I just threw some skinny queer off a bridge. Now I'm gonna gut me a fat one like a hog." The statement meant more than he knew.

Big Nelly almost called Sean's name, but he held it in and let it smolder. The knife flashed before him, but it didn't matter. Nelly focused on center mass, dropped down and hammered forward with a straight, leather-clad right to the body, and in that same moment, lightning struck close by.

The Zombie parried and stabbed the incoming gauntlet with his T-handled knife, but his blade turned against the studded leather, torquing his wrist at an odd angle, and it didn't reduce the impact. Fireworks blossomed in the hater's vision, which then tunneled into black. A machine was helping him breathe when he awoke much later, handcuffed to a hospital bed.

Tíng's expression was melancholy as his hands hardened into deadly Eagle Talon Fists. Then his claws shredded the wind as he advanced, shrieking like the raptor whose attack he mimicked.

Terror was only amused for a second. Then he flexed the thick wall of his abdomen just in time to save his organs from Tíng's tempered fingers, as they rained on the brute like a torrent of railroad spikes.

Terror kept every core muscle rigid, and blocked the potentially lethal strikes aimed for his head and neck, but he couldn't manage a counterattack. The greater Zombie's utility vest was shredded, and pieces of it flew like confetti, until at last the whirlwind subsided. When Tíng spun away and came to a rest, his fingers were numb, and he was breathing hard from the effort. He had a vision of a giant Invincible Toad as Terror stood before him, grinning. The monster stripped off what was left of his ruined, utility vest. Bare to the waist, the fiend's musculature appeared that it might burst through his skin. He had several faded, prison-quality tattoos, including a fist-sized swastika over his heart. His flesh was blistered with angry welts, but he exuded mirth. He wasn't hurt. He was amused to have an opponent that wasn't too easy to kill.

But he wasn't wasting time either. Right shoulder forward, Terror mounted a low, protected offensive. If his winded little adversary didn't move back from his advance, maybe he could get in for a clench—at which point he would gut the little bastard with his bare hands. The prime Zombie was a chemically enhanced war machine, while the little freak was already breaking down.

Tíng hadn't fully caught his breath as he was forced to dodge, parry, and retreat, lest this beast get a grip on him. Marcus wandered in reverse, dozens of yards from Leo and Nelly—who were engaged in their own battles—and into a shallow cul-de-sac on the east side of Amber's abandoned car. Terror followed, steadily trying to dash Tíng's brains out. The little red ballerina was on the run, taking on a blank stare. He was coming undone.

Terror was about to up the tempo and finish this when Tíng's retreat abruptly changed course and slowed down. The little mutt still wasn't counterpunching, but now he evaded using singular fluid movements, one step at a time, instead of constantly back-pedaling. The mirth in Terror's expression hardened into fury as he swarmed Tíng with a prolonged flurry of lethal strikes. But the dancing duelist sidestepped every attack like he knew what was coming. "Goddamned fairy!" Terror roared with gasoline breath.

Tíng was thinking, *It can't be his body that's so hard. That's not possible. It's his energy field—his Ch'i.*

Tíng allowed a cold raindrop to strike his forehead and he heard it plop into the bottomless pool. His arms hung relaxed as blasts of warm air from Terror's fists and boots whisked around his head and bare torso. A smile curled Tíng's lips. A big parasite was tickling him with its wings. *Me, a dragonfly.*

Tíng intercepted a punch that was meant for his face, striking Terror's wrist with The Serpent's Head and torquing it to one side while his other hand, The Serpent's Tail, speared the big Zombie's throat, evoking a gurgling sound. The dancing duelist followed with a kick to Terror's sternum that sent him stumbling backward, gasping for breath.

The deviant who had Amber by the neck could see things quickly going south for him and his crew. He was about to knock the little bitch out and run for it, when he heard the guttural growl of a large animal behind him. He turned, expecting to see a wandering pit bull, but instead saw the tall, shaggy form and reflective eyes of a freakin' wolf snarling at him from the shadows.

Amber felt the goon's hold on her loosen, and in her peripheral she could see that his head was turned. He was distracted. Now was her chance. She straightened her knees, arched her back and thrust her head upward toward the big man's unprotected face. The maneuver produced a solid impact that sounded with a crack. Amber didn't know if she'd broken his jaw or if that had just been his teeth clacking together. Either way, he released her, and stumbled backward toward the wolf-like creature, holding the side of his face with both hands. He got too close, and the beast attacked.

Marcus scanned his surroundings in a full circle, from the apex of the sky down to the toes of his Doc Martens boots, as if he were testing new eyesight. Then he widened his stance and began to spar with nobody. Alternating the Animal Style forms, he flowed through combinations of punches, kicks, parries, and counterattacks, though he struck nothing but the multiplying raindrops. He rotated in place, never travelling in any one direction as his master's words seemed to whisper from the encroaching storm: *You have been long untested, Dragonfly.*

A thin veil of steam enshrouded Tíng's body, misty vortices trailing behind his thrashing arms and legs. He felt an added resistance to his limbs, as if some ether was coalescing there, tickling his fingers as it manifested from the saturated air. Cobwebs of dull light formed an airy sphere of ghostly threads that crackled and arced. Tíng's short wavy hair stood on end.

Terror had caught his breath and he charged from several yards away. The giant killer roared as he launched a flying dropkick at Tíng's head, leading with his massive steel-toe boots. In his heightened state, the dancing duelist could see Terror without looking, for Qīngtíng had thirty thousand eyes. He perceived a malign black shadow sailing toward him, devouring everything around it that was good. So Tíng channeled Ch'i through his hands, and ignited the dark spot with the sphere of light.

The air burned like atomized sulphur in the vanishing space between the two foes, precipitating a blast which Qīngtíng beheld through a web of translucent red polygons. He felt detached, yet held his stance in the physical plane, though his boots slid backward a foot and a half on the wet pavement. Terror's legs were wracked with pins and needles, his knees buckling, plunging into his breadbasket and emptying his lungs as his hulking body cartwheeled through the air and tumbled to a rest several yards away.

Amber winced as she touched the lump on top of her skull, somewhat dazed from the head butt she'd just delivered. The lightning flash reset her awareness and drew her attention. She looked up just in time to see Terror's body hurtling through the air.

Marcus came rushing up as the struggle behind her in the shadows subsided. The shaggy canine beast loped away into the night, while the remaining Zombie hobbled away, still holding the side of his face. Tíng considered putting his boots on the hater's back, but decided to let him go. Then he finally removed his velvety red mask and stuffed it into his jeans pocket. Amber scanned the darkness and glimpsed the wolf-like creature one last time, but it was hard to make out any details under the dim streetlights and intensifying rain shower.

"What was that?" Marcus asked.

She only blinked and shook her head. Tíng pulled her close, and they hugged for a moment before Amber held him at arm's length and asked, "What was *that!*" pointing in the direction from which he'd come.

Marcus knew what she was talking about but he just shrugged. "Uh, lightning?"

Amber gave him a long, searching look. Then she broke away and ran over to her car, searching the ground for her keys.

"O-kay," Marcus said as Leo and Nelly shuffled over to his position. The three men cringed as the angry hybrid lurched backward in an arc and slung off the debris-laden fence it had dragged from the alley. The car stopped and lunged forward, wheeling about and skidding to a stop in an expanding puddle right next to the trio of brawlers. Amber finished pushing out the ragged rim of safety glass with her elbow and yelled, "Come on, let's get out of here!" through her busted out window.

Marcus hustled around the front to claim shotgun while Nelly and Leo went skeptically to the back. Nobody was optimistic about escaping in Amber's two-door, compact car, but Nelly's ride was blocks away, on the other side of the inferno and the newly arriving emergency vehicles.

Amber's only obvious escape route was back through the alley from which she'd come, though it was still strewn with wreckage and partially blocked by a big dumpster which she'd barely scraped by the first time. A more immediate issue arose when Leo and Nelly peered through the hybrid's windows and saw a wet pit bull wrapped in a beach towel curled up in the back seat. Amber glanced back and said defensively, "I'm sorry, but she was hurt." The two big dudes looked at each other over the roof of the car. Marcus hopped out of the front seat and offered it to Leo. All were getting soaked. It was somewhat of a fiasco.

Leo looked to the sky, thinking he heard a chopper. A startling boom echoed from the littered alleyway that was Amber's intended escape route, and the impeding dumpster sprang to life. The heavy steel container took a jolt and spun sideways before charging up the alley, pushing a pile of debris toward the hybrid like the blade of a rampaging bulldozer. All four humans abandoned Amber's poor little car.

The rushing waste receptacle breached the alley, snagged on a curb and tumbled over, tearing its lid asunder before it came to a halt a few feet from the hybrid. Amber stopped at a safe distance, looked back, and gave a sigh of relief that the dog and her car were okay. But she was a bit stunned by the appearance of the She-rex. Mud spackled and rumbling, she'd tossed the dumpster out of her path like a toy.

Bill Cox sat behind the wheel looking like a fox who'd just escaped a brush fire while Jake wiped away tears of laughter in the passenger seat. The country boys lowered their windows as the She-rex rocked to a stop with just a stripe of the dumpster's paint on her welded-pipe front bumper. Leo recognized Brother Bill at once and hustled toward the big truck.

Jake shouted, "Anybody need a ride?!"

"More than you know, sweet cheeks!" Big Nelly hollered as he hustled toward his little redneck buddy in the huge pickup.

Jake blushed and faced forward. Then the skinny rice-farmer popped open his glove box and removed a fifty caliber semi-automatic pistol. Everybody ducked, screamed, or swore as Jake stuck the hand cannon out his window and blasted three deafening shots. Dozens of yards away, the asphalt around Terror erupted and peppered his skin while the alpha Zombie covered his head and buried his face in the gritty wet pavement.

Jake kicked open his door, hopped out into the rain, and walked in the direction which he'd shot. He was still aimed-in, and the weapon looked comically large attached to his wiry arm. A laser sight danced all about Terror's head and shoulders as Jake hollered at him, "You weren't aimin' that peashooter at us, were you, big boy? Now toss it away, or I'll have to blast you all to pieces!"

Terror cursed as he flung away his .38 caliber leg-gun.

"Okay, you take care now. We gotta go!" Jake giggled as he tipped his straw hat, turned and scampered back to the truck, barefoot as always on his nine calloused toes.

Bill turned down the stereo as Leo and Nelly climbed into the back seat. There was ample room for both big men in the She-rex's four-door cab.

When Jake swung back into the truck, Bill winced and said, "Be careful with that thing! How many guns do you have in here? Thank goodness we didn't get pulled over."

"It pays to be prepared," Jake said, smiling as he tossed the bulky handgun haphazardly back into the glove box, causing Bill to flinch again.

Marcus hopped into the hybrid, and had to shake his head at the serene yet watchful pooch in the back seat. Amber whipped around the dumpster and jammed the tortured compact back up the alley—now conspicuously free of obstacles—while the wet Northern buffeted her busted window. Before Marcus could ask, she said, "I made Jaime talk. Then I flew down here like a maniac and saw y'all running away from the boathouse back there. So I drove along the Ship Channel, hoping to get ahead and pick you up. But there weren't any damn streets that turned that way. So I had to turn around and pick one of those stupid blocked alleys."

The light was red at the turn-off to the secluded highway that would take them north, away from the Ship Channel. Amber swore as she laid on the brakes for a hasty stop. Sitting at the intersection directly across from them was an unmarked police cruiser. The driver was just visible enough for Amber and Marcus to watch him point his finger at them like he was firing an imaginary pistol. The pair in the hybrid faced each other and said in unison, "Freakin' Lamonte." Amber made a quick right on red and hit the gas, heading back toward Houston. She and Marcus both looked back, but the sketchy detective made no attempt to follow them.

"Freakin' Ting," Lamonte said to himself, grinning as he watched the hybrid's tail lights speed away down the dark rainy highway.

蚙

Terror saw flickering emergency lights reflecting off the surrounding buildings, and heard sirens multiplying and getting closer. A helicopter approached in the distance. He tried to stand and run, but he stumbled and fell forward onto all fours again. It was all he could manage for now, bruised and bloodied, his equilibrium still addled from being nearly electrocuted. Luckily, everybody had run from the boatyard in the direction of his speedboat, fueled up and ready to go. He scrabbled onto the short dock and undid the mooring lines on his hands and knees. But vertigo struck him again as he tried to climb aboard, and he fell through the widening gap between the boat and the dock.

The water in the Ship Channel was deep, even this close to shore, so there was no bottom for Terror to kick off of. His heavy boots were pulling him down, but he managed to thrash his way to the surface. The current was taking hold of his boat and pulling it farther out, but he swam for the stern with all his might and grabbed onto the small platform at the base of the transom. Terror hung there for a moment, garnering his strength to pull himself aboard, panting through a hateful smile. He would slip away down the coast to a safehouse, and live to revenge another day.

Two fin tips breached the surface, several feet apart, and Terror tried to claw his way onto the boat. Pain flooded his senses as something with immense primal power gripped his leg and dragged him beneath the swirling brine, cutting short his anguished cry.

蜻

Several miles northwest, an old fisherman stood near his truck, which was stuck in a ditch. He swore up and down to a young sheriff's deputy that two huge critters had leapt out from the marsh and run right in front of his pickup.

"Two huge critters?"

"Yessir. Was the damnedest thing too. Hadn't seen neither kind o' beast 'round here since, well I can't remember when. Ya know I used to crew on a dredger, near to here." The old-timer pointed out into the darkness, his eyes wide and bloodshot.

The aroma of stale beer and expired fish bait clung to the old man's truck, and the north wind was fresh by contrast. The cop shined his light out into the night but saw only wetlands. "What *exactly* did you see sir, running across the road?" Thankfully the tow truck had arrived. The deputy was ready to be done here, and go check out the fire everybody was squawking about on the radio.

The old-timer had gotten a good look. They'd been right in his headlights. He was of sound judgment and he was no liar. "Gotta be fifty years, or better," he mumbled pensively.

"What was it that you saw, sir?"

"Was a, a big ol' red wolf, and a...." He shook his head as he stared out into the dark marsh. "Couldn't a been though, looked like somethin' was in his mouth."

The cop holstered his light and asked, "You saw a big red wolf run across the road, and a what else?"

The old feller cleared his throat and said it before he doubted himself any more. "Looked like that wolf was chasin' a, a big black jaguarundi."

"A big black jagger-what?"

Epilogue

Six Months Later

Amber climbed the rutted footpath that led from the sidewalk along Allen Parkway up to the formerly abandoned lot known as "the village." She had parked her hybrid in the small parking lot at the front entrance along Montrose Boulevard, and then walked around the side because this was still her favorite way to enter the property. She reached the top of the trail and stopped to catch her breath, placing a hand on her tummy while she admired the big, wooden, hand-painted sign that was staked into the hill: *Frank's Garden.*

She passed behind the sign, and walked to the tall rusty fence inundated with sprawling creepers. The trumpet vine and morning glory were both blooming, and Frank's Garden was surrounded by a verdant wall of competing orange and blue blossoms. She slipped through the part of the fence that had been cut a decade ago for clandestine entry to the village. What she saw on the other side took her breath away—row after row of seasonal vegetables and fruits maintained and masterminded by Bill's rice-farmer buddy, Jake Bontemps. Amber shook her head, thinking *that dude's got a serious green thumb.*

She strolled past the row crops and small, fragrant trees to the open area where Frank used to tend his sprouting compost heap. She saw Brother Bill there, speaking and gesturing at the open air like he owned the place. *He kind of does.* Bill was talking over the shoulder of his childhood friend, Jake, who was stooped over and tinkering with the little tractor that Bontemps Farms had donated. The antique piece of equipment was well worn, but the motor still purred like a kitten, and Jake had tuned it to run on used vegetable oil collected from local eateries. The exhaust from the rumbling tractor smelled like overcooked French fries, and tended to make peoples' tummies rumble as well. Jake had dubbed it "the fryolator." He saw Amber out of the corner of his eye, turned, and tipped his hat. Brother Bill looked her way and blew her a kiss. She waved and continued to walk toward the main building.

She walked past the compost heap, which was now an extensive fenced-in area, maintained by a small disc-plow mounted on the back of the fryolator. A soil scientist from The Bayou City Conservancy, who was a friend of her friend, Ryan Dylan had tested the dirt and certified it clean. Since early spring, Frank's Garden had been purveying homegrown produce to anybody for a reasonable donation or work exchange. Every day, Jake added plants and traded with other local growers to keep up with demand and variety.

The old loading dock was busy again, fixed with a new wooden ramp and covered with potted seedlings, baskets of harvested produce, and a small fleet of wheelbarrows. The bay doors were fully functional once more, refurbished and repainted the same shade of green as the old steel awning that shaded them from above. The south end of the dock had been designated for leisure, now decked with a half-dozen tables and benches, and bordered by a wooden handrail connected to latticework overhead that was threaded with young, flowering vines.

Amber walked up the steps on the south end of the dock,

and meandered through the patio furniture in the shade of the old shrine. The white hill-country shale edifice, with rust stains radiating from its iron gutters, ladders, and catwalks looked much the same, but the building had undergone quite a non-cosmetic renovation. The stone exterior was solid as always, but the interior had needed some clearing, cleaning, patching, painting, plumbing, wiring, and new fixtures to make it suitable for the public. Nelson Riley Construction had handled the reno, mostly pro bono, plus a sizeable cash donation from Marcus covered a modest solar panel array on the roof. But the *major* contribution had come from Toby Goodspeed himself. After all, he had bought this place from Kristian Klein for one hell of a deal.

Amber walked inside, through the southernmost bay door, and had to stop and smile at the decent crowd of patrons navigating the multitude of wooden displays and shelves bearing fresh produce and indigenous plants. Volunteers worked the second-hand registers at the far end of the space, some of whom were fringe folks that once again spread their bedrolls in the old shrine at night to sleep.

She spied big Leo in the corner, head and shoulders taller than everyone else in the room, and dusty from working outside. He was talking with Jaime, who had taken on a more formal counseling role around here. Amber wouldn't recognize Jaime if she hadn't witnessed his transformation firsthand, clean-shaven and with color in his cheeks. It appeared that he'd totally quit drinking.

She heard a ruckus in the high rafters, and looked up to see a small squadron of sparrows as they descended from the massive steel I-beams and flew back outside through one of the big bay doors. Amber could still hardly believe she'd been able to leverage this huge property on Bill's behalf. The size and location made it quite valuable, but it had been a drop in the bucket for a televangelist like Toby Goodspeed and his American Missionary brand of megachurches. A small price to keep his name clean and his conscience clear. Toby had already skedaddled back to Denver when she'd contacted him. He was done with Houston. And he'd been all too eager to cut this place loose when Amber promised to keep his name out of the mouths of the federal cops investigating Third Coast Harvest and his former associate, Kristian Klein. It had been all over the news.

Amber had conspired with a friend in City Hall, and the priests at La Estrella de Jahweh church, to get Brother William Cox on the fast track to his very own, spanking-new nonprofit charter. Brother Bill had wept and over-hugged everyone present when they'd handed him the deed.

Amber turned and continued to stroll, following the scent of grilled cheese. She passed behind a service counter and through a saloon door back into the small kitchen, where Marcus stood before a pair of electric griddles side by side on the countertop. Many gently sizzling sandwiches were arrayed there. He was hardly minding his work, though. Instead he was watching the news as it played quietly on the little TV mounted up in the corner of the room.

The image was a familiar aerial view of a burned-out husk that was once a large metal building down on the Ship Channel, the Third Coast Harvest boatyard. Then the scene cut to a low-quality, grainy video of three men talking about all kinds of heinous and illegal endeavors: Wilhelm Desange, aka Terror—who was still missing—some cop who had been arrested though Amber couldn't remember his name, and Kristian Klein himself. The video still made Amber's skin crawl. The scene froze just as Klein turned to walk away from the conversation, and unwittingly faced the camera. Klein's mercenary remained largely out of the shot, and could only be seen briefly from behind.

The volume was low but the reporter's voice was clear enough. "—finally enough evidence for a grand jury to indict Kristian Klein, but the billionaire petrochemical magnate has apparently disappeared. A federal judge has issued an order to freeze Klein's assets, as it seems like the beginning of a high-stakes manhunt is underway."

Amber cleared her throat to get Marcus's attention, and he turned and smiled at her. Then he employed the spatula he was holding to quickly flip the remaining grilled cheeses from his griddles onto his big wooden cutting board to cool. The sandwiches were a little dark, but some people like 'em that way. He turned off the griddles, and quickly wiped them down with a dish towel.

He turned to Amber and started to reach for her stomach, but she caught him by the arm and pulled him in for a smooch. They separated and looked each other in the eyes. Marcus saw something of his mother in there, but it wasn't anything physical. Amber caught a glimpse of that aqueous internal refuge where Marcus spent so much of his time.

The news had moved onto a different story, so Marcus grabbed the remote and turned off the TV. Amber had to say it. "So it's only taken, like, six months for them to try and arrest Kristian Klein."

Marcus smiled bitterly. "Baby, you know as well as I do that 'equal protection under the law' means 'equal' to how much money you got."

Amber nodded solemnly. She'd been following the case closely. Enough contraband weapons, drug residue, and paraphernalia had survived the blaze at the Third Coast Harvest boatyard to prosecute a handful of Zombie shrimpers and one dirty cop. But most of the guilt had been hung on Terror, aka Wilhelm Desange, because it was his place of business. Of course, he was still missing, which had Amber still looking over her shoulder from time to time.

When the video had surfaced, the corporate brass in various Houston Chambers of Commerce had dropped Kristian Klein like he was covered in fire ants. So his plan to bury the green levees of Buffalo Bayou under a glorified strip mall had withered and died. A new, eco-friendly plan including more trees, trails, and maybe a skate park was gaining momentum. Klein had to hate that, wherever he was. Amber smiled.

Marcus was using his spatula to artfully arrange the grilled cheeses into his giant Tupperware cake carrier. He asked, "What are you thinking about?"

She continued to smile, letting her eyelids flutter and inhaling the sweet smell of buttery, caramelized bread and molten cheese. "Nothing," she replied.

Marcus waited until she looked at him. Then he handed her a sandwich and said, "It took forever, but they're finally trying to arrest Klein. He'll turn up. Not even a billionaire can hide forever. And if the Terror shows his face again, he better hope the cops get ahold of him before he has a chance to mess with us." Tíng channeled some Shaw Brothers, employing a dubbed-English, *Kung Fu Theater* accent to say, "Hmph, because if he comes looking for trouble, then he better be ready. He just might find some. Yah!" He threw a flurry of punches at the air for emphasis.

She tried not to laugh and choke on her grilled cheese. She swallowed a big bite and said, "Alright, alright, settle down, Bruce Leroy."

Marcus grabbed a bottle of water from the fridge, unscrewed the top, and handed it to her.

"Thanks." She took a drink. "So—"

"So what?"

It had been a while since they'd talked about it, but while they were on the subject, she figured she'd bring it up. "So we still don't know how Pan-terito got his little paws on your video camera."

He shook his head. "I have no idea. Jaime said he just showed up under the bridge, him and his dog. Dropped off the camera like it was no big deal, and then skipped town." Tíng opened a lower cabinet door, moved a heavy stock pot, and retrieved a small toolbox from behind it. He set the box on the counter, popped the lid, and inside, along with a few screwdrivers and a pair of plyers, was Marcus's little pawnshop camera. He ran his fingers over the symmetrical pairs of indentions in the camera's pleather case, as if it had been gripped by two rows of pointed teeth. He shook it off, and put it back in the toolbox.

Jaime had turned the camera over to Marcus and Amber, whereupon she had copied the footage onto a generic disc and sent it to Channel 4. But neither the strange little man, nor his big red dog, had been seen since. Marcus hid the toolbox away again. Then he grabbed his Tupperware full of grilled cheeses for distribution to the folks, the volunteers or anybody who was hungry.

Amber's grilled cheese was toast. She polished off her water too, and then threw the bottle into the recycling bin. She and Marcus walked out of the kitchen, one after the other, and then stopped. The China Man was across the counter, seated in one of the barstools he'd built of reclaimed lumber. A young man from Korea, referred by Brother Bill, was helping him manage the store now.

Marcus slid the Tupperware of sandwiches across the counter to a fringe fellow who'd come to retrieve it for delivery. It was ol' Marty, and Tíng could still hardly believe the old-timer had survived his ordeal down at the Third Coast Harvest. Ol' Marty was made of some tough stuff. The cops had found him wandering the scene near the conflagration that night.

Free from sandwich duty, Marcus grabbed a remote and cranked up the music, since the griddles were turned off now and he could pull a few more amps from the solar cells. The couple walked around from behind the counter, and as they strolled out the bay door, Amber looked back at the China Man and asked, "You coming, Grandfather?"

They walked out and sat at a table on the south end of the

old loading dock, now a sprawling patio shaded by lattice work. Marcus had snagged an extra grilled cheese for Amber, since she was eating for two these days. He smirked when he imagined the little multiracial nymph wiggling around in her belly. Who knew what the poor kid would look like? Asian eyes and a red afro maybe? Amber's parents had threatened to disown her, but that was nothing new. Marcus had a feeling they'd come around when they saw their grandbaby.

The China Man strolled up to their little table, but didn't take a seat. It was a little early, but people were already gathering in the shade alongside the building for his free yoga and meditation class. He had to go, but he patted Amber's shoulder, and told Marcus they would talk later. Then he walked down the steps saying, "Good morning, my friends. The sun has gifted us with another bright day."

Ryan Dylan hadn't been by Frank's Garden in over a week, so he was even more agog than usual as he strode onto the dock from the north side. He shouted, "Hey kids!" when he saw Marcus and Amber. She greeted him with a hug. Then he kissed his fingertips and touched them to her tummy. He and Marcus slapped hands.

Ryan wasted no time. "So is it a boy or a girl? Do we know yet?"

Amber shook her head. "No, not yet." Then she flinched as a large bug flew up and lit on her shoulder. She slowly craned her neck to see what it was. It was a dragonfly, iridescent red, from its searching compound eyes down to the pincer at the tip of its armor-plated tail.

Ryan sighed like he was in love. "Wow, this place is a zoo." He gestured to the shimmering insect without spooking it. "This little guy's actually indigenous to Southeast Asia. I did some post-grad work transplanting dragonfly nymphs into populated areas with mosquito infestations, and some of my associates introduced these into south Louisiana. So they must be catching on."

The sparkling little beast was preening its foreclaws.

"What kind is it, exactly?" Amber asked, trying not to move.

"Oh, he's a beautiful specimen—sparkling red, one of the fastest insects on the planet, *voracious* consumer of parasites *and* they're picky about where they raise babies, so they're a great indicator of water quality—just gorgeous. He's *Crocothemis servilia*, but his common name that I really love is the *Crimson Darter*."

Amber laughed, and the red dragonfly took flight. "Crimson Darter? Sounds like a cheesy superhero name." Marcus grinned, and the two of them shared an odd look.

Ryan had to giggle too. "I know, right?"

The bane of diminutive bloodsuckers hovered for a moment, and then banked east, disappearing out over the rows of tall vegetable plants. Amber thought of the wildflower patch out back, past the tomato vines, and it reminded her of something else she'd been meaning to ask Ryan. "Um, it's just about migration time, isn't it? Have you seen many—"

"No, not many at all, and I don't even want to talk about it," he said, pouting. But he perked up when he heard Bill Cox calling him from out in the yard. Ryan climbed over the rail and hopped down to meet him, and they hugged. Then Bill dragged him away east through the garden. Ryan hadn't seen the new blooms yet.

Farah stood at a trailhead wearing a *cǎomào* and a floral dress, soiled here and there. She withdrew a pinch of Frank's ashes from her little brass urn, and tossed it up into the humid breeze, smiling as she watched it disperse into the field of flowers downwind. She startled as Bill and Ryan dashed by, laughing like children, out into the billowing patch of amethyst-colored blossoms.

Ryan was speechless. So Bill proudly declared the plants to be what Jaime had called them, what Pan had called them, but in English. "They're some kind of a rare, purple hemp flower."

Ryan stooped to inspect the hearty vegetation, and then said, "Or, some people might call this swamp milkweed."

Bill nodded soberly. "Oh, right."

Ryan scrutinized an intricately formed bloom and said, "Although, I've never seen milkweed blossoms quite like this before, so lustrous and asymmetrical. I think you're onto something here—these *are* unique." He stood, smiling. "Anyway, I like the sound of 'rare purple hemp flower' a lot better."

Amber and Marcus stood up on the bench to get a better look when they heard Bill and Ryan screaming out in the back part of the lot. The two full-grown boys were looking up, dancing around and waving at the sky. Above their heads, swarming like a cloud of flame, were myriad monarch butterflies.

蛉令

Kristian Klein was buzzed on scotch though it wasn't even close to noon. His usually bronzed skin looked pale and blemished. He hated being this far from the equator. This wasn't a jail cell, but he felt imprisoned nonetheless, isolated and trapped.

Satellite TV played the Houston news softly in the corner of the vast chamber. A chill hung in the room despite the crackling fire. A goddamn judge had "frozen his assets." Kristian scoffed at the idea, that they believed they could even do such a thing. Klein Chemical was running itself in his absence, and he had enough assets outside the reach of American bureaucrats to live ten lifetimes. He vowed to send an armed emissary to meet this *judge* when the timing was right.

With red-rimmed eyes, Kristian looked out the second-floor window of his dacha at a meadow fringed by evergreen forest still blanketed in snow. He hated to take a chance on squandering his best man, but Klein was sick of dealing with crooked bureaucrats and amateur thugs, sick of waiting for a name. He walked to his desk and called the earpiece of the man standing out in the hall. Then he pressed a button to unlock the heavy oak and steel door.

Klein's driver stepped in, stopped a respectful distance away and stood relaxed. "Sir?"

Kristian wondered how many pounds of weaponry and Kevlar hung beneath the man's broad black coat. "I've got a project for you, Argus. There'd be a big bonus involved."

Argus cracked his head from side to side and flexed his thick fingers. "About time, isn't it, sir?"

Acknowledgments

The idea of completing this book without support from home base is laughable. So, thank you, Clara, for being my biggest fan and you, Ava, for being the muse that keeps me returning to my keyboard. Thanks to all my friends from H-town, especially that circle of readers who've always read my stuff when I've asked them to: Catherine, Megan, Rachel, Todd.

Thanks to Robert John Astle for helping me unravel a story line from a bird's nest of narrative, and to SDP Publishing, Lisa Akoury-Ross, and Cath Lauria for shining this thing up and finding it an audience.

And thanks to the folks I met all those years ago, before a word of this story was written, back when I biked the bayou trails under the bridges and overpasses, carrying a backpack full of sandwiches.

About the Author

A native of the Texas Gulf Coast, Jason Bujnoch has been a farmhand, a waiter, a bartender, a sous chef, a SCUBA Instructor, and a US Marine. But along the way, he's also been a writer on the sly, whispering to himself in the wee hours, tallying life's experiences and fusing them into stories that are almost unbelievable.

A deep admirer of Terry Brooks, Cormac McCarthy, and Jeff Wheeler, Jason is currently working on a trilogy of Urban Fiction and Fantasy novels set in and around Houston. He inhabits Bayou City with his wife, daughter, and too many pets.

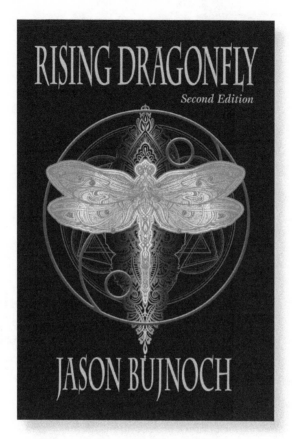

Rising Dragonfly
Second Edition
Jason Bujnoch

Publisher: SDP Publishing
Also available in ebook format

 **SDP Publishing**

www.SDPPublishing.com
Contact us at: info@SDPPublishing.com

CPSIA information can be obtained
at www.ICGtesting.com
Printed in the USA
BVHW071455100821
614083BV00007B/67

9 781736 720400